50 Magical Stories

Compiled by Vic Parker

Miles Kelly

First published in 2011 by Miles Kelly Publishing Ltd
Harding's Barn, Bardfield End Green, Thaxted, Essex, CM6 3PX, UK

This edition printed 2012

2 4 6 8 10 9 7 5 3

Publishing Director Belinda Gallagher
Creative Director Jo Cowan
Editorial Director Rosie McGuire
Editor Carly Blake
Designer Joe Jones
Editorial Assistant Lauren White
Production Manager Elizabeth Collins
Reprographics Stephan Davis
Assets Lorraine King

ISBN 978-1-84810-547-8

Printed in China

British Library Cataloguing-in-Publication Data
A catalogue record for this book is available from the British Library

ACKNOWLEDGEMENTS

The publishers would like to thank the following artists who have contributed to this book:
Advocate Art: Alida Massari
The Bright Agency: Marcin Piwowarski, Tom Sperling
Marsela Hajdinjak

All other artwork from the Miles Kelly Artwork Bank

The publishers would like to thank the following sources for the use of their photographs:
Shutterstock page decorations Dragana Francuski Tolimir
Dreamstime frames Gordan

Every effort has been made to acknowledge the source and copyright holder of each picture.
Miles Kelly Publishing apologises for any unintentional errors or omissions.

Made with paper from a sustainable forest

www.mileskelly.net   info@mileskelly.net

www.factsforprojects.com

Contents

CURIOUS CREATURES

WISHES AND DREAMS

MAGICAL PLACES

ENCHANTMENTS AND TRANSFORMATIONS

MYSTERIOUS MORALS

CURIOUS CREATURES

The Crab that Played with the Sea

From the *Just So* stories
by Rudyard Kipling

BEFORE THE HIGH and Far-Off Times, O my Best Beloved, came the Time of the Very Beginnings, and that was in the days when the Eldest Magician was getting Things ready. First he got the Earth ready, then he got the Sea ready, and then he told all the Animals that they could come out and play. And the Animals said, "O Eldest Magician, what shall we play at?"

And he said, "I will show you." He took the Elephant and said, "Play at being an Elephant," and the Elephant played. He took the Beaver and said,

"Play at being a Beaver," and the Beaver played. He
took the Cow and said, "Play at being a Cow," and
the Cow played. He took the Turtle and said, "Play
at being a Turtle," and the Turtle played. One by one
he took all the beasts and birds and fishes and told
them what to play at.

Towards evening, there came up the Man, with
his own best beloved little girl-daughter sitting upon
his shoulder, and the Man said, "See that you make
all the Animals obedient to me."

Now, while the Man and the Eldest Magician
were talking together, Pau Amma
the Crab, who was next in the
game, scuttled off sideways
and stepped into the sea,
saying to himself, "I will play
my play alone in the deep
waters, and I will never be obedient
to this son of Adam." Nobody saw him
go away except the little girl-daughter.

And the play went on till there were no more Animals left without orders, and the Eldest Magician wiped the fine dust off his hands and walked about the world to see how the Animals were playing.

He went North, East, West and South, and by and by the Eldest Magician met the Man on the banks of the Perak river, and said, "Ho! Son of Adam, are all the Animals obedient to you?"

"Yes," said the Man.

"Is all the Earth obedient to you?"

"Yes," said the Man.

"Is all the Sea obedient to you?"

"No," said the Man. "Once a day and once a night the Sea runs up the Perak river and drives the sweet-water back into the forest, so that my house is made wet. Once a day and once a night it runs down the river and draws all the water after it, so that there is nothing left but mud, and my canoe is upset. Is that the play you told it to play?"

"No," said the Eldest Magician. "That is a new and a bad play. Launch your canoe and we will find out who is playing with the Sea."

They stepped into the canoe – the little girl-daughter came with them – and they pushed out on the Perak river and far out into the ocean. Then the Eldest Magician stood up and shouted, "Ho! Beasts, birds, and fishes, which one of you is playing with the Sea?"

Then all the beasts, birds, and fishes said together, "Eldest Magician, we play the plays that you taught us to play – we and our children's children. But not one of us plays with the Sea."

Then the little girl-daughter put up her little soft brown arms with the beautiful white shell bracelets and said, "O Eldest Magician! When my father here talked to you at the Very Beginning, one beast went away naughtily into the Sea before you had taught him his play. He was round and he was flat, and his eyes grew upon stalks, and he walked sideways like this, and he was covered with strong armour upon his back."

And the Eldest Magician said, "How wise are little children! Give me the paddle!"

So he took the paddle and paddled till they came to the place called Pusat Tasek – the Heart of the Sea. Then the Eldest Magician slid his arm up to the shoulder through the deep warm water, and touched the broad back of Pau Amma the Crab. Then the Eldest Magician called out, "What are you doing, Pau Amma?"

And Pau Amma, deep down below, answered, "Once a day and once a night I go out to look for my food. Once a day and once a night I return. Leave me alone."

Then the Eldest Magician said, "Listen, Pau Amma. When you go out from your cave the waters of the Sea pour down into Pusat Tasek. When you come back and sit in Pusat Tasek, the waters of the Sea rise. If you are not afraid, come up and we will talk about it."

"I am not afraid," said Pau Amma, and he rose to the top of the sea, huge in the moonlight. No animal was as big as Pau Amma, for Pau Amma was King of all the crabs. "I didn't know I was so important," he said, rolling his eyes and waving his legs.

The Eldest Magician laughed. "You are not so important after all, Pau Amma," he said. And he made a Magic with just the little finger of his left hand – and lo and behold, Pau Amma's hard, rusty-copper-black shell fell off him as a husk falls off a coconut, and Pau Amma was left all soft.

Then Pau Amma said, "What shall I do? I am so enormous that

I can only hide in Pusat Tasek, and if I go anywhere else, all soft as I am now, the sharks and the dogfish will eat me. And if I go to Pusat Tasek, all soft as I am now, though I may be safe, I can never stir out to get my food, and so I shall die. "Then he waved his legs and lamented.

Then the Eldest Magician made a Magic with all five fingers of his right hand, and lo and behold, Best Beloved, Pau Amma grew smaller and smaller and smaller, till at last there was only a little coppery crab swimming in the water alongside the canoe.

And the girl-daughter took pity on him and gave him a pair of her scissors, and then Pau Amma was happier. He waved them in his little arms, and opened them and shut them and snapped them, and said, "I can eat nuts. I can crack shells. I can dig holes. I can climb trees. I can breathe in the dry air, and I can find a safe Pusat Tasek under every stone. I did not know I was so important!"

And the Eldest Magician said, "I will give you

back your shell, Pau Amma, for eleven months of the year, but on the twelfth month of every year it shall grow soft again, to remind you and all your children that I can make magics, and to keep you humble, Pau Amma."

And from that day to this, you can see when you go to the beach, how all Pau Amma's babies make little Pusat Taseks for themselves under every stone and bunch of weed on the sands, and you can see them waving their little scissors. But once a year all Pau Ammas have to shake off their hard armour and be soft – to remind them of what the Eldest Magician could do.

The Mermaid and the Boy

From Andrew Lang's *Brown Fairy Book*

LONG AGO, there lived a king who ruled over a country by the sea. Once, he had to leave his wife to visit his subjects in some distant islands. The king set off on the long sea voyage, but his ship soon ran upon a rock, and was stuck fast.

Suddenly a mermaid was seen dancing on the waves which threatened every moment to dash the ship to pieces. "There is only one way to free yourselves," she said to the king, "and that is to give me your solemn word that you will deliver to me the first child that is born to you."

Just then a huge wave broke with great force on the ship's side, and the king's crew fell on their knees and begged him to save them.

So he promised, and this time a wave lifted the vessel clean off the rocks, into the open sea.

In the fullness of time, a year after the king had returned home, he was overjoyed when the queen gave birth to a baby boy. But from that moment, he and the queen lived in terror, wondering if their son was to be snatched away.

When the prince was sixteen, the king and his wife decided that for his own sake, it would be best to send him into the world, for then perhaps the mermaid would never find him. The prince was delighted at the thought of adventures.

He prepared a knapsack, bade farewell to his parents and set out.

All day he walked, till evening drew in. He was just about to stretch himself out on a soft mossy bank under a tree, when there was a fearful roar and a lion stood before him.

"Give me some food," said the lion, "it is past my supper time, and I am very hungry."

The boy was so thankful that the lion did not want to eat him, that he gladly picked up his knapsack and held out some bread and a flask of wine.

"I must be off now," remarked the lion, when he was done, "but if you are in any danger just wish yourself a lion and you will become one on the spot. One good turn deserves another, you know."

The prince thanked him for his kindness, and the two then bade each other farewell.

Next day, the boy again walked until evening drew in. Then he prepared a sleeping place in some ferns. Suddenly there was a crashing noise and the boy saw a huge black bear thundering towards him.

"'I am hungry," cried the bear. "Give me something to eat."

From his knapsack the prince took out his second flask of wine and another loaf of bread.

"I must go now," said the bear, when he was done, "but when you are in any danger just wish yourself a bear and you will become one. One good turn deserves another, you know."

And the boy and the bear bade each other farewell.

On the third day, the prince once again walked until evening drew in, whereupon he threw himself down under a tree to rest. Then, he heard a great buzzing over his head.

"I am hungry," said a bee in a cross voice. "Give me something to eat."

The boy took his last loaf and flask out of his knapsack and laid them on the ground, and they had supper together.

"I must be off," said the bee when he was done. "But if you are in danger just wish yourself a bee and you will become one. One good turn deserves another, you know." And the bee departed.

Next day, the boy walked and walked until he entered a great city. He listened to the people gossiping and heard much talk about the king's only daughter, who was extremely beautiful.

The prince waited until everyone had gone to bed, then he wished himself a bee, and flew through the keyhole in the front door of the palace, up the great stairs, past the guards, and through the keyhole into the princess's chamber. Then he turned into a man again.

The princess, who was awake, was so startled that she couldn't even scream – she just sat up in bed gazing at him in silent terror.

"Do not be afraid," he said, "I shall not hurt you." And he began to praise her gardens, of which he had also heard the people speak, and the birds and flowers which she loved, till the princess's anger softened, and she answered him with gentle words. Indeed, she was so charmed by the prince that she vowed she would marry him, and confided to him that in three days her father would be off to the wars, leaving his sword in her room. If any man could find it and bring it to him he would receive her hand as a reward.

At this point the youth jumped up hastily saying: "Of course I shall ride with the king to the war, and if I do not return, take your violin every evening to the seashore and play on it."

Just as the princess had foretold, in three days the king set out for the war with a large following, and among them was the young prince. They had left the city many miles behind them, when the king suddenly discovered that he had forgotten his sword, and though each and every one of his attendants immediately offered theirs, he declared that he could fight with none but his own.

"The first man who brings it to me from my daughter's room," cried he, "shall not only have her to wife, but after my death shall reign in my stead."

At this the young prince, a Red Knight, and several more turned their horses to ride as fast as the wind back to the palace. But suddenly a better plan entered the prince's head, and, letting the others pass him, he wished himself a lion. Then on he bounded, uttering such dreadful roars that the horses were frightened and grew unmanageable, and he easily outstripped them, and soon reached the gates of the palace. Here he hastily changed himself into a bee, and flew straight into the princess's room, where he became a man again. She showed him where the sword hung concealed behind a curtain, and he

26

took it down, saying as he did so: "Be sure not to forget what you have promised to do."

The princess made no reply, but smiled sweetly, and slipping a golden ring from her finger she broke it in two and held half out to the prince, while the other half she put in her pocket. He kissed it, and ran down the stairs with the sword.

On his way back to the king, he stopped at a stream. Unbuckling the sword, he flung himself on the ground for a long drink. Unluckily, the mermaid happened at that moment to be floating on the water not very far off, and knew he was the boy who had been given her before he was born. So she floated gently up, seized his arm, and the waves closed over them both. Hardly had they disappeared, when the Red Knight came by – he could scarcely believe his eyes when he saw the king's sword on the bank. He fastened it to his belt and carried it off to the king.

When the war was over and the king and his

company returned, the princess saw to her great dismay that her true love was not among them. Moreover, the king told the poor princess that the Red Knight had won her fairly, and that the wedding would take place the very next day.

That evening, taking her violin under her arm, the princess crept down to the shore as she had promised.

"Listen!" said the mermaid to the prince, who was lying stretched on a bed of seaweeds at the bottom of the sea. "Listen! That is your old love playing."

"I hear nothing," answered the youth, who did not look happy. "Take me up higher, where the sounds can reach me."

So the mermaid took him on her shoulders and bore him right up to the surface. "Can you hear now?" she asked.

As soon as the prince thrust his head and shoulders into the air, he wished himself a bee, and flew straight into the pocket of the princess. The mermaid looked in vain for him all night, but he never came back, and never more did he gladden her eyes.

But the princess felt that something strange was about her, and returned quickly to the palace, where the young man at once resumed his own shape. Oh, what joy filled her heart at the sight of him! But there was no time to be lost, and she led him right into the great hall, where the king and his nobles were sitting feasting.

"Behold the gallant prince who fetched your sword by the powers of his great magic!" the princess announced. To prove it, the prince turned himself into a lion, and the Red Knight quaked with fear. Then the prince turned himself into a bear, and the Red Knight hid behind the princess. Then the prince turned himself into a bee, and stung the Red Knight repeatedly until he fled the palace, never to be seen again.

How the king and his nobles laughed with joy!

The princess drew out her half of the golden ring
and showed how it fitted the prince's half perfectly.
And next day, there was indeed a marriage feast for
the princess and her true prince.

The King of the Polar Bears

From *American Fairy Tales*
by L Frank Baum

THE KING of the Polar Bears lived among the icebergs in the deep cold of the far north country. He was old, monstrous big, and very wise. His body was thickly covered with long, white hair that glistened silver under the midnight sun. His claws were strong and sharp, that he might walk over the smooth ice or grasp and tear the fishes and seals upon which he fed.

The seals were afraid of him, but the gulls – both white and grey – loved him because he left the remnants of his feasts for them.

Often his subjects, the polar bears, came to him for advice when they were ill or in trouble, but they kept away from his hunting grounds, lest they might arouse his anger.

The wolves, who sometimes came as far north as the icebergs, whispered among themselves that the King of the Polar Bears was a magician. For no earthly thing seemed able to harm him – he never failed to secure plenty of food, and he grew bigger and stronger day by day.

Yet the time came when this monarch of the north met man, and his wisdom failed him.

He came out of his cave among the icebergs one day and saw a boat moving through a strip of water uncovered by the shifting of the summer ice. In the boat were men.

The great bear had never seen such creatures before, and advanced sniffing the strange scent with aroused curiosity.

When the king came near the water's edge a man

stood up in the boat and
with a queer instrument
made a loud 'Bang!'
The polar bear felt a
shock, his brain became
numb, his thoughts deserted
him, his great limbs shook
and gave way beneath him
and his body fell heavily
upon the hard ice.

That was all he
remembered for a time.

When he awoke he was smarting with pain on
every inch of his huge bulk, for the men had cut
away his hide with its glorious white hair and
carried it with them to a distant ship.

Above him circled thousands of his friends, the
gulls, wondering if their benefactor were really dead
and it was proper to eat him. But when they saw
him raise his head and groan and tremble they knew

he still lived, and one of them said to his comrades: "The wolves were right. The king is a great magician, for even men cannot kill him. But he suffers greatly for lack of covering. Let us repay his kindness to us by each giving him as many feathers as we can spare."

One after another they plucked with their beaks the softest feathers from under their wings, and, flying down, dropped them gently upon his body.

Then they called to him in a chorus: "Our feathers are as soft and beautiful as your own shaggy hair. They will guard you from the cold winds and warm you while you sleep."

And the King of the Polar Bears had courage to bear his pain and lived and was strong again.

The rest of that summer and all through the six months of night the king left his icy cavern only to fish or catch seals for food. He felt no shame at his feathery covering, but it was still strange to him, and he avoided meeting any of his brother bears.

When the moon fell away from the sky and the sun came to make the icebergs glitter with the gorgeous tintings of the rainbow, two of the polar bears arrived at the king's cavern to ask his advice about the hunting season. But when they saw his great body covered with feathers instead of hair they began to laugh, and one said: "Our mighty king has become a bird! Who ever before heard of a feathered polar bear?"

Then the king gave way to wrath. He advanced upon them with deep growls and stately tread and with one blow of his monstrous paw stretched the mocker lifeless at his feet.

The other ran away to his fellows and carried the news of the king's strange appearance. The result was a meeting of all the polar bears upon a broad field of ice, where they talked gravely of the remarkable change that had come upon their monarch.

"He is, in reality, no longer a bear," said one, "nor

can he justly be called a bird. But he is half bird and half bear, and so unfit to remain our king."

"I will fight him," growled a particularly huge bear. " I — Woof — the strongest of our race! I will be King of the Polar Bears instead."

The others nodded agreement, and dispatched a messenger to the king to say he must fight the great Woof and beat him, if he would stay ruler.

When the king heard this he visited his friends, the gulls, and told them of the coming battle. "I shall conquer," he said, proudly. "Yet my people are in the right, for only a hairy one like themselves can hope to command their obedience."

The queen gull said: "I met an eagle yesterday, who had flown over a big city of men. The eagle told me he had seen a monstrous polar bear skin thrown over the back of a carriage that rolled along the street. That skin must have been yours, oh king, and if you wish I will send one hundred of my gulls to the city to bring it back to you."

"Let them go!" said the king, gruffly. And the hundred gulls were soon flying rapidly southward.

For three days they flew straight as an arrow, until they came to scattered houses, to villages, and to cities. Then their search began.

The gulls were brave, cunning and wise. Upon the fourth day they reached the great metropolis, and hovered over the streets until a carriage rolled along with a great white bear robe thrown over the back seat. Then the birds swooped down and, seizing the skin in their beaks, flew quickly away.

They were late. The king's great battle was upon the seventh day, and they must fly swiftly to reach the Polar regions by that time.

Meanwhile the bird-bear was preparing for his fight. He sharpened his claws in the small crevasses of the ice. He caught a seal and tested his big yellow teeth by crunching its bones between them. And the queen gull set her band to pluming the king bear's feathers until they lay smoothly upon his body.

But every day they cast anxious glances into the southern sky, watching for the hundred gulls to bring back the king's own skin.

The seventh day came, and all the polar bears in that region gathered around the king's cavern. Among them was Woof, confident of his success.

"The bird-bear's feathers will fly fast enough when I get my claws upon him!" he boasted, and the others laughed and encouraged him.

The king was sad at not having recovered his skin, but he resolved to fight bravely without it. He advanced from his cavern with a kingly bearing, and when he faced his enemy he gave so terrible a growl that Woof's heart stopped beating for a moment, and he began to realise that a fight with the wise and mighty king of his race was no laughing matter.

After exchanging a few heavy blows with his foe Woof's courage returned, and he decided to dishearten his adversary by bluster.

"Come nearer, bird-bear!" he cried, "So that I may pluck your plumage!"

Filled with rage, the king ruffled his feathers till he seemed to be twice his actual size. He struck Woof a blow which cracked his skull like an egg-shell and he fell prone upon the ground.

While the assembled bears stood looking with fear and wonder at their fallen champion the sky became darkened.

One hundred gulls flew down from above and dropped upon the king's body a skin covered with pure white hair that glittered in the sun like silver.

And behold! The bears saw before them the well-known form of their wise and respected master, and with one accord they bowed their shaggy heads in homage to the mighty King of the Polar Bears.

The Egg

An extract from *The Phoenix and the Carpet*
by E Nesbit

*Five children — Cyril, Anthea, Robert, Jane, and the youngest, 'the Lamb',
are in their playroom. Their mother recently bought a new carpet for the room.
It was delivered rolled up, and when the children laid it out, they found inside a
strange golden egg, which they have placed on the mantelpiece…*

I WISH they taught magic at school," Jane sighed. "I
believe if we could do a little magic it might make
something happen."

"I wonder how you begin?" Robert looked round
the room, but he got no ideas from the faded green
curtains, or the drab Venetian blinds, or the worn
brown oil-cloth on the floor. Even the new carpet
suggested nothing, though its pattern was a very
wonderful one, and always seemed as though it were

just going to make you think of something.

"I could begin right enough," said Anthea, "I've read about it. But I believe it's wrong in the Bible."

"It's only wrong in the Bible because people might use it to hurt other people. We don't want to hurt anybody, and what's more, we jolly well couldn't if we tried. Let's get the *Ingoldsby Legends*. There's a thing about Abra-cadabra there," said Cyril, yawning.

"I'll get *Ingoldsby*," said Anthea. "You turn up the hearthrug."

So they traced strange figures on the linoleum, where the hearthrug had kept it clean. They traced them with chalk that Robert had nicked from the top of the mathematical master's desk at school. And they chanted all the gloomiest songs they could think of. And, of course, nothing happened.

So then Anthea said, "I'm sure a magic fire ought to be made of sweet-smelling wood, and have magic gums and essences and things in it."

"I don't know any sweet-smelling wood, except

cedar," said Robert, "but I've got some ends of cedar-wood lead pencil."

So they burned the ends of lead pencil. And still nothing happened.

"Let's burn some of the eucalyptus oil we have for our colds," said Anthea.

And they did. It certainly smelled very strong. And they burned lumps of camphor out of the big chest. It was very bright, and made lots of horrid black smoke, which looked very magical indeed. But still nothing happened. Then they got some clean tea-cloths from the dresser drawer in the kitchen, and waved them over the magic chalk-tracings, and sang 'The Hymn of the Moravian Nuns at Bethlehem', which is very impressive. And still nothing happened. So they waved more and more wildly, and then Robert's tea-cloth accidentally caught the golden egg and whisked it off the mantelpiece, and it fell into the fender and rolled under the grate.

"Oh, crikey!" said more than one voice.

And everyone instantly fell down flat on their fronts to look under the grate, and there lay the egg, glowing in a nest of hot ashes.

"It's not smashed, anyhow," said Robert, and he put his hand under the grate and picked up the egg. But the egg was much hotter than anyone would have believed it could possibly get in such a short time, and Robert had to drop it with a cry of "Bother!" It fell on the top bar of the grate, and then bounced right into the glowing red-hot heart of the fire.

"The tongs!" cried Anthea. But, alas, no one could remember where they were. Everyone had forgotten that the tongs had last been used to fish up the doll's teapot from the bottom of the water-butt, where the Lamb had dropped it. So the nursery tongs were resting between the water-butt and the dustbin.

"Never mind," said Robert, "we'll get it out with the poker and the shovel."

"Oh, stop," cried Anthea. "Look at it! Quick, look! Look! Look! I do believe something IS going to happen!"

For the egg was now red-hot, and inside it something was moving. Next moment there was a soft cracking sound, the egg burst in two, and out of it came a flame-coloured bird.

It rested a
moment among
the flames, and as
it rested there the
four children could
see it growing bigger and
bigger under their eyes.

Every mouth was a-gape,
every eye a-goggle.

The bird rose in its nest of
fire, stretched its wings, and flew
out into the room. It flew round and
round, and then round again, and where it
passed the air was warm. Then it perched on the
fender. The children looked at each other. Then
Cyril put out a hand towards the bird. It put
its head on one side and looked up at him,
just as you may have seen a parrot do when
it is getting ready to speak, so that the
children were hardly astonished

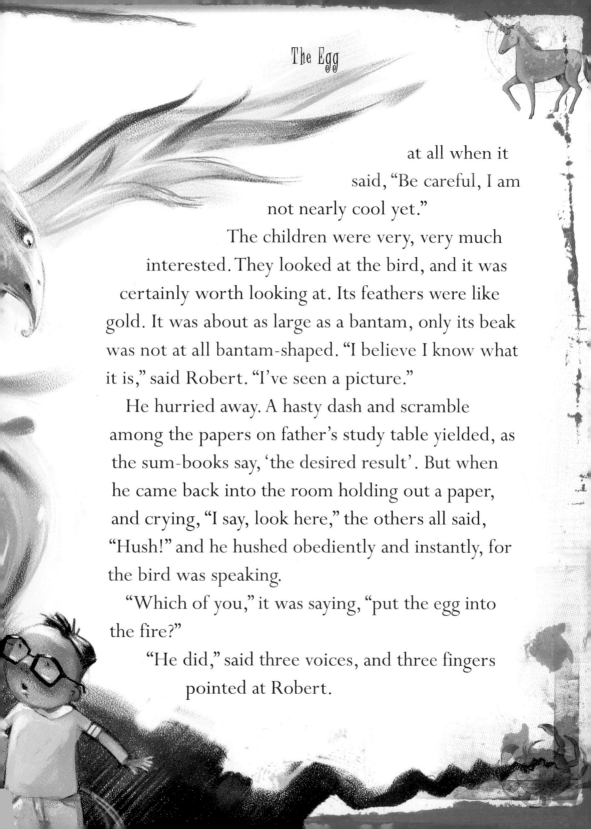

at all when it said, "Be careful, I am not nearly cool yet."

The children were very, very much interested. They looked at the bird, and it was certainly worth looking at. Its feathers were like gold. It was about as large as a bantam, only its beak was not at all bantam-shaped. "I believe I know what it is," said Robert. "I've seen a picture."

He hurried away. A hasty dash and scramble among the papers on father's study table yielded, as the sum-books say, 'the desired result'. But when he came back into the room holding out a paper, and crying, "I say, look here," the others all said, "Hush!" and he hushed obediently and instantly, for the bird was speaking.

"Which of you," it was saying, "put the egg into the fire?"

"He did," said three voices, and three fingers pointed at Robert.

The bird bowed – at least, it was more like that than anything else.

"I am your grateful debtor," it said with a high-bred air.

The children were all choking with wonder and curiosity – all except Robert. He held the paper in his hand, and he KNEW. He said so. He said:

"I know who you are."

And he opened and displayed a printed paper, at the head of which was a little picture of a bird sitting in a nest of flames.

"You are the Phoenix," said Robert, and the bird was quite pleased.

The Emperor's Nightingale

From *Tales of Wonder Every Child Should Know*
by Kate Douglas Wiggin and
Nora Archibald Smith

THE EMPEROR OF CHINA lived in the most beautiful palace in the world, surrounded by such a beautiful, large garden that the gardener himself did not quite know where it ended. If you kept on far enough, you came to a mighty forest which stretched down so close to the sea that the poor fishermen in their boats could sail under the overhanging branches.

In one of these boughs a nightingale lived, and so beautiful was its song that the sailors would stop to listen on their way out to spread their nets.

"Heavens! How gloriously that bird sings!" they would exclaim.

Travellers came from all over the world to see the emperor's city and his palace and garden, but when they heard the nightingale, they would say: "That is most beautiful of all." And when the travellers reached their homes again, they told all their friends of the wonderful things they had seen and heard, and wise people wrote books, in which they did not forget to tell of the nightingale. Even the poets wrote verses about this nightingale that lived in the wood by the sea.

And then, one by one, the books travelled over the world, until some at last reached the hands of the emperor, who sat in his golden chair and read them, nodding his head with pleasure, for he was charmed with the beautiful descriptions of his city and castle and garden. Then he read the words: 'The nightingale is the most lovely thing of all!'

"What is this?" he said. "The nightingale!

I have never heard of such a bird, yet there seems to be one in my empire – and in my own garden! Imagine learning of such a thing for the first time from a book!"

Thereupon he summoned his chamberlain to find the bird.

"I must hear the nightingale," the emperor demanded. "I command it to perform for me this evening."

The chamberlain raced up and down stairs and through all the corridors again, accompanied by half the court, all searching for the nightingale.

At length they came to the kitchen, where a poor little scullery-maid at once exclaimed: "Why, yes, I know it well – and it sings beautifully!"

So the girl led the chamberlain and all the court into the wood.

"Listen!" said the girl. "There it sits up in the branches," and she pointed to a tiny bird clinging to a spray of thorn.

"I should never have believed it would look like that," exclaimed the chamberlain. "It looks so simple and so pale, it must be frightened at the sight of so many grand people."

"Dear nightingale," called the little girl, "our most noble emperor desires you to sing to him."

"Oh, certainly, with pleasure," promised the nightingale, and accompanied everyone back through the wood.

When the little bird began to sing in the splendid palace, he sang so gloriously that the emperor's eyes filled with tears which overflowed and ran down his cheeks. The emperor was so delighted that he commanded the nightingale to live at court, in its own cage, with permission to fly out twice a day, and once during the night. On these trips it was accompanied by twelve servants, each of whom held a silken cord attached to its leg, so that really there could not be the slightest pleasure for it in such a flight. As for the city, wherever you went, you met people talking of the wonderful bird, and news of it spread even further than before.

One day a gift arrived at the palace, addressed to the emperor, with the words, "A nightingale from the Emperor of Japan," written on the outside of the casket.

A wonderful work of art lay within, a clockwork nightingale, encrusted in diamonds and rubies and pearls, and fashioned in the shape of a real bird. When it had been wound up it sang, and its glittering tail moved up and down in time to the notes. A ribbon hung around its neck, and on it these words were written: "The Emperor of Japan's nightingale is nothing compared to that of the Emperor of China."

"How perfect!" everyone cried, and the emperor immediately bestowed the title of the King's Imperial Nightingale Bringer on the courier who had brought the bird.

"Now we must hear them sing a duet together. How beautiful it will sound!" they all said. But it did not sound so well as they had expected, for the real bird sang in a natural way, and just whatever came into its little throat, and the artificial bird could only sing a waltz.

So then the new one had to sing by itself and obtained quite as much applause as the real one had done. Besides, it looked so much handsomer, glittering and gleaming like bracelets and breast-pins.

Over and over again, for quite thirty-three times, it sang the same tune and yet was not tired. The courtiers would have liked to hear it again even, only the emperor said "No, it's the real bird's turn now, let us ask it to sing."

But where was the nightingale? Not a soul had

seen it fly out of the open window back to its own green woods.

"Well, well! Whatever has become of it?" exclaimed the emperor. And all the courtiers united in saying it was a most ungrateful creature.

"After all," they said, "we still have the better bird," and with that the new one had to sing his song for the thirty-fourth time.

And so the real nightingale was sent into exile, and the imitation one slept on a satin cushion very close to the emperor's bed. All the jewels and precious stones that had been showered on it as presents were arranged around the edge of the cushion, and it was given the title of the Emperor's Own Court Singer.

A whole year passed by in this fashion, and at last the emperor and his court and all the Chinese people knew every turn and trill of the nightingale's song by heart.

One evening the emperor lay in his bed listening

to the bird, which was singing its very best. Suddenly it stopped with a jerk, and bang! Something had snapped in its inside, and all its wheels ran down with a whirr, and then there was a dead silence.

The emperor sprang out of bed and sent for the court physician, but he could do nothing. Then a watchmaker was fetched, and after he had talked a lot, and examined the inside a great deal, he was able to put it in something like working order again.

"You must not use it too much," he said, "it is nearly worn out, and one can never put in fresh works again and be sure of the music being as good as before."

At this there was great mourning all over the country, for the imitation bird must only be allowed to sing once a year in future, and even that might prove too much for it.

After five years had passed the emperor fell very ill. All the people felt sad, for they were really extremely fond of him, and now it was said he could not possibly live.

White and cold the old emperor lay in his great tall bed, and all the courtiers thought he was dead, and ran away to greet their new king. But the emperor was yet alive – though barely. He lay still upon the magnificent bed, with its heavy velvet draperies and gorgeous golden tassels. High up, through the open window, the moon shone in upon him and the imitation nightingale lay in its casket by the bed.

A terrible weight seemed pressing on the emperor's chest, and he opened his eyes to see Death himself sitting there before him, whispering to him to come.

"Music! I want music! So I cannot hear the call of Death," gasped the emperor. But the imitation bird was silent, for until someone wound it up, it could not sing, and there was no one to do it. And Death still sat gazing at him with hollow, hungry eyes.

Suddenly a silvery note floated in at the open window. It was the voice of the real nightingale as it sat upon a bough outside. It had heard the emperor was ill, and had come back to comfort him and fill him with hope.

And as its song gained strength and rose and fell in delicious trills, the warm life blood began to flow anew in the emperor's veins, and Death was filled with a yearning to be in his own garden, and passed like a grey mist out of the open window.

"Deep, deep thanks I give you," said the emperor. "Merciful little bird! It was you I banished from my presence and my kingdom. And yet, you have charmed Death from my heart! You must never leave me – but you shall only sing when you desire, and I will break the artificial bird into a million pieces."

"No, spare it," said the nightingale. "It did its best as long as it was able, so keep it as before. I cannot build my nest within the castle, but I will often

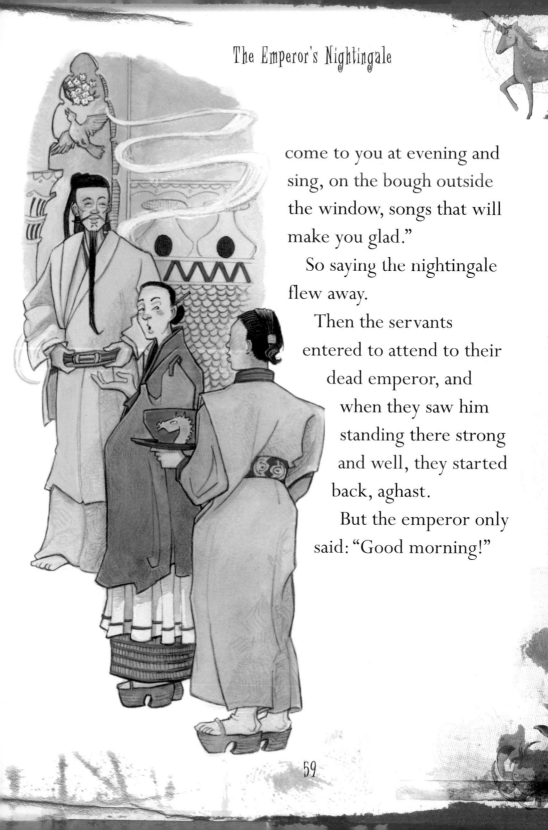

come to you at evening and sing, on the bough outside the window, songs that will make you glad."

So saying the nightingale flew away.

Then the servants entered to attend to their dead emperor, and when they saw him standing there strong and well, they started back, aghast.

But the emperor only said: "Good morning!"

The Unicorn

From *Tales of Wonder Every Child Should Know*
by Kate Douglas Wiggin and
Nora Archibald Smith

FRITZ, FRANZ, AND HANS were charcoal-burners who
lived with their mother in the depths of a forest.
Once upon a time they had been well off, but their
father had died and all their money had been used
up. Now their house was a poor hut and they
scarcely had enough food for barely one meal a day.
Fritz and Franz were, unfortunately, selfish,
unpleasant lads, but Hans always had a cheerful
smile or word, and did all in his power to help his
mother to keep in good spirits.

One day, at dinner time, they were startled by a

knock at the door. Fritz growled out, in his usual surly tone, "Come in." The door opened, and a huntsman came in, who had been shooting game in the forest.

"Good morning, good friends," he said, in a cheerful tone. "Could you provide me with a cup of water and a mouthful of something to eat? I have forgotten to bring anything with me, and am ravenously hungry, and far from home."

Fritz and Franz threw a scowling glance from under their eyebrows and continued munching at their hunks of bread. Hans, however, was more polite. He invited the visitor to sit down, then filled a cup from a spring of delicious, cool water, which rose near the hut. He handed his own coarse crust to the stranger, saying he was sorry that there was nothing better to offer him.

"Thank you," said the stranger, courteously. He made short work of them, rolling the crumbs which fell from the crust into a hard pellet. Then he rose to go. "Well, I thank you heartily for your hospitality," said the huntsman, "now I will give you a word of advice. One of you lads should go and seek the sparkling golden water, which turns everything it touches into gold."

Fritz and Franz pricked up their ears at this, and both at once demanded where this sparkling golden water was to be found. The stranger replied: "The sparkling golden water is to be found in the forest of dead trees, on the farther side of those blue mountains in the far distance." Then, bowing to his hosts, he stepped toward the door.

Hans, opened it for him and, obeying a sign from the stranger, followed him a little way from the hut. Then the stranger, taking from his pocket the little black bread pellet, said, "Keep this pellet carefully, and when you seek the sparkling golden water, as I know you will, don't forget to bring it with you." So saying, the stranger waved his hand to Hans, and, plunging into the thicket, disappeared.

Hans slipped the pellet into his pocket and re-entered the hut, where he found his brothers in loud dispute about the sparkling golden water – for each wanted to make a fortune for themselves. At last it was decided, after a great deal of squabbling, that Fritz as the eldest should go in search first, and accordingly next day he set out. As he had no money he was forced to beg at the doors of the cottages and farmhouses which he passed, for food and shelter for the night. Eventually he found himself approaching a vast forest of enormous trees, which lifted leafless, sapless branches to the sky, and every breath of wind rattled them together like the bones of a skeleton. Suddenly there was a terrible roaring sound and out of the forest rushed a huge unicorn with a spiral golden horn on his forehead.

"What seek you here?" asked the unicorn, in a voice of thunder.

Fritz stammered out that he sought the sparkling golden water.

The unicorn stamped furiously
on the ground with his right forefoot.
"Say this instant," he cried, "what it is
that you want with the sparkling golden
water!"

"I want to get money to buy land and
become a count," Fritz was just able to
gasp out.

The unicorn said nothing – he simply lowered
his head, and with his golden horn tossed
Fritz three hundred and forty-five
feet in the air. Up went Fritz like
a sky-rocket, and down he
came, through the branches of
one of the trees until he
reached the point where they
joined the trunk. The tree was
hollow here, and Fritz tumbled down
to the bottom of the trunk and found
himself a prisoner. While he was feeling his arms

64

and legs, to find out if any bones were broken or not, he had the satisfaction of hearing the unicorn, as he trotted back into the forest, muttering: "So much for you and your countship!"

Franz, Hans, and their mother waited and waited for Fritz to come back. Six weeks passed, and two months, and three months, and no Fritz. Then Franz's patience came to an end. "I won't wait here starving any longer," said he. "Fritz has forgotten all about us. I'll get the sparkling golden water and become Burgomaster." So off he set, following the same road as Fritz.

Eventually, Franz, very hungry and sulky, reached the verge of the forest of dead trees. Out came the unicorn and asked his business. On

Franz replying that he wanted the sparkling golden
water to buy the house and post of Burgomaster, the
unicorn tossed him into the air, and he tumbled into
the same tree as Fritz. Then the unicorn trotted
back into the forest, muttering, for Franz's benefit:
"So much for you and your Burgomastership!"

The months passed by, but no news came to Hans
and his mother of Fritz and Franz. Eventually there
was nothing for it but to leave his mother in the care
of a kindly neighbour and go and see if he could find
out what had become of them. By making enquiries
Hans easily found the road which they had taken. At
last he, too, found himself on the verge of the forest
of dead trees and face to face with the golden-
horned unicorn. But in reply to the usual question,
given in the usual tone of thunder, Hans replied,
coolly, "I seek my brothers, Fritz and Franz."

"They are where you will never find them," said
the unicorn, "so go home again."

"If I cannot find my brothers," said Hans, firmly,

"I will not go home without the sparkling golden water."

"What do you want with the sparkling golden water, which is in my charge?" asked the unicorn, in his terrible voice.

"I want to buy food and wine and comforts for my mother, who is very ill," answered Hans, undaunted. But his eyes filled with tears as he thought of his mother.

The unicorn spoke more gently.

"Have you," he asked, "the crystal ball? Because without it I cannot allow you to pass to the sparkling golden water."

"The crystal ball!" echoed Hans. "I never heard of such a thing."

"That's a pity," said the unicorn, gravely. "I'm afraid you will have to go home without the water. But, stay, feel in your pockets. You may have had the ball, and put it somewhere, and have forgotten it."

"No," Hans said to the unicorn, "I have nothing in

my pocket, except this pellet," and he was about to throw it away when the unicorn called out to him to stop.

"Why," the unicorn went on, "this is the crystal ball – look!"

Hans did look, and sure enough he found in his hand a tiny globe of crystal.

"Your possession of the crystal ball makes me your servant," declared the unicorn. "It is my duty to carry you to the fountain of sparkling golden water, if you wish to go."

So Hans clambered onto the unicorn's back and

68

grasped his mane. Then the unicorn gave a bound that carried him over the tops of the highest trees. Three such bounds did he take, and then he paused and said to Hans, "Now you may open your eyes." Hans found himself in a desolate, rocky valley, in the middle of which there sprang up a fountain of water, which sparked with such intense brilliancy that Hans was unable at first to look upon it.

"There, master," said the unicorn, turning his head, "this is the fountain of sparkling golden water. Dismount, and fill your flask. But take care that you do not allow your hand to touch the water. If it does it will be turned into gold, and will never become flesh and blood again."

Hans slipped quickly from his seat and, flask in hand, approached the fountain. He tried to be as careful as he possibly could be when filling the flask, but, despite his greatest care, the top joint of his little finger briefly touched the golden water, and in an instant it became gold. However, he had his flask full of sparkling golden water, the flask itself was now, of course, golden, and he felt that the top joint of his little finger was really a small price to pay for all this.

"Where now, master?" said the unicorn when Hans got back.

"Take me to my brothers!" Hans asked. And the unicorn sprang away.

In the blink of an eye they were back in the dead forest. The unicorn led Hans to the tree in which his brothers were imprisoned, where they had been surviving on beetles, worms and rainwater. With one or two powerful blows with his horn, the unicorn made a hole large enough for the unhappy prisoners to creep out. Two more sheepish, miserable wretches than those half-starved brothers of his, Hans had never seen. They fell at his feet and thanked him again and again for delivering them, and they promised never to do anything unkind or selfish again.

So did the brothers keep their promise? And did the sparkling golden water make Hans and his mother wealthy and happy? Well, that's another story...

Dapplegrim

From *Tales of Wonder Every Child Should Know*
by Kate Douglas Wiggin and
Nora Archibald Smith

ONCE ON A TIME there was a rich couple who had
twelve sons. When the youngest was grown up,
he said he wouldn't stay any longer at home, but be
off into the world to try his luck.

When he had walked a good bit, he came to a
king's palace, where he asked for a place, and got it.
Now, the king's daughter had been carried off into
the hill by a troll. The king had no other children, so
he and all his land were in great grief and sorrow,
and the king gave his word that anyone who could
set her free should have the princess and half the

kingdom. But there was no one who could do it, though many tried.

When the lad had been there a year or so, he longed to go home again, and back he went, but his father and mother were dead, and his brothers had shared everything between them. All that was left were twelve old mares up on the hill.

However, the lad was quite content. He thanked his brothers, and went to where the twelve mares were out at grass. One of them had a big dapple-grey foal, which was so sleek that the sun shone from its coat.

"A fine fellow you are, my little foal," said the lad.

"Yes," said the foal, "but you wait for another year to pass, and then see how big and sleek I'll be."

When the lad came back the following year, the foal had indeed grown. He had become such a big horse that he had to lie down before the lad could mount upon him — and it was hard work to climb up even then.

When he came riding home to his brothers, they all clapped their hands and shouted, for such a horse they had never heard of or seen before. The lad said they could keep the twelve mares on the hill, if they would get him the best shoes they could find for his horse, and the grandest saddle and bridle. At the thought of more such splendid foals, the brothers gladly agreed. So the lad got such strong shoes under his horse that the stones flew high aloft as he rode away across the hills, and he had a golden

saddle and a golden bridle, which gleamed and
glistened a long way off.

When the lad and Dapplegrim, for that was the
horse's name, reached the palace, the king stared
and stared. "Nay," said he, "such a man and such a
horse I never saw in all my life." The king was
delighted to welcome the extraordinary lad and his
steed back into his household. In fact, he gave him as
much meadow-hay and oats as his horse could cram,
and all the other knights had to lead
their horses out of the stable that
Dapplegrim might have it all
to himself.

It wasn't long before all the others in the king's household began to be jealous of the lad, and there was no end to the bad things they would have done to him, if they had only dared. At last they thought of telling the king that he had been boasting he was man enough to set the king's daughter free – whom the troll had long since carried away into the hill – if he only chose. The king called the lad before him, and said he had heard what the lad had said, so now he must go and do it. If he succeeded, the king's daughter and half the kingdom should be his, and that promise would be faithfully kept. If he failed, he should be killed.

The lad kept on saying he never said any such thing, but it was no good – the king wouldn't even listen to him. And so the end of it was that he was forced to say he'd go and try.

So he went into the stable, down in the mouth and heavy-hearted, and told Dapplegrim why he was in such doleful dumps.

"This might be done, perhaps," said Dapplegrim. "But you must first have me well shod. You must go and ask for ten pounds of iron and twelve pounds of steel for the shoes, and one smith to hammer and another to hold."

Yes, the lad did that, and got for answer, "Yes." He got both the iron and the steel, and the smith, and so Dapplegrim was shod very well, and off went the lad from the courtyard in a cloud of dust.

But when he came to the hill into which the princess had been carried, the difficulty was how to get up the steep wall of rock where the troll's cave was in which the princess had been hidden. For you must know the hill stood straight up and down right on end, as upright as a house wall, and as smooth as a sheet of glass.

The first time the lad went at it he got a little way up, but then Dapplegrim's forelegs slipped, and down they went, with a sound that crashed like thunder on the hill.

The second time he rode at it he got some way further up, but then one foreleg slipped, and down they went with a sound like a landslip.

But the third time Dapple said: "Now we must show our mettle," and went at it again till the stones flew heaven-high about them, and so they got up.

Then the lad rode right into the cave at full speed, and caught up the princess, and threw her over his saddle-bow, and out and down again before the troll had time even to get on his legs.

"Thanks you shall have for freeing my princess," said the king to the lad, when he brought the princess into the hall and made his bow.

"She ought to be mine as well as yours, for you're a word-fast man, I hope," said the lad.

"Ay, ay!" said the king. "But first we'll have one trial more, just to see whether you're fated to have her. First, she shall hide herself twice, and then you shall hide yourself twice. If you can find out her hiding-place, and she can't find out yours, why, then, you're fated to have her, and so you shall have her."

"That's not in the bargain, either," said the lad, "but we must try, since it must be so." And so the princess went off to hide herself first.

So she turned herself into a duck, and lay swimming on a pond that was close to the palace. But the lad only ran down to the stable, and asked Dapplegrim what she had done with herself.

"Oh, you only need take your gun," said Dapplegrim, "and go down to the brink of the pond, and aim at the duck which lies swimming about there, and she'll soon show herself."

So the lad snatched his gun and ran off to the pond. "I'll just take a pop at this duck," he said, and began to aim at it.

"Nay, nay, dear friend, don't shoot. It's I," said the princess.

So he found her once.

The second time the princess turned herself into

a loaf of bread, and laid herself on the table amongst four other loaves, and so like was she to the others, that no one could say which was which.

But the lad went again down to the stable to Dapplegrim, and said how the princess had hidden herself again, and he couldn't tell at all what had become of her.

"Oh, just take and sharpen a good bread-knife," said Dapplegrim, "and do as if you were going to cut in two the third loaf on the left hand of those four loaves which are lying on the dresser in the king's kitchen, and you'll find her soon enough."

Yes, the lad was down in the kitchen in no time, and began to sharpen the biggest bread-knife he could lay his hands on. Then he caught hold of the third loaf on the left hand, and put the knife to it, as though he were going to cut it in two.

"I'll just have a slice off this loaf," he said.

"Nay, dear friend," said the princess, "don't cut. It's I."

So he found her twice.

Then he was to go and hide, but he and Dapplegrim had settled it so well beforehand that it wasn't easy to find him. First he turned himself into a fly, and hid himself in Dapplegrim's left nostril, and the princess went about hunting for him everywhere, high and low. At last she wanted to go into Dapplegrim's stall, but he began to bite and kick, so that she daren't go near him, and so she couldn't find the lad.

"Well," she said, "since I cannot find you, you must show where you are yourself." In a trice the lad stood there on the stable floor.

The second time Dapplegrim told him just what to do. The lad turned himself into a clod of earth, and stuck himself between Dapple's hoof and shoe on the near forefoot. So the princess hunted up and down, out and in, everywhere. At last she came into the stable, and wanted to go into Dapplegrim's loose box. This time he let her come up to him, and she pried high and low, but under his heels she couldn't come, for he stood firm as a rock on his feet, and so she couldn't find the lad.

"Well, you must just show yourself, for I'm sure I can't find you," said the princess, and as she spoke the lad stood by her side on the stable floor.

"Now you are mine indeed," said the lad, "for now you can see I'm fated to have you." This he said both to the father and daughter.

"Yes, it does seem that it is so fated," said the king, "and so it must be."

Then everything was made ready for the wedding

with great splendour and promptitude, and the lad
and the princess got on Dapplegrim's back, and
then, as you may guess, they were not long on their
way to church.

The Butterfly that Stamped

From the *Just So* stories
by Rudyard Kipling

SULEIMAN-BIN-DAOUD was wise. He understood what the beasts said, what the birds said, what the fishes said, and what the insects said. He understood what the rocks said deep under the earth when they bowed in towards each other and groaned, and he understood what the trees said when they rustled in the morning.

Suleiman-bin-Daoud was strong. Upon the third finger of the right hand he wore a ring. When he turned it once, magical creatures called Djinns came out of the earth to do whatever he told them. When he turned it twice, Fairies came down from the sky to do whatever he told them. When he turned it three times, the very great angel Azrael of the Sword came and told him the news of the three worlds, Above – Below – and Here.

Suleiman-bin-Daoud married ever so many wives. He married nine hundred and ninety-nine wives, besides his Head Queen, the Most Beautiful Balkis. They all lived in a great golden palace in the middle of a lovely garden with fountains.

Some of the wives were nice, but some were simply horrid, and the horrid ones quarrelled with the nice ones and made them horrid too, and then they would all quarrel with Suleiman-bin-Daoud, and that was horrid for him. But Balkis the Most Beautiful never quarrelled with Suleiman-bin-Daoud. She loved him too much. She sat in her rooms in the Golden Palace, or walked in the Palace garden, and was truly sorry for him.

Whenever the nine hundred and ninety-nine

wives quarrelled too much, Suleiman-bin-Daoud walked by himself in one part of the beautiful Palace gardens. One day, when they had quarrelled for three weeks, Suleiman-bin-Daoud went out for peace and quiet, and among the orange trees he met Balkis the Most Beautiful, very sorrowful because Suleiman-bin-Daoud was so worried. And she said to him, "O my Lord and Light of my Eyes, turn the ring upon your finger and show these Queens of Egypt and Mesopotamia and Persia and China that you are the great and terrible King."

But Suleiman-bin-Daoud shook his head and said, "I must not use my power for the purpose of showing off. I shall continue to endure my fate."

So he went on between the lilies and the roses and the heavy-scented ginger-plants that grew in the garden, till he came to a great camphor-tree. But Balkis hid among the tall irises and the spotted bamboos behind the camphor-tree, so as to be near her own true love.

Presently two Butterflies flew under the tree, quarrelling. Suleiman-bin-Daoud heard one say to the other, "How dare you talk to me like this! Don't you know that if I stamped with my foot all Suleiman-bin-Daoud's Palace and this garden here would immediately vanish in a clap of thunder."

Then Suleiman-bin-Daoud forgot his nine hundred and ninety-nine bothersome wives, and laughed, till the camphor-tree shook. And he held out his finger and said, "Little man, come here."

The Butterfly was dreadfully frightened, but he managed to fly up to the hand of Suleiman-bin-Daoud, and clung there, fanning himself.

Suleiman-bin-Daoud bent his head and whispered very softly, "Little man, what made you tell that awful fib to your wife? For doubtless she is your wife."

The Butterfly picked up his courage and said, "O King, you know what wives are like. She has been quarrelling with me all the morning. I said that to quiet her."

And Suleiman-bin-Daoud said, "May it quiet her. Go back to your wife, little brother, and let me hear what you say."

Back flew the Butterfly to his wife, who was all of a twitter behind a leaf, and she said, "And what did he say? Oh, what did he say?"

"Well," said the Butterfly, fanning himself most importantly, "between you and me, my dear, he asked me not to stamp, and I promised I wouldn't."

"Gracious!" said his wife, and sat quite quiet, but Suleiman-bin-Daoud laughed till the tears ran down his face at the impudence of the bad little Butterfly.

Balkis the Most Beautiful stood up behind the tree and smiled to herself, for she had heard all this talk. She thought, 'Maybe I can yet save my Lord from these quarrelsome Queens,' and she held out her finger and whispered softly to the Butterfly's Wife, "Little woman, come here." Up flew the Butterfly's Wife, very frightened, and clung to Balkis's white hand. Balkis bent her beautiful head down and whispered, "Little woman, do you believe what your husband has just said?"

The Butterfly's Wife picked up her courage and said, "O Queen, you know what men-folk are like. They get angry over nothing at all and they never mean half they say. If it pleases my husband to believe that I believe he can make Suleiman-bin-Daoud's Palace disappear by stamping his foot, I'm sure I don't care. He'll forget all about it tomorrow."

"Little sister," said Balkis, "you are quite right, but next time he begins to boast, take him at his word.

Ask him to stamp, and see what will happen. He'll be very much ashamed."

Away flew the Butterfly's Wife to her husband, and in five minutes they were quarrelling worse than ever.

"Remember!" said the Butterfly. "Remember what I can do if I stamp my foot."

"I dare you to do it," said his wife. "Stamp! Stamp! Stamp!"

The Butterfly, very hot and puffy, came whirling back to the King and said, "She wants me to stamp! You know nothing will happen, and she'll never again believe a word I say!'

"No, little brother," said Suleiman-bin-Daoud, who was laughing most joyously. And he turned the ring on his finger and, lo and behold, four huge Djinns came out of the earth!

"Slaves," said Suleiman-bin-Daoud, "when this gentleman on my finger stamps his left front forefoot you will make my Palace and these gardens disappear in a clap of thunder. When he stamps again you will bring them back carefully."

Away flew the Butterfly to his wife, who was crying, "I dare you to do it! Stamp now!"

Balkis saw the four vast Djinns stoop down to the four corners of the gardens with the Palace in the middle, and she clapped her hands softly and said, "At last Suleiman-bin-Daoud will do for the sake of a Butterfly what he ought to have done long ago for his own sake, and the quarrelsome Queens will be frightened!"

The butterfly stamped. The Djinns jerked the Palace and the gardens a thousand miles into the air, there was a most awful thunder-clap, and everything grew inky-black.

The Butterfly was nearly as frightened as his wife, and Suleiman-bin-Daoud laughed so much that it was several minutes before he found breath enough to whisper to the Butterfly, "Stamp again, most great magician."

So he stamped once more, and that instant the Djinns let down the Palace and the gardens, without even a bump.

The Butterfly's Wife lay on her side under the camphor-tree waggling her wings and panting, "Oh, I'll be good! I'll be good!"

Suleiman-bin-Daoud could hardly speak for laughing.

Then came a terrible noise. All the nine hundred and ninety-nine Queens ran out of the Palace shrieking. They hurried down the great marble steps below the fountain, one hundred abreast, and the Most Wise Balkis went forward to meet them and said, "What is your trouble, O Queens?"

They stood on the marble steps one hundred abreast and shouted, "Suddenly our Palace disappeared, and we were left sitting in a thick and noisome darkness!"

Then Balkis said, "It is nothing, O Queens! A Butterfly has made complaint against his wife because she quarrelled with him, and it has pleased our Lord Suleiman-bin-Daoud to teach her a lesson. Come and see."

The Queens ran down the steps, and beneath his camphor-tree, still weak with laughing, they saw the Most Wise King Suleiman-bin-Daoud rocking back and forth with a Butterfly on either hand. Then all the Queens except Balkis fell flat on their faces, for they said, "If these things are done when a Butterfly is displeased with his wife, what shall be done to us who have vexed our King with our loud-speaking and open quarrelling through many days?"

Then they put their veils over their heads, and they all went up to the Palace and lived happily ever afterwards – including Suleiman-bin-Daoud and his equally wise wife, Balkis.

The Frog

From Andrew Lang's *Violet Fairy Book*

ONCE UPON A TIME there was a woman who had three sons. They were farmers, and the soil on which they lived was fruitful, and yielded rich crops. One day they all three told their mother they meant to get married. To which their mother replied: "Do as you like, but see that you choose good housewives – and, to make certain of this, take these three skeins of flax, and give it to them to spin. Whoever spins the best will be my favourite daughter-in-law."

Now the two eldest sons had already

chosen their wives, so they took the flax and carried it off with them, to have it spun as she had said. But the youngest son was puzzled what to do with his skein, as he knew no girl to whom he could give it to be spun. He wandered hither and thither, asking the girls that he met if they would undertake the task, but none would do so. Then he went out into the country and, seating himself on the bank of a pond, began to cry bitterly.

Suddenly there was a noise close beside him, and a frog jumped out of the water and asked him why he was crying. The youth told her of his trouble, and the frog said: "Do not weep. Give me the thread, and I will spin it for you." And, having said this, she took it out of his hand, and flopped back into the water, and the youth went back, not knowing what would happen next.

In a short time the two elder brothers came home, bringing with them the linen that had been spun by their chosen wives to show their mother. But the youngest brother was greatly troubled, for he had nothing to show. Sadly he took himself to the pond and, sitting down on the bank, began to weep.

Flop! And the frog appeared out of the water close beside him.

"Take this," she said, "here is the linen that I have spun for you."

You may imagine how delighted the youth was. He took the linen straight back to his mother, who declared she had never seen linen so beautifully spun. Indeed, she said it was far finer and whiter than the webs that the two elder brothers had brought home.

Then she turned to her sons and said: "But this is not enough, my sons, I must have another proof as to what sort of wives you have chosen. In the house there are three puppies. Each of you take one, and give it to the woman whom you mean to bring home as your wife. She must train it and bring it up.

Whichever dog turns out the best, its mistress will be my favourite daughter-in-law."

So the young men set out on their different ways, each taking a puppy with him. The youngest, not knowing where to go, returned to the pond, sat down once more on the bank, and began to weep.

Flop! And close beside him, he saw the frog. "Why are you weeping?" she said. Then he told her his difficulty, and that he did not know to whom he should take the puppy. "Give it to me," she said, "and I will bring it up for you." And she took the little creature out of his arms and disappeared with it into the pond.

The weeks and months passed, till one day the mother said she would like to see how the dogs had been trained by her future daughters-in-law. The two eldest sons departed, and returned shortly, leading with them two great mastiffs, who growled so fiercely, and looked so savage, that the mere sight of them made the mother tremble with fear.

The youngest son went to the pond and called on the frog to come to his rescue.

In a minute she was at his side, bringing with her the most lovely little dog, which she put into his arms. It sat up and begged with its paws, and went through the prettiest tricks, and was almost human in the way it understood and did what it was told.

In high spirits the youth carried it off to his mother. As soon as she saw it, she exclaimed: "This is the most beautiful little dog I have ever seen. You are indeed fortunate, my son, you have won a pearl of a wife."

Then, turning to all three, she said: "Here are three shirts. Take them to your chosen wives. Whoever sews the best will be my favourite daughter-in-law."

So the young men set out once more, and again, this time, the work of the frog was much the best and the neatest.

This time the mother said: "Now that I am

content with the tests I gave, I want you to go and fetch home your brides, and I will prepare the wedding-feast."

You may imagine what the youngest brother felt on hearing these words. Whence was he to fetch a bride? Would the frog be able to help him in this new difficulty? With bowed head, and feeling very sad, he sat down on the edge of the pond.

Flop! And once more the faithful frog was beside him. "What is troubling you?" she asked him, and then the youth told her everything. "Will you take me for a wife?" she asked.

"What should I do with you as a wife?" he replied, wondering at her strange proposal.

At this the frog disappeared. The next minute the youth beheld a lovely little chariot, drawn by two tiny ponies, standing on the road. The frog was holding the carriage door open for him to step in. "Come with me," she said. And he got up and followed her into the chariot.

As they drove along the road they met three witches. The first of them was blind, the second was hunchbacked, and the third had a large thorn in her throat. When the three witches beheld the chariot, with the frog seated pompously among the cushions, they broke into such fits of laughter that the eyelids of the blind one burst open, and she recovered her sight, the hunchback rolled about on the ground in merriment till her back became straight, and in a roar of laughter the thorn fell out of the throat of the third witch. Their first thought was to reward the frog, who had unconsciously been the means of curing them of their misfortunes.

The first witch waved her magic wand over the frog, and changed her into the loveliest girl that had ever been seen. The second witch waved the wand over the tiny chariot and ponies, and they were turned into a beautiful large carriage with prancing horses, and a coachman on the seat. The third witch gave the girl a magic purse, filled with money. Having done this, the witches disappeared, and the youth with his lovely bride drove to his mother's home.

Great was the delight of the mother at her youngest son's good fortune. A beautiful house was built for them, she was the favourite daughter-in-law, everything went well with them, and they lived happily ever after.

The Half-Chick

From Andrew Lang's *Green Fairy Book*

ONCE UPON A TIME there was a handsome black Spanish hen, who had a large brood of chickens. They were all fine, plump little birds, except the youngest. When he first chipped his shell his mother could scarcely believe her eyes, he was so different from the twelve other fluffy, downy, soft little chicks who nestled under her wings. This one looked just as if he had been cut in two. He had only one leg, and one wing, and one eye, and he had half a head and half a beak. His mother shook her head sadly and said: "My youngest born can never grow up tall and handsome like his brothers. They will go out into the world and rule over poultry yards of their own, but this poor little fellow will always have to stay at home with his mother." And she called him Medio Pollito, which is Spanish for half-chick.

Now though Medio Pollito was such an odd, helpless-looking little thing, his mother soon found that he was not at all willing to remain under her wing and protection. Medio Pollito had a roving spirit in spite of his one leg, and as he grew older he became more self-willed and disobedient.

One day, he strutted up to his mother with the peculiar little hop and kick which was his way of walking, and cocking his one eye at her in a very bold way he said: "Mother, I am tired of this life in a dull farmyard, with nothing but a dreary maize field to look at. I'm off to Madrid to see the king."

"To Madrid, Medio Pollito!" exclaimed his mother. "Why, you silly chick, it would be a long journey for a grown-up cock, and a poor little thing like you would be tired out before you had gone half the distance. No, no, stay at home with your mother, and some day, when you are bigger, we will go on a little journey together."

But Medio Pollito had made up his mind, and he would not listen to his mother's advice, nor to the prayers and entreaties of his brothers and sisters.

"What is the use of our all crowding each other up in this poky little place?" he said. "When I have a fine courtyard of my own at the king's palace, I shall perhaps ask some of you to come and pay me a short visit," and scarcely waiting to say goodbye to his family, away he stumped down the high road that led to Madrid.

A little later in the day, as he was taking a short cut through a field, he passed a stream. Now the stream was all choked up, and overgrown with weeds and water-plants, so that its waters could not flow freely.

"Oh! Medio Pollito," it cried, as the half-chick hopped along its banks, "do come and help me by clearing away these weeds."

"Help you, indeed!" exclaimed Medio Pollito, tossing his head, and shaking the few feathers in his tail. "Do you think I have nothing to do but to waste my time on such trifles? Help yourself, and don't trouble busy travellers. I am off to Madrid to see the king," and hoppity-kick, hoppity-kick, away stumped Medio Pollito.

A little later he came to a fire that had been left by some gipsies in a wood. It was burning very low, and would soon be out.

"Oh! Medio Pollito," cried the fire, in a weak, wavering voice as the half-chick approached, "in a few minutes I shall go quite out, unless you put some sticks and dry leaves upon me. Do help me, or I shall die!"

"Help you, indeed!" answered Medio Pollito. "I have other things to do. Gather sticks for yourself, and don't trouble me. I am off to Madrid to see the king," and hoppity-kick, hoppity-kick, away stumped Medio Pollito.

The next morning, as he was getting near Madrid, he passed a large chestnut tree, in whose branches the wind was caught and entangled. "Oh! Medio Pollito," called the wind, "do hop up here, and help me to get free of these branches. I cannot come away, and it is so uncomfortable."

"It is your own fault for going there," answered Medio Pollito. "I can't waste all my morning stopping here to help you. Just shake yourself off, and don't hinder me, for I am off to Madrid to see the king," and hoppity-kick, hoppity-kick, away stumped Medio Pollito in great glee, for the towers and roofs of Madrid were now in sight.

When he entered the town he saw the king's palace, and he determined to hop up to the front gate and wait there until the king came out. But as he was hopping past one of the back windows the king's cook saw him. "Here is the very thing I want," he exclaimed, "for the king has just sent a message to say that he must have chicken broth for his dinner," and opening the window he stretched out his arm, caught Medio Pollito, and popped him into the broth-pot that was standing near the fire. Oh! How wet and clammy the water felt as it went over Medio Pollito's head, making his feathers cling to his side.

"Water!" he cried in his despair. "Do not wet me like this."

"Ah! Medio Pollito," replied the water, "you would not help me when I was a little stream away on the fields, now you must be punished."

Then the fire began to burn and scald Medio

Pollito, and he danced and hopped from one side of the pot to the other, trying to get away from the heat, and crying out in pain: "Fire! Do not scorch me like this!"

"Ah! Medio Pollito," answered the fire. "You would not help me when I was dying away in the wood. You are being punished."

Then the cook lifted up the lid of the pot to see if the broth was ready for the king's dinner.

"Look here!" he cried in horror. "This chicken is quite useless. It is burned to a cinder. I can't send it up to the royal table." He opening the window and threw Medio Pollito into the street. But the wind caught him up and whirled him through the air.

"Oh, wind!" he gasped out. "If you hurry me along like this you will kill me. Do let me rest a moment."

"Ah! Medio Pollito," replied the wind, "when I was caught in the branches of the chestnut tree you would not help me. Now you are punished." And he

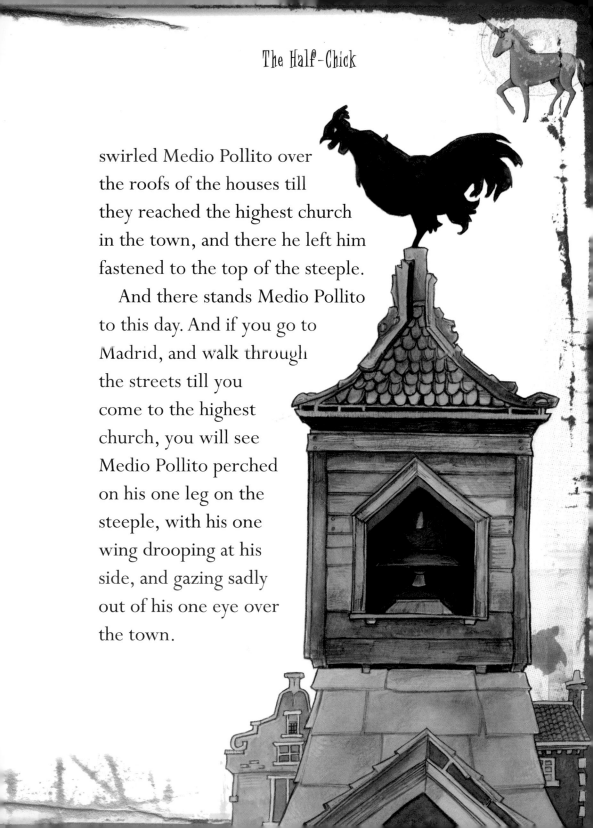

swirled Medio Pollito over
the roofs of the houses till
they reached the highest church
in the town, and there he left him
fastened to the top of the steeple.

And there stands Medio Pollito
to this day. And if you go to
Madrid, and walk through
the streets till you
come to the highest
church, you will see
Medio Pollito perched
on his one leg on the
steeple, with his one
wing drooping at his
side, and gazing sadly
out of his one eye over
the town.

WISHES AND DREAMS

The Stone-cutter

From Andrew Lang's *Crimson Fairy Book*

ONCE UPON A TIME there lived a stone-cutter, who went every day to a great rock in the side of a big mountain and cut out slabs. He understood very well the kinds of stones wanted for different purposes, and as he was a careful workman he had plenty of customers. For a long time he was quite contented, and asked for nothing better than what he had.

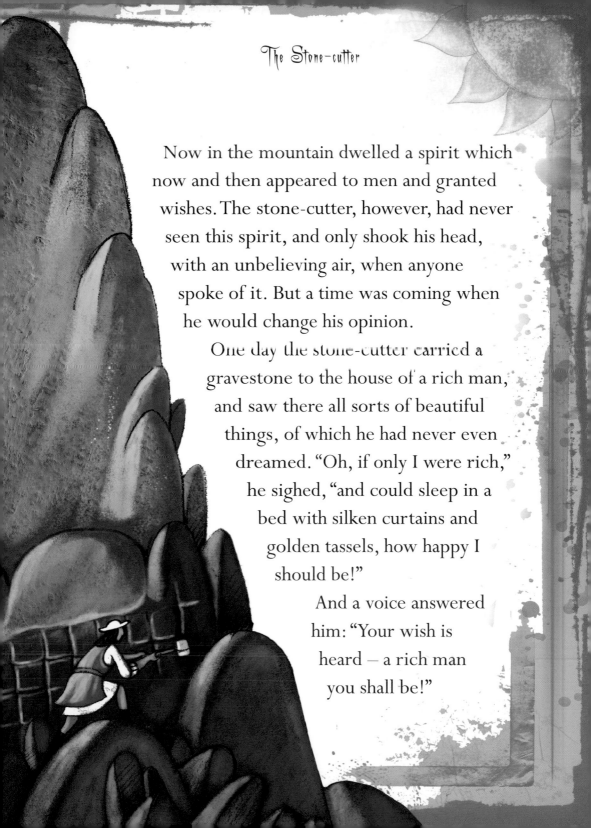

Now in the mountain dwelled a spirit which now and then appeared to men and granted wishes. The stone-cutter, however, had never seen this spirit, and only shook his head, with an unbelieving air, when anyone spoke of it. But a time was coming when he would change his opinion.

One day the stone-cutter carried a gravestone to the house of a rich man, and saw there all sorts of beautiful things, of which he had never even dreamed. "Oh, if only I were rich," he sighed, "and could sleep in a bed with silken curtains and golden tassels, how happy I should be!"

And a voice answered him: "Your wish is heard — a rich man you shall be!"

The stone-cutter looked round, but could see nobody. He thought it was all his fancy, and picked up his tools and went home. But when he reached the little house where he lived, he stood still with amazement, for instead of his wooden hut was a stately palace filled with splendid furniture, and most splendid of all was the bed, in every respect like the one he had envied. He was nearly beside himself with joy, and in his new life the old one was soon forgotten.

It was now the beginning of summer, and each day the sun blazed more fiercely. One morning the heat was so great that the stone-cutter could scarcely breathe, and he determined he would stay at home till the evening. It was rather dull, for he had never learned how to amuse himself, and he was peeping through the closed blinds to see what was going on in the street, when a little carriage passed by, drawn by servants dressed in blue and silver. In the carriage sat a prince, and over his head a golden

umbrella was held, to protect him from the sun's
bright rays.

"Oh, if I were only a prince!" said the stone-cutter
to himself, as the carriage vanished round the
corner. "Oh, if only I could go in such a carriage and
have a golden umbrella held over me, how happy I
should be!"

And the voice of the mountain spirit answered.
"Your wish is heard – a prince you shall be."

And a prince he was. Before his carriage rode one
company of men and another behind it. Servants
dressed in scarlet and gold bore him along, the
coveted umbrella was held over his head, everything
heart could desire was his.

But yet it was not enough.

He looked round still for something to wish for,
and when he saw that in spite of the water he
poured on his grass the rays of the sun scorched it,
and that in spite of the umbrella held over his head
each day his face grew browner and browner, he

cried in his anger: "The sun is mightier
than I. Oh, if I were only the sun!"

And the mountain spirit answered: "Your
wish is heard – the sun you shall be."

And the sun he was, and felt himself proud in
his power. He shot his beams above and below, on
earth and in heaven. He burned up the grass in the
fields and scorched the faces of princes as well as of
poorer folk. But in a short time he began to grow
tired of his might, for there seemed nothing left for
him to do. Discontent once more filled his soul, and
when a cloud covered his face, and hid the earth
from him, he cried in his anger: "Does the cloud
hold captive my rays, and is it mightier than I? Oh,
that I were a cloud, and mightier than any!"

And the mountain spirit answered: "Your wish is
heard – a cloud you shall be!"

And a cloud he was. He caught the
sun's beams and held them, and to his joy
the earth grew green again and flowers
blossomed. But that was not enough for
him, and for days and weeks he poured forth
rain till the rivers overflowed their banks, and the
crops of rice stood in water. Towns and villages were
destroyed, only the great rock on the mountain side
remained unmoved. The cloud was amazed and
cried out: "Is the rock, then, mightier than I? Oh, if I
were only the rock!"

And the mountain spirit answered: "Your wish is
heard – the rock you shall be!"

And the rock he was. Proudly he stood, and
neither the heat of the sun nor the force of the rain
could move him. "This is better than all!" he said to
himself. But one day he heard a strange noise at his

feet, and when he looked down to see what it could be, he saw a stone-cutter driving tools into his surface. Even while he looked, a trembling feeling ran all through him, and a great block broke off and fell upon the ground. Then he cried in his wrath: "Is a mere child of earth mightier than a rock? Oh, if I were only a man!"

And the mountain spirit answered: "Your wish is heard. A man once more you shall be!"

And a man he was, and in the sweat of his brow he toiled again at his trade of stone-cutting. His bed was hard and his food scanty, but he had learned to be satisfied with it, and did not long to be something or somebody else. And as he never asked for things he had not got, or desired to be greater and mightier than other people, he was happy at long last, and he heard the voice of the mountain spirit no longer.

A Grand Transformation Scene

An extract from *Vice Versa* by F Anstey

*Dick Bultitude is a Victorian schoolboy. The school holidays are
at an end, and his father, Paul, is saying goodbye as Dick is about to
set off back to boarding school, where he is very unhappy.*

MR BULTITUDE selected from the coins before
him a florin, two shillings, and two sixpences,
which he pushed across to his son, who looked at
them with disappointment.

"That's a lot of pocket money for a young fellow
like you," Mr Bultitude observed. "Don't buy
anything foolish with it, and if, towards the end of
the term you want a little more, and write an
intelligible letter asking for it, and I think proper to
let you have it – why, you'll get it, you know."

Dick had not the courage to ask for more, much as he longed to do so, so he put the money in his purse. There, he seemed to find something which had escaped his memory, for he took out a small parcel and unfolded it.

"I nearly forgot," he said, "I didn't like to take it without asking you, but may I have it?"

"Eh?" said Mr Bultitude, sharply. "What's that? Something else – what is it you want now?"

"It's only that stone Uncle Marmaduke brought Mamma from India – the thing, he said, they called a 'Pagoda stone', or something, out there."

"Pagoda stone? The boy means Garudâ Stone. I should like to know how you got hold of that – you've been meddling in my drawers, now, haven't you? A thing I will not put up with, as I've told you over and over again."

"No, I haven't," said Dick, "I found it in a tray in the drawing-room — but I may have it, mayn't I?" he persisted.

"Have it? You may certainly not. What could you possibly want with a ridiculous thing like that? Give it to me."

Dick handed it over reluctantly. It was not much to look at, a little square tablet of greyish green stone, pierced at one angle, and having on two of its faces faint traces of mysterious letters or symbols, which time had made very difficult to distinguish.

It looked harmless enough as Mr Bultitude took it — there was no kindly hand to hold him back, no warning voice to hint that there might possibly be sleeping within that small marble block the pent-up energy of long-forgotten Eastern magic, ready to awake into action at the first words which had power to stir it.

Paul Bultitude put on his glasses to examine the stone more carefully, for it was some time since he had last seen or thought about it. Then he looked up and said once more, "What use would a thing like this be to you?"

Dick would have considered it a very valuable prize indeed. He could have shown it to admiring friends under the desk during boring lessons, he could have played with it and invented astonishing legends of its powers, and when he had grown tired of it at last, he could have swapped it for something else. But he could not find either courage or words to explain himself. So he only said awkwardly, "Oh, I don't know, I would just like it."

"Well, any way," said Paul, "you certainly won't have it. It must be worth something, whatever it is, as the only thing your Uncle Marmaduke was ever known to give to anybody."

"Isn't it a talisman, a charm, though?" said Dick.

"I'm sure I can't tell you," yawned Paul, "how do you mean?"

"I don't know, only Uncle Marmaduke once said

something about it. Maybe it cures people of things – though I tried it once on my chilblains, and it wasn't a bit of good. If you would only let me have it, perhaps I might find out, you know."

"You might," said his father drily, "but you won't have the chance. If it has a secret, I will find it out for myself…and, by the way, I hear your taxi arriving – at last."

There was a sound of wheels outside, and, as Dick heard them, he grew desperate to ask for something else, something even more important. He got up and moved timidly towards his father.

"Father," he said, "there's something I want to say. Do let me ask you now."

"Well, what is it?" said Paul. "Make haste, you haven't much time."

"It's this. I want you to…to let me leave Grimstone's at the end of the term."

"Let you leave Grimstone's!" said Paul angrily. "What do you mean? It's an excellent school!"

"I'd like to go to Marlborough, or Harrow, or somewhere," whimpered Dick. "My friend Jolland's going to Harrow at Easter. The head, Dr Grimstone, is nice enough to pupils he likes, but he doesn't like me – he's always blaming me for something – and I hate some of the other boys there, and altogether it's awful. Do let me leave!"

"It's all ridiculous nonsense, I tell you," said Paul angrily. "You will stay at Grimstone's for as long as I say, and there's an end of that!"

At this, Dick began to sob, which was more than his father could bear. To do Paul justice, he had not meant to be quite so harsh, and, a little ashamed, he sought to justify himself by running through all the reasons why Grimstone's was such a good school.

"Now, you know, it's no use to cry like that," he began. "It's the usual thing for boys at school, I'm quite aware, to go about fancying they're very hard done by, and miserable, and all the rest of it! It's one of those things all boys have to go through. And you mark my words, my boy, when they grow up and go out into the world, they look back at school as the happiest time of their life!"

"Well," said Dick, "then I hope it won't be the happiest time in mine! You may have been happy at the school you went to, perhaps, but I don't believe you would very much care about being a boy again like me, and going back to Grimstone's!"

Paul still had the stone in his hand as he replied, smirking, "Perhaps you will believe me, when I tell you that, old as I am, I only wish that I could be a boy again, going back to school, like you."

As he spoke, he felt a shiver, followed by a curious shrinking sensation all over. And the armchair in which he sat seemed to have grown so much bigger all at once. He felt a passing surprise, but decided it must be his imagination, and went on as before.

"I should like it, my boy, but what's the good of wishing? I'm an old man and you're a young boy, and there's nothing anyone can...What the devil are you giggling about?"

For Dick, after some seconds of half-frightened and open-mouthed staring, had suddenly burst into a violent fit of sniggering, which he was trying hard to stop.

This naturally annoyed Mr Bultitude, and he went on with immense dignity, "I'm not aware that I've been saying anything particularly ridiculous. You seem to be amused?"

"Don't!" gasped Dick. "It, it isn't anything you're saying... it's, it's...oh, can't you feel any difference?"

"The sooner you go back to school the better!" said Paul angrily. "I've had quite enough of this.

Leave the room this instant!"

Dick, however, remained where he was, choking and shaking with laughter, while his father sat stiffly on his chair, and tried to ignore his son's strange behaviour.

At last his patience gave out, and he said coldly, "Now, perhaps, you will be good enough to let me know what the joke is?"

Dick's voice was hoarse with laughter as he spoke. "Haven't you found out yet? Go and look at yourself in the mirror!"

Mr Bultitude walked to the mirror, wondering whether he had a smudge on his face or something wrong with his collar and tie. But no sooner had Paul met his reflection than he started back in horror – then returned and stared again, and again.

Surely, surely, this could not be he!

He had expected to see his own familiar, portly presence there – but somehow, look as he would, the mirror insisted upon reflecting the figure of his son Dick! Besides, the reflection opposite him moved when he moved, returned when he returned, copied his every gesture!

He turned round upon his son in anger. "You've been playing some of your tricks with this mirror," he cried fiercely. "What have you done to it?"

"Done! How could I do anything to it?"

"Then," stammered Paul, " do you mean to tell me you can see any — changes to my appearance? Tell me the truth now!"

"I should think so!" said Dick. "It's very queer, but just look here," and he came over to the mirror and placed himself by the side of his horrified father. "Why," he said, with another giggle, "we're as like as two peas!"

They were indeed. The glass

reflected now two small boys, each with chubby cheeks and golden hair, both dressed, too, exactly alike, in Eton jackets and broad white collars. The only difference to be seen between them was that, while one face wore an expression of intense glee and satisfaction, the other – the one which Mr Bultitude was beginning to fear must belong to him – was lengthened and drawn with dismay and bewilderment.

"Dick," said Paul faintly, "what is all this? What has happened?"

"I'm sure I don't know, I haven't done anything!" protested Dick. "You can't be me, because here I am, you know. And you're not yourself, that's very plain."

"Never mind who I am," said Paul angrily. "I feel just the same as I always did. Tell me when you first began to notice any change."

"It was just as you were talking about going to school and all that. You said you only wished… Why of course – it must be the stone that did it!"

"Stone! What stone?" said Paul. "I don't know what you're talking about."

"Yes, you do – the Garudâ Stone! You've got it in your hand still. Don't you see? It is a real talisman after all! How amazing!"

"How perfectly absurd!"

"Well, something has definitely happened to you, hasn't it? And it must have been done somehow," argued Dick.

"I was holding the confounded thing, certainly," said Paul, "here it is. But what could I have said to start it? What has it done this to me for?"

"I know!" cried Dick. "Don't you remember? You said you wished you were a boy again, like me. So you are, you see, exactly like me!"

"Wished!" echoed Mr Bultitude. "Why, to be sure," he said, "of course – I never thought of that.

The thing's a wishing stone – it must be! You have to hold it, I suppose, and then say what you wish aloud, and there you are. If that's the case, I can soon put it all right by simply wishing myself back again."

He took the stone, and got into a corner by himself where he began repeating the words, "I wish I was back again," and "I wish I was the man I was five minutes ago," and "I wish all this had not happened," and so on, until he was very exhausted and red in the face. He tried with the stone held in his left hand, as well as his right, sitting and standing, under all the various conditions he could think of, but absolutely nothing came of it – he was just as exasperatingly boyish and youthful as ever at the end of it.

"I don't like this," he said at last, giving it up with a rather crestfallen air. "It seems to me that this diabolical invention has got out of order somehow – I can't make it work any more!"

"Perhaps," suggested Dick, who still looked

gleeful, "perhaps it's one of those talismans that only give you one wish, and you've had it, you know?"

"Then it's all over!" groaned Paul. "What the devil am I to do? Suppose your sister or one of the servants comes in and sees me like this! If I don't see my way out of this soon, I shall go raving mad!" And he paced restlessly up and down the room with his brain on fire.

All at once, an idea came to him. He was forced to agree that, improbable and fantastic though it might appear, there must be some magic power in this Garudâ Stone. It was plain too that the talisman would no longer work for him. But perhaps it would grant a wish for someone else? If Dick took the stone and wished that his father would return back to normal, maybe everything would be put right.

Mr Bultitude explained his plan to Dick at once.

"I may as well try," Dick said, with a mischievous sparkle in his eye, "give the stone to me."

"Take it," said Paul, desperately. "Take it, and wish

your poor old father himself again!"

Dick took the stone, and held it thoughtfully in his hand for some moments.

"I suppose," he asked, "when you are yourself again, things would go on just as usual?"

"I… I hope so."

"I mean you will go on sitting here, and I shall go off to Grimstone's?"

"Of course, of course," said Paul, "don't ask so many questions. I'm sure you quite understand what has to be done, so get on. We might be found like this any minute."

"That settles it," said Dick.

"Settles what?" asked Mr Bultitude, struck by something peculiar in the boy's manner.

"Well, I've thought of something fairer. You see, you wished to be a boy just like me. Well, if I wish to be a man just like you were ten minutes ago, before you took the stone, that will put things all right again, won't it?"

"Are you mad?" cried Paul, horrified at this proposal. "Why that would be worse than ever! Give me back that stone. I can't trust you with it."

But Dick was too quick for him. Slipping off the table, he planted himself firmly on the hearthrug, with the hand that held the stone clenched behind his back, and the other raised in self-defence.

"I wish I was a man like you were just now!" he cried in triumph.

And as he spoke, Mr Bultitude had the bitterness of seeing his son swell into the exact copy of his former self!

The transformed Dick began to skip and dance round the room in glee. "It's all right, you see," he said. "The old stone's as good as ever. You can't say anyone would ever know, to look at us."

And then he threw himself panting into a chair, and began to laugh excitedly at the success of his brilliant idea.

The Stars in the Sky

From *More English Fairy Tales* by Joseph Jacobs

ONCE UPON A TIME, there was a lassie who wept all day to have the stars in the sky to play with. She wouldn't have this, and she wouldn't have that, but it was always the stars she would have. So one day, off she went to find them. And she walked and walked, till by and by she came to a mill-dam.

"Goode'en to ye," says she, "I'm seeking the stars in the sky to play with. Have you seen any?"

"Oh, yes," said the mill-dam. "They shine in my face o' nights till I can't sleep for them. Jump in and perhaps you'll find one."

So she jumped in, and swam about and swam about, but ne'er a one could she see. So she went on till she came to a brooklet.

"Goode'en to ye, Brooklet," says she. "I'm seeking the stars in the sky to play with. Have you seen any?"

"Yes, indeed," said the Brooklet. "They glint on my banks at night. Paddle about and maybe you'll find one."

So she paddled and paddled, but ne'er a one did she find. So on she went till she came to the Good Folk.

"Goode'en to ye, Good Folk," says she. "I'm looking for the stars in the sky to play with. Have ye seen e'er a one?"

"Why, yes," said the Good Folk. "They shine on the grass here o' night. Dance with us and maybe you'll find one."

And she danced and danced, but ne'er a one did she see. So down she sat and wept.

"Oh dearie me," says she, "I've swam and I've

paddled and I've danced, and if ye'll not help me I shall never find the stars in the sky to play with."

But the Good Folk whispered together, and one of them took her by the hand and said, "Go forward – and mind you take the right road. Ask Four Feet to carry you to No Feet at all, and tell No Feet at all to carry you to the stairs without steps, and if you can climb that…"

"Oh, shall I be among the stars in the sky then?" cried the lassie.

"If you'll not be, then you'll be elsewhere," said the Good Folk, and set to dancing again.

So on she went again with a light heart, and by and by she came to a saddled horse, tied to a tree.

"Goode'en to ye, Beast," said she. "I'm seeking the stars in the sky to play with. Will you give me a lift, for all my bones are an-aching."

"Nay," said the horse, "I know naught of the stars in the sky, and I'm here to do the bidding of the Good Folk, not my own will."

"Well," said she, "it's from the Good Folk I come, and they bade me tell Four Feet to carry me to No Feet at all."

"That's another story," said he, "jump up and ride with me."

So they rode and rode, till they got out of the forest and found themselves at the edge of the sea. And on the water was a wide glistening path running straight out towards a beautiful thing that rose out of the water and went up into the sky, and was all the colours in the world, blue and red and green, and wonderful to look at.

"Now get you down," said the horse. "I've brought ye to the end of the land, and that's as much as Four Feet can do."

"But," said the lassie, "where's No Feet at all, and where's the stair without steps?"

"I know not," said the horse. "Goode'en to ye." And off he went.

The lassie stood and looked at the water, till a

strange kind of fish came swimming up to her feet.

"Goode'en to ye, big fish," says she. "I'm looking for the stars in the sky, and for the stairs that climb up to them. Will ye show me the way?"

"Nay," said the fish, "I can't unless you bring me word from the Good Folk."

"Yes, indeed," said she. "They said Four Feet would bring me to No Feet at all, and No Feet at all would carry me to the stairs without steps."

"Ah, well," said the fish, "that's all right then. Get on my back and hold fast."

And off he went — *kerplash!* — into the water, along the silver path, towards the bright arch. And the nearer they came, the brighter the sheen of it, till she had to shade her eyes.

And as they came to the foot of it, she saw it was a broad bright road, sloping up and away into the sky, and at the far, far end of it she could see wee shining things dancing about.

"Now," said the fish, "here you are, and yon's the stair. Climb up, if you can, but hold on fast." And off he splashed through the water.

So she climbed and climbed, but ne'er a step higher did she get. The light was before her and around her, and the water behind her, and the more she struggled the more she was forced down into the dark and the cold, and the more she climbed, the deeper she fell.

But she climbed and climbed, till she got dizzy in the light and shivered with the cold, and dazed with the fear – and she let clean go, and sank down… down… down…

And – *bang!* – she landed on hard boards, and found herself sitting, weeping and wailing, by the bedside at home all alone.

The Three Wishes

From *More English Fairy Tales* by Joseph Jacobs

ONCE UPON A TIME there lived a poor woodman in a great forest, and every day of his life he went out to fell timber. So one day he started out, and his wife filled his wallet and slung his bottle on his back, that he might have meat and drink in the forest. He had marked out a huge old oak, which he could chop into many good planks. When he had reached it, he took his axe and swung it round his head to fell the tree at one stroke. Suddenly, there stood before him a fairy who prayed and beseeched him to spare the tree. He was dazed with

wonderment and couldn't
open his mouth to utter a word.
When he found his tongue at last,
he said, "Well, I'll do as you ask."

"Thank you," answered the fairy, "and to
show I'm grateful, I'll grant you your next
three wishes, be they what they may." With that,
the fairy vanished.

The woodman slung his wallet over his shoulder
and his bottle at his side, and off he started home.
But the way was long, and the poor man was
regularly dazed with the wonderful thing that had
befallen him, and when he got home there was
nothing in his noddle but the wish to sit down and
rest. Down he sat by the blazing fire.

"Isn't my supper ready yet?" said he to his wife.

"No, not for a couple of hours," said she.

"Ah!" groaned the woodman. "I wish I'd a good
link of black pudding here before me."

No sooner had he said it, when *clatter*, *clatter*,

rustle, *rustle*, what should come down the chimney but a link of the very finest black pudding.

"What's all this?" his wife said, gawping in bewilderment.

Then the woodman remembered the fairy and told his wife what had happened.

"Oh, you are a fool," she burst out. "I wish the pudding were on your nose, I do indeed."

Before you could say 'Jack Robinson', there the woodman sat, and his nose was the longer for a link of black pudding.

He gave a pull, but it stuck, and she gave a pull, but it stuck, and they both pulled till they had nearly pulled the nose off, but it stuck and stuck.

"What's to be done now?" said he.

"Well… I suppose it doesn't look all that bad," replied his wife.

Then the woodman saw that if he wished, he should wish quickly, and wish he did, that the black pudding might come off his nose. Well! There it lay in a dish on the table, and if the woodman and his wife didn't ride in a golden coach, or dress in silk and satin, why, they had at least as fine a black pudding for their supper as anyone would want.

Beautiful as the Day

An extract from *Five Children and It*
by E Nesbit

*Five children — Cyril, Anthea, Robert, Jane, and the youngest,
a baby whom they call 'the Lamb'— have moved house from
London to the countryside of Kent.*

THE CHILDREN had explored the gardens and the outhouses thoroughly before tea, and they saw quite well that they were certain to be happy at the White House. It was on the edge of a hill, with a wood behind it and the chalk-quarry on one side and the gravel-pit on the other. And it was at the gravel-pit that IT happened…

One day, the children decided to take their buckets and spades to dig in the pit, pretending they were at the seaside. They built a big castle, of course. Then Cyril wanted to dig out a cave to play smugglers in, but the others thought it might bury them alive, so it ended in all spades going to work to dig a hole through the castle to Australia. The children dug and they dug and they dug, and their hands got sandy and hot and red, and their faces got damp and shiny. The hole soon grew so deep that Jane begged the others to stop.

"Suppose the bottom gave way suddenly," she said, "and you tumbled out among the Australians, all the sand would get in their eyes."

"Yes," said Robert, "and they would probably hate us, and not let us see the kangaroos, or opossums, or eucalyptus trees, or emus, or anything."

Cyril and Anthea knew that Australia was not quite so near as all that, but they agreed to stop using the spades and go on with their hands. This was quite easy, because the sand at the bottom of the hole was soft and fine and dry, like sea-sand. And there were little shells in it.

Nevertheless, Cyril had soon had quite enough. "It's beastly hot in this Australian hole," he puffed. "Let's go and look for bigger shells – I think that little cave looks likely, and I see something sticking out there like a bit of wrecked ship's anchor."

The others agreed, but Anthea carried on digging the hole, because she liked to finish a thing once she had begun it.

The cave was disappointing – there were no shells, and the wrecked ship's anchor turned out to be only the broken end of a pickaxe handle, and the cave party were just making up their minds that the sand makes you thirstier when it is not by the seaside, and someone had suggested going home for some lemonade, when Anthea suddenly gave a loud scream:

"Cyril! Come here! Oh, come quick! It's alive! It'll get away! Quick!" They all hurried back to her.

"It's a rat, I shouldn't wonder," said Robert. "Father says they infest old places – and this must be old if the sea was here thousands of years ago."

"Perhaps it is a snake," said Jane, shuddering.

"Oh, don't be silly!" said Anthea. "It's not a rat, it's MUCH bigger. And it's not a snake. It's got feet – I saw them – and fur! And I – it sounds silly, but it said something. It really and truly did."

"What?" Cyril challenged.

"It said, 'You leave me alone'."

But Cyril just observed that his sister must have gone off her nut, and he and Robert dug with spades while Anthea stood on the edge of the hole, jumping up and down. They dug carefully, and presently everyone could see that there really was something moving in the bottom of the Australian hole.

Then Anthea cried out, "I'm not afraid. Let me dig," and fell on her knees and began to scratch like a dog does when he has suddenly remembered where it was that he buried his bone.

"Oh, I felt fur," she cried, half laughing and half crying. "I did indeed! I did!" when suddenly a dry husky voice in the sand made them all jump back, and their hearts jumped nearly as fast as they did.

"Leave me alone," it said. And now everyone heard the voice and looked at the others to see if they had too.

"But we want to see you," said Robert bravely.

"I wish you would come out," said Anthea, also taking courage.

"Oh, well – if that's your wish," the voice said, and the sand stirred and spun and scattered, and something brown and furry and fat came rolling out into the hole and all the sand fell off it, and it sat there yawning and rubbing the ends of its eyes with its hands.

"I believe I must have dropped asleep," it said, stretching itself.

The children stood round the hole in a ring, looking at the creature they had found. Its eyes were on long horns like a snail's eyes, and it could move them in and out like telescopes. It had ears like a bat's ears, and its tubby body was shaped like a spider's and covered with thick soft fur. Its legs and arms were furry too, and it had hands and feet rather like a monkey's.

"What on earth is it?" Jane said. "Shall we take it home with us?"

The thing turned its strange eyes to look at her, and said: "Does she always talk nonsense, or is it only the rubbish on her head that makes her silly?"

and it looked scornfully at Jane's hat as it spoke.

"She doesn't mean to be silly," Anthea said gently. "None of us do, whatever you may think! Don't be frightened – we don't want to hurt you, you know."

"Hurt ME!" it said. "ME frightened? Why, you talk as if I were nobody in particular." All its fur stood out like a cat's when it is going to fight.

"Well," said Anthea, still kindly, "perhaps if we knew who you are in particular we could think of something to say that wouldn't make you cross. Everything we've said so far seems to have. Who are you? Don't get angry! Because we don't know."

"You don't know?" it said. "Well, I knew the world had changed – but – well, really – do you mean to tell me seriously you don't know a Psammead when you see one?"

"A Sammyadd? That's Greek to me."

"So it is to everyone," said the creature sharply. "Well, in plain English, then, a SAND-FAIRY. Don't you know a Sand-fairy when you see one?'

It looked so grieved and hurt that Jane hastened to say, "Of course I see you are, now. It's quite plain now one comes to look at you."

"You came to look at me, several sentences ago," it said crossly, beginning to curl up again in the sand.

"Oh – don't go away again! Do talk some more," Robert cried. "I didn't know you were a Sand-fairy, but I knew directly I saw you that you were much the wonderfullest thing I'd ever seen."

The Sand-fairy seemed a shade less disagreeable after this.

"It isn't talking I mind," it said, "as long as you're reasonably civil. But I'm not going to make polite conversation for you. If you talk nicely to me, I might answer you, I might not. Now say something."

Of course no one could think of anything to say, but at last Robert thought of 'How long have you lived here?' and he said it at once.

"Oh, ages – several thousand years," replied the Psammead.

"Tell us all about it. Do."

"It's all in books."

"You aren't!" Jane said. "Oh, tell us everything you can about yourself! We don't know anything about you, and you are so nice."

The Sand-fairy smoothed his long rat-like whiskers and smiled.

"Do please tell!" said the children all together.

It drew its eyes in and said: "How very sunny it is today – quite like the old times. It used to be very nearly all sand where I lived, and coal grew on the trees, and the periwinkles were as big as tea-trays – you can still find them now, they're turned into stone. We Sand-fairies used to live on the seashore, and the children would come along with their little flint-spades and flint-pails, and they would make castles for us to live in. That's thousands of years ago, but I hear that even now children still build castles on the sand. It's difficult to break yourself of a habit."

"But why did you stop living in the sand castles?" asked Robert.

"It's a sad story," said the Psammead gloomily. "It was because they would build moats to the castles, and the nasty wet bubbling sea used to come in, and of course as soon as a Sand-fairy got wet it caught cold, and generally died. And so there got to be fewer and fewer."

"And did YOU get wet?" Robert enquired.

The Sand-fairy shuddered. "Only once," it said. "The very end of the twelfth hair of my top left whisker – I feel the place still if the weather is damp. It was only once, but it was quite more than enough for me.

"I went away as soon as the sun had dried my poor dear whisker. I scurried away to the back of the beach, and dug myself a house deep in warm dry sand, and there I've been ever since. And the sea changed its lodgings afterwards. And now I'm not going to tell you another thing."

"Just one more, please," said the children. "Can you give wishes now?"

"Of course," said it, "didn't I give you yours a few minutes ago? You said, 'I wish you'd come out,' and then I did."

"Oh, please, mayn't we have another?"

"Yes, but be quick about it. I'm tired of you."

I daresay you have often thought what you would do if you had three wishes given you, and have despised the old man and his wife in the black-pudding story, and felt certain that if you had the chance you could think of three really useful wishes without a moment's hesitation. These children had often talked this matter over, but, now the chance had suddenly come to them, they could not make up their minds.

"Quick," said the Sand-fairy crossly. No one could think of anything, only Anthea did manage to remember a private wish of her own and Jane's which they had never told the boys. She knew the boys would not think much of it — but still it was better than nothing.

"I wish we were all as beautiful as the day," she said in a great hurry.

The children looked at each other, but each could see that the others were not any better-looking than usual. The Psammead pushed out its long eyes, and seemed to be holding its breath and swelling itself out till it was twice as fat and furry as before. Suddenly it let its breath go in a long sigh.

"I'm really afraid I can't manage it," it said apologetically, 'I must be out of practice."

The children were horribly disappointed.

"Oh, DO try again!" they said.

"Well," said the Sand-fairy, "the fact is, I was keeping back a little strength to give the rest of you your wishes with. If you'll be contented with one wish a day amongst the lot of you I daresay I can screw myself up to it. Do you agree to that?"

"Yes, oh yes!"'said Jane and Anthea. The boys

nodded. They did not really believe the Sand-fairy could do it.

It stretched out its eyes farther than ever, and swelled and swelled and swelled.

"I do hope it won't hurt itself," said Anthea.

"Or crack its skin," Robert said anxiously.

Everyone was very much relieved when the Sand-fairy, after getting so big that it almost filled up the hole in the sand, suddenly let out its breath and went back to its proper size.

"That's all right," it said, panting heavily. "It'll come easier tomorrow."

"Did it hurt much?" asked Anthea.

"Only my poor whisker, thank you," said he, "but you're a kind and thoughtful child. Good day."

It scratched suddenly and fiercely with its hands and feet, and disappeared in the sand. Then the children looked at each other, and each child suddenly found itself alone with three perfect strangers, all radiantly beautiful.

The Magical Mug

An extract from *The King of the Golden River*
by John Ruskin

*Three brothers, Hans, Schwartz, and Gluck (the youngest), are goldsmiths who
live in Treasure Valley, high up in the mountains of Austria. The two elder brothers
are unpleasant and wicked, and one day they cruelly decide to melt down Gluck's
only precious possession — a golden mug which has the face of a bearded man
upon it — and they put it in the furnace...*

IT WAS JUST at the close of the day, and, when
the goldsmith Gluck sat down at the window, he
saw the rocks of the mountain-tops, all crimson and
purple with the sunset, and there were bright
tongues of fiery cloud burning and quivering about
them, and the river, brighter than everything around
it, fell, in a waving column of pure gold, from
precipice to precipice, with a broad rainbow

stretched across it, flushing and fading alternately in the wreaths of spray.

"Ah!" said Gluck aloud. "If that river were really all gold, what a nice thing it would be!"

"No, it wouldn't, Gluck," said a clear, metallic voice, close at his ear.

"Bless me, what's that?" exclaimed Gluck, jumping up. There was nobody there. He looked round the room, and under the table, and a great many times behind him, but there was certainly nobody there, and he sat down again at the window. This time he didn't speak, but he couldn't help wishing again that the river were really all gold.

"Not at all, my boy," said the same voice, louder than before.

"Bless me!" said Gluck again. "What is that?" He looked again into all the corners and cupboards, and then began turning round and round, as fast as he could, in the middle of the room, thinking there was somebody behind him, when the same voice struck again on his ear. It was singing now very merrily "Lala-lira-la" – no words, only a soft melody. Gluck looked out of the window. No, it was certainly in the house. Upstairs and downstairs. No, it was certainly in that very room. "Lala-lira-la."

All at once it struck Gluck that it sounded louder near the furnace. He ran to the opening and looked in. Yes, he saw right, it seemed to be coming, not only out of the furnace, but out of the pot. He uncovered it, and ran back in a great fright, for the pot was certainly singing! He stood in the farthest corner of the room, with his hands up, and his mouth open, for a minute or two.

Then the singing stopped and the voice said: "Hello!"

Gluck was too utterly shocked to answer.

"Hello! Gluck, my boy," came the voice again.

This time, Gluck summoned all his energies, walked straight up to the furnace and looked in. There, in the crucible, was the gold of his mug, all melted. But on the surface of the golden liquid lay the red nose and the sharp eyes of his old friend on the mug, a thousand times redder and sharper than ever he had seen them in his life.

"Come, Gluck, my boy," said the voice out of the molten gold, "I'm all right; pour me out."

But Gluck was too much astonished to do anything of the kind.

"Pour me out, I say," said the voice, rather gruffly. Still Gluck couldn't move.

"Will you pour me out?" said the voice. "I'm hot." Gluck finally sprang into action, took hold of the crucible, and sloped it so as to pour out the contents. At first liquid gold and steam poured out, but after a moment there emerged, first the well-known head of his friend the mug, then a pair of arms stuck akimbo, then some coat-tails, and finally a pair of pretty little yellow legs.

And standing there before him on the floor was a golden dwarf, about a foot and a half high.

"That's right!" said the dwarf, stretching out first his legs, and then his arms, and then shaking his head up and down, and as far round as it would go, apparently to see if he was quite correctly put together, while Gluck stood in speechless amazement.

The dwarf was dressed in a slashed doublet of gleaming spun gold. Over this, his hair and beard fell almost to the ground, in a wave of curls. The features of his face were rather coarse and even coppery in colour, which made the dwarf look as though he was a very determined and fiery-tempered person.

When the dwarf had finished checking himself over, he turned his small, sharp eyes full on Gluck, and stared at him. "No, it wouldn't, Gluck, my boy," said the little man.

This was certainly rather an abrupt way to begin conversation. Gluck supposed that it might be a comment on his earlier thoughts about wishing that the river were really gold. But whether it was or wasn't, Gluck wasn't about to argue with the dwarf.

"Wouldn't it, sir?" said Gluck, very mildly and submissively indeed.

"No," said the dwarf, conclusively. "No, it wouldn't." And with that, he pulled his cap hard over his brows, and took three steps down the room, turned and took three steps back, lifting his legs very high, and setting them down very hard.

This pause gave time for Gluck to collect his thoughts. "Sir," he asked, rather hesitatingly, "were you my mug?"

On which the little man span round, walked

straight up to Gluck, and drew himself up to his full height. "I," said the little man, "am the king of the Golden River." Whereupon he turned about again, and paced up and down once more.

Gluck thought he should say something. "I hope Your Majesty is very well?" he asked.

"Listen!" said the little man, not bothering to reply. "I am the king of what you mortals call the Golden River. I had been enchanted into the shape of a mug by a stronger, evil king, from whose wicked spell you have just freed me. I know you are a good lad, unlike your wicked brothers, and I would like to help you, so listen to what I say.

"Whoever shall climb to the top of that mountain from which you see the Golden River spring, and shall cast into the stream at its source three drops of holy water, for him, and for him only, the river shall turn to gold. But no one failing in his first attempt can have another go, and anyone who casts unholy water into the river will become a black stone."

So saying, the king of the Golden River turned away, and deliberately walked into the centre of the hottest flame of the furnace. His figure became red, white, transparent, dazzling – a blaze of intense light which rose, trembled, and disappeared. The king of the Golden River had evaporated.

"Oh!" cried poor Gluck, running to look up the chimney after him, "Oh dear, dear, dear me! My mug! My mug! My mug!"

The Cinder-Maid

From *Europa's Fairy Book* by Joseph Jacobs

ONCE UPON A TIME there was a king who had an only son, who was about to come of age. So the king sent round a herald to blow his trumpet and call out, "O yea, O yea, O yea, know ye that His Grace the king will give, on Monday week, a royal ball to which all maidens of noble birth are summoned, and be it furthermore known that at this ball His Highness the prince will select a lady to be his bride. God save the king."

Now there was among the nobles of the king's court one who had married twice. By the first marriage he had one daughter. His wife died, and as the girl was growing up her father married again — a lady with two daughters.

His new wife, instead of caring for his first daughter, thought only of her own and favoured them in every way. She would give them beautiful dresses but none to her stepdaughter, who had only to wear the cast-off clothes of the other two. The noble's daughter was set to do all the drudgery of the house, and had nothing to sleep on but the heap of cinders raked out in the scullery, and that is why they called her Cinder-Maid. And no one took pity on her and she would go and weep at her mother's grave where she had planted a hazel tree, under which she sat.

You can imagine how excited everyone was when they heard the herald's proclamation. "What shall we wear, Mother?" cried out the two daughters, and they all began talking about dresses. But when the father suggested that Cinder-Maid should also have a dress they all cried out: "What, Cinder-Maid going to the king's ball? Why, look at her, she would only disgrace us all." And so her father held his peace.

Now when the night came for the royal ball Cinder-Maid had to help the two sisters to dress in their fine dresses and saw them drive off in the carriage with her father and their mother. But she went to her own mother's grave and sat beneath the hazel tree and wept.

Then a little bird on the tree called out to her:

170

Cinder-Maid, Cinder-Maid, shake the tree,
Open the first nut that you see.

So Cinder-Maid shook the tree and the first nut
that fell she took up and opened, and what do you
think she saw? A beautiful silk dress as blue as the
heavens, all embroidered with stars, and two little
lovely shoes made of shining copper. And when she
had dressed herself the hazel tree opened and from
it came a coach all made of copper with four milk-
white horses, with coachman and footmen all
complete. And as she drove away the little bird
called out to her:

Be home, be home ere mid-o'night
Or else again you'll be a fright.

When Cinder-Maid entered the ballroom she was
the loveliest of all the ladies, and the prince, who
had been dancing with her stepsisters, would dance
only with her. But as it came towards midnight
Cinder-Maid remembered what the little bird had
told her and slipped away to her carriage. And when

the prince missed her he went to the guards at the palace door and told them to follow the carriage. But Cinder-Maid when she saw this, called out:

Mist behind and light before,
Guide me to my father's door.

And when the prince's soldiers tried to follow her there came such a mist that they couldn't see their hands before their faces. So they couldn't find which way Cinder-Maid went.

When her father and stepmother and two sisters came home after the ball they could talk of nothing but the lovely lady: "Ah, would not you have liked to have been there?" said the sisters to Cinder-Maid as she helped them to take off their fine dresses. "There was a most lovely lady with a dress like the heavens and shoes of bright copper, and the prince would dance with none but her, and when midnight came she disappeared and the prince could not find her. He is going to give a second ball in the hope that she will come again. Perhaps she will not, and then we will have our chance."

When the time of the second royal ball came round the same thing happened as before. The sisters teased Cinder-Maid, saying, "Wouldn't you like to come with us?" and drove off again as before. And Cinder-Maid went again to the hazel tree over her mother's grave and cried.

And then the little bird on the tree called out:

Cinder-Maid, Cinder-Maid, shake the tree,
Open the first nut that you see.

But this time she found a dress all golden brown like the earth, embroidered with flowers, and her shoes were made of silver, and when the carriage came from the tree, lo and behold, that was made of silver too, drawn by black horses with trappings all of silver, and the lace on the coachman's and footmen's liveries was also of silver. When Cinder-Maid went to the ball the prince would dance with none but her, and when midnight came round she fled as before. But the prince, hoping to prevent her

running away, had ordered the soldiers at the foot
of the staircase to pour out honey on the stairs so
that her shoes would stick in it. But Cinder-Maid
leaped from stair to stair and got away just in time,
calling out as the soldiers tried to follow her:

Mist behind and light before,

Guide me to my father's door.

And when her sisters got home they told her once
more of the beautiful lady that had come in a silver
coach and silver shoes and in a dress all embroidered
with flowers: "Ah, wouldn't you have liked to have
been there?" said they.

Once again the prince gave a ball in the hope that
his unknown beauty would come to it. All happened
as before – as soon as the sisters had gone Cinder-
Maid went to the hazel tree over her mother's grave
and wept. And then the little bird appeared and said:

Cinder-Maid, Cinder-Maid, shake the tree,

Open the first nut that you see.

And when she opened the nut, in it was a dress of

silk as green as the sea with waves upon it, and her shoes this time were made of gold, and when the coach came out of the tree it was also made of gold, with gold trappings for the horses and for the retainers. And as she drove off the little bird from the tree called out:

Be home, be home ere mid-o'night
Or else again you'll be a fright.

Now this time, when Cinder-Maid came to the ball, she was as desirous to dance only with the prince as he with her, and so, when midnight came round, she had forgotten to leave till the clock began to strike, one – two – three – four – five – six, and then she began to run away down the stairs as the clock struck, eight – nine – ten.

But the prince had told his soldiers to put tar upon the lower steps of the stairs, and just as the clock struck eleven her shoes stuck in the tar, and when she jumped to the foot of the stairs one of her golden shoes was left behind. Then the clock struck

TWELVE, and the golden coach, with its horses and footmen, disappeared, and the beautiful dress of Cinder-Maid changed again into her ragged clothes and she had to run home with only one golden shoe.

You can imagine how excited the sisters were when they came home and told Cinder-Maid all about it, how the beautiful lady had come in a golden coach in a dress like the sea, with golden shoes, and how all had disappeared at midnight except the golden shoe. "Ah, wouldn't you have liked to have been there?" said they.

Now when the prince found out that he could not keep his lady-love nor trace where she had gone he spoke to his father and showed him the golden shoe, and told him that he would never marry anyone but the maiden who could wear that shoe. So the king, his father, ordered the herald to take round the golden shoe upon a velvet cushion and sound the trumpet and call out: "O yea, O yea, O yea, be it known unto you all that whatsoever lady of noble birth can fit this shoe upon her foot shall become the bride of His Highness the prince and our future queen. God save the king."

And when the herald came to the house of Cinder-Maid's father the eldest of her two step-sisters tried on the golden shoe. But it was much too small for her, as it was for every other lady that had tried it up to that time. And the herald asked, "Have you no other daughter?"

And the sisters cried out, "No, sir."

But the father said, "Yes, I have another daughter."

And the sisters cried out, "Cinder-Maid, Cinder-Maid, she could not wear that shoe."

But the herald said, "As she is of noble birth she has a right to try the shoe." So the herald went down to the kitchen and found Cinder-Maid, and when she saw her golden shoe she took it from him and put it on her foot, which it fitted exactly. Then she took the other golden shoe from underneath the cinders where she had hidden it and put that on too.

Then the herald knew that she was the true bride of his master, and he sent for the prince at once.

When the prince saw Cinder-Maid's face, he knew at once that she was the lady of his love. So he took her behind him upon his horse, and as they rode to the palace, the little bird from the hazel tree cried out:

Some squashed their heel, and some squished their toe,
But she sat by the fire who could wear the shoe.

And so they were married and they lived happy ever afterwards.

An Unexpected Opening

An extract from *The Brass Bottle* by F Anstey

Horace Ventimore is a young man living in Victorian times in London.
He buys an antique bottle, which turns out to be much
more than he had bargained for…

HORACE WENT UP to his sitting-room. It was quite dark and he had to light his oil-lamps. After he had done so, the first object he saw was the long-necked jar which he had bought that afternoon, and which stood on the floor near the mantelpiece.

"It's uglier than I thought," he said to himself. "What an idiot I was to waste money on it! I wonder if there is anything inside? I'll have to find out before I go to bed."

He grasped it and tried to twist the cap off, but it remained firm, which was not surprising, seeing that it was thickly coated with a crust like cooled, hard lava from a volcano.

"I must get some of that off first, and then try again," he decided, and after foraging downstairs, he returned with a hammer and chisel, with which he chipped away the crust till the line of the cap was revealed, together with a clumsy-looking metal knob that seemed to be a catch. He fiddled with this for some time, and again attempted to wrench off the lid. Then he gripped the vessel between his knees and used all his strength. The cap was beginning to give way, very slightly. One last wrench – and it came off in his hand so suddenly that he fell backwards and hit his head on the floor with a thump.

He had a vague impression of the bottle lying on its side, with dense volumes of hissing, black smoke pouring out of its mouth and towering up in a gigantic column to the ceiling. He was also aware of a strong smell, before he fainted clean away.

When he opened his eyes the room was still thick with smoke. As it cleared, Horace saw the figure of a stranger – an elderly man wearing an Eastern robe and headdress of a dark-green hue. He stood there with uplifted hands, loudly uttering something in a strange language.

Horace, being still somewhat dazed, felt no surprise. He thought that his landlady must have rented out the next-door apartment at last. His new neighbour must have noticed the smoke and rushed in to offer help.

"Awfully good of you to come in, sir," he said, as he scrambled to his feet. "I don't know what's happened exactly, but there's no harm done. I dare say you've been rather startled. So was I, when I opened that bottle."

"Tell me," pronounced the stranger in a booming voice, "was it thy hand that removed the seal, O young man of kindness and good works?"

"I certainly did open it," said Horace, "though I don't know where the kindness comes in – for I've no notion what was inside the thing."

"I was inside it," said the curious stranger, calmly.

"So you were inside that bottle, were you?" said Horace with a smile. "How amazing!" He realised that his new neighbour must be slightly mad, and it would probably be best to play along with him.

"Dost thou doubt that I speak truth? I tell thee that I have been confined in that accursed vessel for countless centuries. Know that he who now addresses thee is Fakrash-el-Aamash, one of the Green Jinn. And I dwelt in the Palace of the Mountain of the Clouds above the City of Babel in the Garden of Irem, which thou doubtless knowest by repute?"

"I fancy I have heard of it," said Horace, as if it were an address in the phone book. "Delightful neighbourhood."

"But now, by thy means, my deliverance hath been accomplished. Demand whatever you wish, therefore, and thou shalt receive."

"My dear Mr Fakrash," Horace replied, "I've done nothing – nothing at all – and if I had, I couldn't possibly accept any reward for it."

'Tomorrow,' thought Horace, 'I'll speak to the landlady, and get her to send for a doctor and have this old boy put under proper care – he really isn't fit to live on his own!'

"The hour is late and I will leave thee awhile," proclaimed the stranger. "But I will return and serve you. May thy days be ever fortunate!" And as he finished speaking, he seemed, to Horace's speechless amazement, to slip through the wall behind him. At all events, he had left the room somehow – and Horace found himself alone.

He rubbed the back of his head, which began to be painful. "He can't really have vanished through the wall," he said to himself. " I must be over-excited this evening – hardly surprising, with all that has happened. The best thing I can do is to go to bed at once."

Which he accordingly proceeded to do.

The Tinder-box

Hans Christian Andersen

A SOLDIER CAME MARCHING along the high road. He had been to war, and was returning home. As he walked, he met an old witch. She said to him, "Good evening. You are a very fine soldier, so you shall have as much money as you could ever want for. Do you see that large tree?" and she pointed to a tree which stood nearby. "Well, it is hollow inside. Climb to the top and you will see a hole, through which you can let yourself down. I will tie a rope round you, so that I can pull you up again when you call out to me."

"But what am I to do, down there in the tree?" asked the soldier.

"Get money," she replied, "for you will find yourself in a large hall, lighted up by three hundred lamps. You will then see three doors, which can be easily opened, for the keys are in all the locks. On entering the first of the chambers, to which these doors lead, you will see a large chest, standing in the middle of the floor, and upon it a dog seated, with a pair of eyes as large as teacups. But you need not be at all afraid of him. I will give you my blue checked apron, which you must spread upon the floor, and then boldly seize hold of the dog, and place him upon it. You can then open the chest, and take from it as many pence as you please, they are only copper pence, but if you would rather have silver money, you must go into the second chamber. Here you will find another dog, with eyes as big as mill-wheels, but do not let that trouble you. Place him upon my apron, and then take what money you please. If, however, you like gold best, enter the third chamber, where there is another chest full of it. The dog who sits on this chest is very dreadful – his eyes are as big as a tower, but do not mind him. If he also is placed upon my apron, he cannot hurt you. Then you may take from the chest what gold you please."

"That sounds good," said the soldier, "but what am I to give you, you old witch? For, of course, you do not mean to tell me all this for nothing."

"No," said the witch, "but I do not ask for a single penny. Only promise to bring me an old tinder-box, which my grandmother left behind last time she went down there."

"Very well, I promise that I will. Now tie the rope round my body."

"Here it is," replied the witch, "and here is my blue checked apron."

As soon as the rope was tied, the soldier climbed up the tree, and let himself down through the hollow to the ground beneath. He found all as the witch had said. The dogs were indeed terrifying! But he handled them as the witch had described. In the first chamber, he filled his pockets with pieces of copper. In the second chamber, he threw away all the coppers he had taken, and filled his pockets and his knapsack with silver instead. But in the third chamber, he threw away all the silver, and filled his pockets, knapsack cap and boots with gold instead, so that he could scarcely walk. He found the tinder-box and called up through the tree: "Now pull me out, you old witch."

So the witch drew him up, and he stood again in the high road.

"Now you have the money," said the witch, "give me the tinder-box."

"Tell me what you are going to do with it," said the soldier, "or I will draw my sword and cut off your head."

"No," said the witch.

So the soldier immediately cut off her head, and there she lay on the ground. Then he tied up all his money in her apron, and slung it on his back like a bundle, put the tinder-box in his pocket, and walked off to the nearest town. There, he put up at the best inn, and ordered a dinner of all his favourite dishes, for now he had plenty of money.

The next day, he bought some good clothes and proper boots, so that our soldier soon became known as a fine gentleman, and the people visited him, and told him all the wonders that were to be seen in the town, and of the king's beautiful daughter, the princess.

"Where can I see her?" asked the soldier.

"She is not to be seen at all," they said. "She lives in a large copper castle, surrounded by walls and towers. No one but the king himself can pass in or out, for there has been a prophecy that she will marry a common soldier, and the king cannot bear to think of such a marriage."

"I should like very much to see her," thought the soldier, but he could not obtain permission to do so.

However, he passed a very pleasant time – went to the theatre, drove in the king's garden, and gave a great deal of money to the poor, which was very good of him, for he remembered what it had been in olden times to be without a shilling. Now he was rich, had fine clothes, and many friends, who all declared he was a fine fellow and a real gentleman, and all this gratified him exceedingly. But his money would not last for ever, and as he spent and gave away a great deal daily, and received none, he found himself at last with only two shillings left. So he was obliged to leave his elegant rooms, and live in a little garret under the roof, where he had to clean his own boots, and even mend them with a large needle. None of his friends came to see him, there were too many stairs to mount up.

One dark evening, he had not even a penny to buy a candle. Then all at once he remembered that there was a piece of candle stuck in the tinder-box which he had brought from the old tree. He found the tinder-box, but no sooner had he struck a few sparks from the flint and steel, than the door flew open and the dog with eyes as big as teacups, whom he had seen while down in the tree, stood before him, and said, "What orders, master?"

"Hello," said the soldier, "bring me some money."

The dog was gone in a moment, and presently returned, carrying a large bag of coppers in his mouth.

The soldier very soon discovered that if he struck the flint once, the dog who sat on the chest of copper money made his appearance, if twice, the dog came from the chest of silver, and if three times, the dog with eyes like towers, who watched over the gold. The soldier soon had plenty of money, so he returned to his elegant rooms, and reappeared in his fine clothes, and that his friends knew him again directly, and made as much of him as before.

After a while he began to think it was very strange that no one could get a look at the princess. 'Everyone says she is very beautiful,' thought he to himself, 'but what is the use of that if she is to be shut up in a copper castle surrounded by so many towers.' He struck his tinder-box and in a moment the dog, with eyes as big as teacups, stood before him. "It is midnight," said the soldier, "yet I should very much like to see the princess, if only for a moment."

The dog disappeared instantly, and before the soldier could even look round, he returned with the princess. She was lying on the dog's back fast asleep, and looked so lovely, that everyone who saw her would know she was a real princess. The soldier could not help kissing her.

Then the dog ran back with the princess. In the morning, at breakfast with the king and queen, she told them of the strange dream she had had during the night, of a dog and a soldier, that she had ridden on the dog, and been kissed by the soldier.

The next night one of the old ladies of the court was set to watch by the princess's bed, to discover whether it really had been a dream, or what else it might be.

The soldier longed very much to see the princess once more, so he sent for the dog again in the night to fetch her, and to run with her as fast as ever he could. But the old lady ran after him as quickly as he did, and watched as he carried the princess into a large house. She thought it would help her to remember the place if she made a large cross on the door with a piece of chalk. Then she went home to bed, and the dog presently returned with the princess. But when he saw that a cross had been made on the door of the house where the soldier lived, the dog took another piece of chalk and made crosses on all the doors in the town, so that the lady-in-waiting might not be able to find out the right door.

Early the next morning the king and queen

accompanied the lady and all the officers of the household, to see where the princess had been. Of course, there were crosses on all the doors in every direction, so it was useless to search.

But the queen was a very clever woman. She took her large gold scissors, cut a piece of silk into squares, and made a neat little bag. This bag she filled with buckwheat flour, and tied it round the princess's neck, and then she cut a small hole in the bag, so that the flour might be scattered on the ground as the princess went along.

During the night, the dog came again and carried the princess on his back, and ran with her to the soldier, who now loved her very much, and wished that he had been a prince, so that he might have her for a wife.

The dog did not observe how the flour ran out of the bag all the way from the castle wall to the soldier's house, and even up to the window, where he had climbed with the princess. Therefore in the morning the king and queen found out where their daughter had been, and the soldier was taken up and put in prison.

The very next day, the soldier saw through the iron grating of the little window how the people were hastening out of the town to see him hanged. He heard the drums beating, and saw the soldiers marching. Every one ran out to look at them, and a shoemaker's boy, with a leather apron and slippers on, galloped by so fast, that one of his slippers flew off and struck against the wall where the soldier sat looking through the iron grating.

"Run to the inn where I have been living," the soldier cried out to the shoemaker's boy. "Bring me my tinder-box and I will give you four shillings — but be quick about it."

And the shoemaker's boy did exactly that.

Then the soldier was led out through the crowd to the gibbet, where the king and the queen sat on splendid thrones opposite to the judges and the

whole council. The soldier was made to climb the
ladder, but as they were about to place the rope
around his neck, he said that an innocent request
was often granted to a poor criminal before he
suffered death. He wished very much to smoke a
pipe, as it would be the last pipe he should ever
smoke in the world.

The king could not refuse this request, so the
soldier took his tinder-box, and struck fire, once,
twice, thrice, and there in a moment stood all the
dogs – the one with eyes as big as teacups, the one
with eyes as large as mill-wheels, and the third,
whose eyes were like towers.

"Help me now, that I may not be hanged," cried
the soldier. And the dogs fell upon the judges and all
the councillors, seized one by the legs, and another
by the nose, and tossed them many feet high in the
air, so that they fell down and were dashed to
pieces.

The largest dog seized the king, as well as the

queen, and threw them after the others. Then the soldiers and all the people were afraid, and cried, "Good soldier, you shall be our king, and you shall marry the beautiful princess."

So they placed the soldier in the king's carriage, and the three dogs ran on in front and cried "Hurrah!" and the little boys whistled through their fingers, and the soldiers presented arms. The princess came out of the copper castle, and became queen, which was very pleasing to her. The wedding festivities lasted a whole week, and the dogs sat at the table, and stared with all their eyes.

The Lad Who Went to the North Wind

From *Popular Tales from the Norse*
by Sir George Webbe Dasent

ONCE ON A TIME there was an old widow who
had one son, and as she was poorly and weak,
her son had to go up into the safe to fetch meal for
cooking. But when he got outside the safe, and was
just going down the steps, there came the North
Wind, puffing and blowing, caught up the meal, and
so away with it through the air. Then the lad went
back into the safe for more, but when he came out
again on the steps, the North Wind came again and
carried off the meal with a puff, and, more than
that, he did so the third time.

At this the
lad got very angry.
He determined to look
up the North Wind and ask
for his meal back. So off he
went, but the way was long, and he
walked and walked, but at last he came to the North
Wind's house.

"Good day!" said the lad. "Thank you for coming
to see us yesterday."

"Good day!" answered the North Wind,
in a voice that was loud and gruff. "And
thanks for coming to see me. What do
you want?"

"I only wished to ask you to be so
good as to let me have back that
meal which you took from me," said
the lad, "for we haven't very much to
live on, and if you're to go on
snapping up the last morsel we have,

201

there'll be nothing for it but for us to starve."

"I haven't got your meal," said the North Wind, "but if you are in such need, I'll give you a cloth which will get you everything you wish, if you only say, 'Cloth, spread yourself, and serve up all kind of good dishes!'"

With this the lad was well content.

As the way was so long he couldn't get home in one day, so he turned into an inn on the way, and when they were going to sit down to supper he laid the cloth on a table which stood in the corner, and said, "Cloth, spread yourself, and serve up all kinds of good dishes." He had scarce said so before the cloth did as it was bid, and all who stood by thought it a fine thing, but most of all the landlady. So, when all were fast asleep at dead of night, she took the lad's cloth, and put another in its stead, just like the one he had got from the North Wind, but which couldn't so much as serve up a bit of dry bread.

When the lad woke, he took his cloth and went off with it, and that day he got home to his mother. "Now," said he, "I've been to the North Wind's house, and a good fellow he is, for he gave me this cloth, and when I only say to it, 'Cloth, spread yourself, and serve up all kinds of good dishes,' I get any sort of food I please."

"All very true, I daresay," said his mother, "but seeing is believing, and I shan't believe it till I see it for myself."

So the lad made haste, drew out a table, laid the cloth on it, and said: "Cloth, spread yourself, and serve up all kinds of good dishes."

But not even a piece of dry bread did the cloth serve up.

"Well," said the lad, "there's no help for it but to go to the North Wind again," and away he went.

Late in the afternoon, he came to where the North Wind lived.

"Good evening!" said the lad.

"Good evening!" said the North Wind.

"I want my rights for that meal of ours which you took," said the lad, "for, as for that cloth I got, it isn't worth a penny."

"I've got no meal," said the North Wind, "but yonder you have a ram which coins nothing but golden ducats as soon as you wish: 'Ram, ram! Make money!'"

So the lad thought this a fine thing.

It was too far to get home that day, so he turned in for the night to the same inn where he had slept before. Before he called for anything, he tried the truth of what the North Wind had said of the ram, and found it all right, but, when the landlord saw that, he thought it was a famous ram, and, when the lad had fallen asleep, he took another which couldn't coin gold ducats, and changed the two.

Next morning off went the lad, and when he got home to his mother, he said: "After all, the North Wind is a jolly fellow, for now he has given me a ram which can coin golden ducats if I only say 'Ram, ram! Make money!'"

"All very true, I daresay," said his mother, "but I shan't believe any such stuff until I see the ducats made for myself."

"Ram, ram! Make money!" said the lad, but if the ram made anything, it wasn't money.

So the lad went back again to the North Wind, and blew him up, and said the ram was worth nothing, and he must have his rights for the meal.

"Well!" said the North Wind. "I've nothing else to give you, except for that old stick in the corner yonder, but it is a stick of that kind that if you wish,

'Stick, stick! Lay on!' it lays on till you say: 'Stick, stick! Now stop!'"

As the way was long, the lad turned in this night too to the landlord, but as he could pretty well guess how things stood as to the cloth and the ram, he lay down at once on the bench and began to snore, as if he were asleep.

Now the landlord, who easily saw that the stick must be worth something, hunted up one which was like it, and when he heard the lad snore, was going to change the two. But, just as the landlord was about to take it, the lad bawled out: "Stick, stick! Lay on!"

So the stick began to beat the landlord, till he jumped over chairs, and tables, and benches, and yelled and roared: "Oh my!

206

Oh my! Bid the stick be still, else it will beat me to death, and you shall have back both your cloth and your ram."

When the lad thought the landlord had got enough, he said: "Stick, stick! Now stop!"

Then he took the cloth and put it into his pocket, and went home with his stick in his hand, leading the ram by a cord round its horns.

And so he got his rights for the meal he had lost.

MAGICAL PLACES

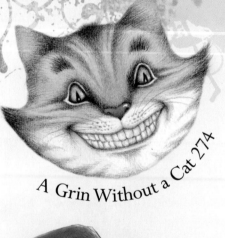

A Grin Without a Cat 274

The Three Golden Apples 280

Shipwreck on Lilliput 294

The Deliverers of Their Country 304

The Council with the Munchkins

An extract from *The Wonderful Wizard of Oz*
by L Frank Baum

*Dorothy lives in a farmhouse in Kansas which is one day whisked
into the air by a tornado – with her and her little dog Toto inside!
It drops down into a wonderful land called Oz...*

DOROTHY SAT UP and noticed that the house was not moving. Nor was it dark, for the bright sunshine came in at the window, flooding the little room. She sprang from her bed and, with Toto at her heels, ran and opened the door.

The little girl gave a cry of amazement and looked about her, her eyes growing bigger and bigger at the wonderful sights she saw.

The cyclone had set the house down very gently – for a cyclone – in the midst of a country of marvellous beauty. There were lovely patches of grass all about, with stately trees bearing rich and luscious fruits. Banks of gorgeous flowers were on every hand, and birds with rare and brilliant plumage sang and fluttered in the trees and bushes. A little way off was a small brook, rushing and sparkling along between green banks, and murmuring in a voice very grateful to a little girl who had lived so long on the dry, grey prairies.

While she stood looking eagerly at the strange and beautiful sights, she noticed coming towards her a group of the queerest people she had ever seen. They were not as big as the grown folk she had always been used to, but neither were they very small. In fact, they seemed about as tall as Dorothy, who was a well-grown child for her age, although they were, so far as looks go, many years older.

Three were men and one a woman, and all were oddly dressed. They wore round hats that rose to a small point a foot above their heads, with little bells

around the brims that tinkled sweetly
as they moved. The hats of the men were
blue, the little woman's hat was white,
and she wore a white gown that hung in
pleats from her shoulders. Over it were
sprinkled little stars that glistened in the
sun like diamonds. The men were dressed
in blue, of the same shade as their hats,
and wore well-polished boots. The men,
Dorothy thought, were about as old as
Uncle Henry, for two of them had
beards. But the little woman was doubtless much
older. Her face was covered with wrinkles, her hair
was nearly white, and she walked rather stiffly.

When these people drew near the house where
Dorothy was standing in the doorway, they paused
and whispered among themselves, as if afraid to
come farther. But the little old woman walked up to
Dorothy, made a low bow and said, in a sweet voice:
"You are welcome, most noble Sorceress, to the land

of the Munchkins. We are so grateful to you for having killed the Wicked Witch of the East, and for setting our people free from bondage."

Dorothy listened to this speech with wonder. What could the little woman possibly mean by calling her a sorceress, and saying she had killed the Wicked Witch of the East? Dorothy was an innocent, harmless little girl, who had been carried by a cyclone many miles from home, and she knew very well that she had never killed anything in all her life.

But the little woman evidently expected her to answer, so Dorothy said, with hesitation, "You are very kind, but there must be some mistake. I have not killed anything."

"Your house did, anyway," replied the little old woman, with a laugh, "and that is the same thing. She pointed to the corner of the house.

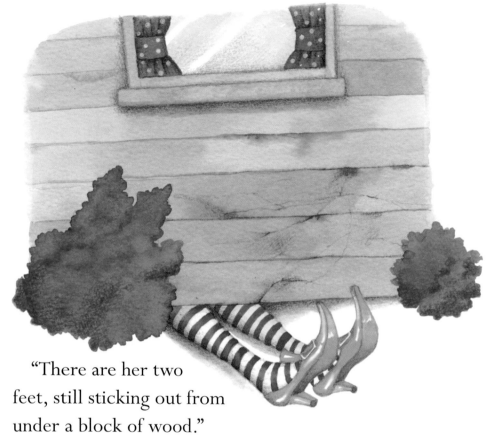

"There are her two feet, still sticking out from under a block of wood."

Dorothy looked, and gave a little cry of fright. There, indeed, just under the corner of the great beam the house rested on, two feet were sticking out, shod in silver shoes with pointed toes.

"Oh, dear! Oh, dear!" cried Dorothy, clasping her hands together in great dismay. "The house must have fallen on her. Whatever shall we do?"

"There is nothing to be done," said the little woman calmly.

"But who was she?" asked Dorothy.

"She was the Wicked Witch of the East, as I said," answered the little woman. "She has held all the Munchkins in bondage for many years, making them slave for her night and day. Now they are all set free, and are grateful to you for the favour."

"Who are the Munchkins?" enquired Dorothy.

"They are the people who live in this land of the East where the Wicked Witch ruled."

"Are you a Munchkin?" asked Dorothy.

"No, but I am their friend, although I live in the land of the North. When they discovered that the Witch of the East was dead the Munchkins sent a swift messenger to me, and I came at once. I am the Witch of the North."

"Oh, gracious!" cried Dorothy. "Are you a real witch?"

"Yes, indeed," answered the little woman. "But I am a good witch, and the people love me. I am not as powerful as the Wicked Witch was who ruled here, or I should have set the people free myself."

"But I thought all witches were wicked," said the girl, who was half frightened at facing a real witch.

"Oh, no, that is a great mistake. There were only four witches in all the Land of Oz, and two of them, those who live in the North and the South, are good witches. I know this is true, for I am one of them myself, and cannot be mistaken. Those who dwelled in the East and the West were, indeed, wicked witches, but now that you have killed one of them, there is but one Wicked Witch in all the Land of Oz – the one who lives in the West."

"But," said Dorothy, after a moment's thought, "Aunt Em has told me that the witches were all dead – years and years ago."

"And who is Aunt Em?" enquired the little old woman, gently.

"She is my aunt and she lives in Kansas – where I came from."

The Witch of the North seemed to think for a time, with her head bowed and her eyes upon the ground. Then she looked up and said, "I do not know where Kansas is, for I have never heard that country mentioned before. But tell me, is it a civilised country?"

"Oh, yes," replied Dorothy.

"Then that accounts for it. In the civilised countries I believe there are no witches left, nor wizards, nor sorceresses, nor magicians. But, you see, the Land of Oz has never been civilised, for we are cut off from all the rest of the world. Therefore we still have witches and wizards among us."

"Who are the wizards?" asked Dorothy.

"Oz himself is the Great Wizard," answered the Witch, sinking her voice to a whisper. "He is more powerful than all the rest of us together. He lives in the City of Emeralds."

Dorothy was going to ask another question, but just then the Munchkins, who had been standing silently by, gave a loud shout and pointed to the corner of the house where the Wicked Witch had been lying.

"What is it?" asked the little old woman, and looked, and began to laugh. The feet of the dead Witch had disappeared entirely, and nothing was left but the silver shoes.

"She was so old," explained the Witch of the North, "that she dried up quickly in the sun. That is the end of her. But the silver shoes are yours, and you shall have them to wear." She reached down and picked up the shoes, and after shaking the dust out of them handed them to Dorothy.

"The Witch of the East was proud of those silver shoes," said one of the Munchkins, "and there is some charm connected with them, but what it is we never knew."

Dorothy carried the shoes into the house and

placed them on the table. Then she came out again to the Munchkins and said: "I am anxious to get back to my aunt and uncle, for I am sure they will worry about me. Can you help me find my way?"

The Munchkins and the Witch first looked at one another, and then at Dorothy, and then they shook their heads.

"At the East, not far from here," said one, "there is a great desert, and none could live to cross it."

"It is the same at the South," said another, "for I have been there and seen it. The South is the country of the Quadlings."

"I am told," said the third man, "that it is the same at the West. And that country, where the Winkies live, is ruled by the Wicked Witch of the West, who would make you her slave if you passed her way."

"The North is my home," said the old lady, "and at its edge is the same great desert that surrounds this Land of Oz. I'm afraid, my dear, you will have to live with us."

Dorothy began to sob at this, for she felt lonely among all these strange people. Her tears seemed to grieve the kind-hearted Munchkins, for they immediately took out their handkerchiefs and began to weep also. As for the little old woman, she took off her cap and balanced the point on the end of her nose, while she counted "One, two, three" in a solemn voice. At once the cap changed to a slate, on which was written in big, white chalk marks:

LET DOROTHY GO TO THE CITY OF EMERALDS.

The little old woman took the slate from her nose, and having read the words on it, asked, "Is your name Dorothy, my dear?"

"Yes," answered the child, looking up and drying her tears.

"Then you must go to the City of Emeralds. Perhaps Oz will help you."

"Where is this city?" asked Dorothy.

"It is exactly in the centre of the country, and is ruled by Oz, the Great Wizard I told you of."

"Is he a good man?" enquired the girl anxiously.

"He is a good Wizard. Whether he is a man or not I cannot tell, for I have never seen him."

"How can I get there?" asked Dorothy.

"You must walk. It is a long journey, through a country that is sometimes pleasant and sometimes dark and terrible. However, I will use all the magic arts I know of to keep you from harm."

"Won't you go with me?" pleaded the girl, who had begun to look upon the little old woman as her only friend.

"No, I cannot do that," she replied, "but I will give you my kiss, and no one will dare injure a person who has been kissed by the Witch of the North."

She came close to Dorothy and kissed her gently on the forehead. Where her lips touched the girl they left a round, shining mark, as Dorothy found out soon after.

"The road to the City of Emeralds is paved with yellow brick," said the Witch, "so you cannot miss it.

When you get to Oz do not be afraid of him, but tell your story and ask him to help you. Goodbye, my dear."

The three Munchkins bowed low to her and wished her a pleasant journey, then walked away through the trees. The Witch gave Dorothy a friendly nod, whirled around on her left heel three times, and disappeared, much to the surprise of Toto, who barked after her loudly when she had gone, but had been afraid even to growl while she stood by.

But Dorothy, knowing her to be a witch, had expected her to disappear in just that way, and was not surprised in the least.

The Mines

An extract from *The Princess and the Goblin*
by George MacDonald

*A young princess called Irene knows nothing of the menacing goblins who
live under the nearby mountains – until one day she and her nanny stay out
late and are chased by a hideous creature. They are rescued by a boy called
Curdie, who knows all about goblins because he works in the mountain mines.
One night, when Curdie is working alone, he comes across yet more of them,
and decides to follow them to see what they are plotting…*

THE WORK WAS HARD, for it is very warm
underground, but some of the miners, when
they wanted to earn a little more money for a
particular purpose, would stop behind the rest and
work all night. You could not tell night from day
down there, for no light of the sun ever came into
those gloomy regions. Some who had thus remained
behind during the night, although certain there were

none of their companions at work, would declare
the next morning that they heard, every time they
halted for a moment to take breath, a tap-tapping all
about them, as if the mountain were then more full
of miners than ever it was during the day, and some
in consequence would never stay overnight, for all
knew those were the sounds of the goblins. They
worked only at night, for the miners' night was the
goblins' day. Indeed, most of the miners were afraid
of the goblins, for there were stories about what the
goblins would do to any miners they found. The
more courageous of them, however, stayed in the
mine all night again and again, and although they
had several times encountered a few stray goblins,
had never yet failed in driving them away. The chief
defence against them was poetry, for they hated
verse of every kind, and some kinds they could not
endure at all. I suspect they could not make any
themselves, and that was why they disliked it so
much. At all events, those who were most afraid of

them were those who could neither make verses themselves nor remember the verses that other people made for them, while those who were never afraid were those who could make verses for themselves, for although there were certain old rhymes which were very effectual, yet it was well known that a new rhyme, if of the right sort, was even more distasteful to them, and therefore more effectual in putting them to flight.

That night, Curdie was the only one who remained in the mine. At about six o'clock the rest went away, everyone bidding him good night, and telling him to take care of himself.

For some time he worked away briskly, throwing all the ore he had dug on one side behind him, to be ready for carrying out in the morning. He heard a good deal of goblin-tapping, but it all sounded far away in the hill, and he paid it little heed. Towards midnight he began to feel rather hungry, so he dropped his pickaxe, got out a lump of bread which in the morning he had laid in a damp hole in the rock, sat down on a heap of ore, and ate his supper. Then he leaned back for five minutes' rest before beginning his work again, and laid his head against the rock. He had not kept the position for one minute before he heard something which made him sharpen his ears. It sounded like a voice inside the rock. After a while he heard it again. It was a goblin voice – there could be no doubt about that – and this time he could make out the words.

"Hadn't we better be moving?" it said.

A rougher and deeper voice replied: "There's no hurry. That wretched little mole won't be through tonight, if he work ever so hard. He's not by any means at the thinnest place."

Curdie realised they were wrong – it could be but a thin partition which now separated them. If only he could get through in time to follow the goblins as they retreated! A few blows would doubtless be sufficient – just where his ear now lay, but if he attempted to strike there with his pickaxe, he would only put the goblins on their guard and hasten their departure. He therefore began to feel the wall with his hands, and soon found that some of the stones were loose enough to be drawn out with little noise. Laying hold of a large one with both his hands, he drew it gently out, and let it down softly.

"What was that noise?" said the older voice.

Curdie blew out his light, lest it should shine through and give him away.

"Maybe it was a stone carried down by the brook inside," said a voice which Curdie guessed must be a female goblin.

"Perhaps," said the younger voice.

Curdie kept quite still. After a little while,

hearing nothing but the sounds of the goblin family's preparations for departure, mingled with an occasional word of direction, he put in his hand to feel. It went in a good way and touched something soft. He had but a moment to feel it over, it was so quickly withdrawn: it was a goblin foot! The owner of it gave a cry of fright.

"What's the matter, Helfer?" asked his mother.

"A beast came out of the wall and licked my foot."

"Nonsense! There are no wild beasts in our country," said his father.

"But it was, father. I felt it."

The Mines

"Nonsense, I say."

"But I did feel it, father."

"I tell you to hold your tongue."

Curdie suppressed his laughter, and lay still as a mouse – but no stiller, for every moment he kept nibbling away with his fingers at the edges of the hole. He was slowly making it bigger, for here the rock had been very much shattered with the blasting.

There seemed to be a good many in the family, to judge from the mass of confused talk which now and then came through the hole, but when all were speaking together, and just as if they had bottle-brushes – each at least one – in their throats, it was not easy to make out much that was said. At length he heard once more what the father goblin was saying.

"Now, then," he said, "get your bundles on your backs. Make haste. I must go to the meeting at the palace tonight. When that's over, we can come back and clear out the last of the things before our enemies return in the morning. Now light your torches and come along."

A sound of many soft feet followed, but soon ceased. Then Curdie flew at the hole like a tiger, and tore and pulled. The sides gave way, and it was soon large enough for him to crawl through. He would not betray himself by rekindling his lamp, but the torches of the retreating company, which he found departing in a straight line up a long avenue from the door of their cave, threw back light enough to afford him to see.

He darted after them like a greyhound. When he reached the corner and looked cautiously round, he saw them again at some distance down another long passage. None of the galleries he saw that night bore signs of the work of man – or of goblin either. Stalactites, far older than the mines, hung from their roofs, and their floors were rough with boulders and large, round stones, showing that there water must

have once run. He waited again at this corner till
they had disappeared round the next, and so
followed them a long way through one passage after
another. The passages grew more and more lofty,
and were more and more covered in the roof with
shining stalactites.

In a moment or two, keeping after the goblins
round another corner, he started back in
amazement. He was at the entrance of a magnificent
cavern, of an oval shape, once probably a huge
natural reservoir of water. It rose to a tremendous
height, but the roof was composed of such shining
materials, and the multitude of torches carried by
the goblins who crowded the floor lighted up the
place so brilliantly, that Curdie could see to the top
quite well. But he had no idea how immense the
place was until his eyes had got accustomed to it,
which was not for a good many minutes. The rough
projections on the walls, and the shadows thrown
upwards from them by the torches, made the sides

of the chamber look as if they were crowded with statues upon brackets and pedestals, reaching in irregular tiers from floor to roof. The walls themselves were, in many parts, of gloriously shining substances, some of them gorgeously coloured besides, which powerfully contrasted with the shadows.

It was the great palace of the goblins.

And at the far end, high above the heads of the multitude, sitting on a terrace-like ledge, was the goblin king and his court.

The Giant Builder

A Norse tale from *In the Days of Giants*
by Abbie Farwell Brown

AGES AND AGES AGO, when the world was first made, the gods decided to build a beautiful city high above the heavens, the most glorious and wonderful city that ever was known. Asgard was to be its name, and it was to stand on Ida Plain under the shade of Yggdrasil, the great tree whose roots were underneath the earth.

First of all they built a house with a silver roof, where there were seats for all the twelve chiefs. In the midst, and high above the rest, was the wonder throne of Odin the All-Father, whence he could see everything that happened in the sky or on the earth or in the sea. Next they made a fair house for Queen Frigg and her lovely daughters. Then they built a smithy, with great hammers, tongs, anvils, and bellows, where the gods could work at their favourite trade, the making of beautiful things out of gold, which they did so well that folk name that time the Golden Age. Afterward, as they had more leisure, they built separate houses for all the Æsir, each more beautiful than the preceding, for of course they were continually growing more skilful.

They saved Father Odin's palace until the last, for they meant this to be the largest and the most splendid of all. Gladsheim, the home of joy, was the name of Odin's house, and it was built all of gold, set in the midst of a wood whereof the trees had leaves of ruddy gold – like an autumn-gilded forest. For the safety of All-Father it was surrounded by a roaring river and by a high picket fence, and there was a great courtyard within. The glory of Gladsheim was its wondrous hall, radiant with gold,

the most lovely room that time has ever seen.
Valhalla, the Hall of Heroes, was the name of it, and
it was roofed with the mighty shields of warriors.
The ceiling was made of interlacing spears, and
there was a portal at the west end before which
hung a great grey wolf, while over him a fierce eagle
hovered. The hall was so huge that it had five
hundred and forty gates, through each of which

eight hundred men could march abreast. Indeed, there needed to be room, for this was the hall where every morning Odin received all the brave warriors who had died in battle on the earth below, and there were many heroes in those days. A happy life it was for the heroes, and a happy life for all who dwelled in Asgard, for this was before trouble had come among the gods, following the mischief of Loki.

This is how the trouble began. From the beginning of time, the giants had been unfriendly to the Æsir, because the giants were older and huger and more wicked. Besides, they were jealous because the good Æsir were fast gaining more wisdom and power than the giants had ever known. The giants hated the Æsir, and tried all in their power to injure them and the men of the earth below, whom the Æsir loved and cared for. The gods had already built a wall around Midgard, the world of men, to keep the giants out. Between Asgard and the giants flowed Ifing, the great river on which ice

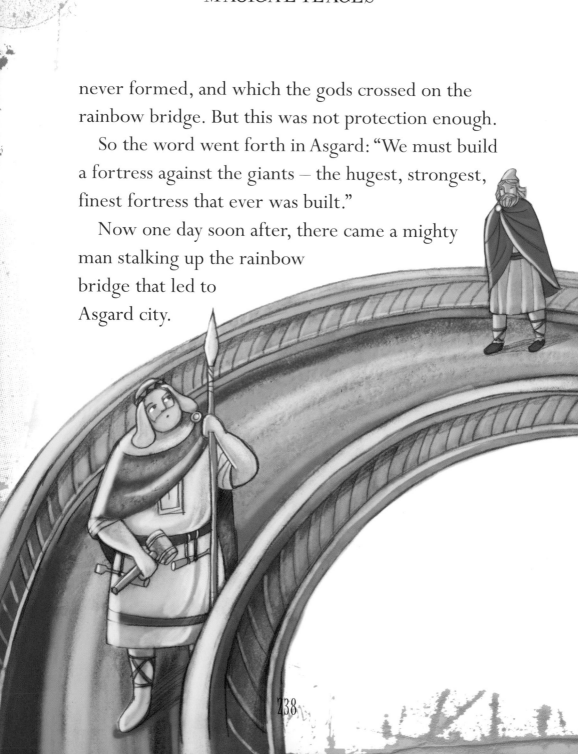

never formed, and which the gods crossed on the rainbow bridge. But this was not protection enough.

So the word went forth in Asgard: "We must build a fortress against the giants – the hugest, strongest, finest fortress that ever was built."

Now one day soon after, there came a mighty man stalking up the rainbow bridge that led to Asgard city.

The Giant Builder

"Who goes there!" cried Heimdal the watchman, whose eyes were so keen that he could easily see for one hundred miles around, and whose ears were so sharp that he could hear the grass growing in the meadow and the wool on the backs of the sheep. "Who goes there! There is no person who may enter Asgard if I say no."

"I am a builder," said the stranger, who was a huge fellow with sleeves rolled up to show the iron muscles of his arms. "I am a builder of strong towers, and I have heard that the folk of Asgard need one to help them raise a fair fortress in their city."

Heimdal looked at the stranger narrowly, for there was something about him which his sharp eyes did not like. But he made no answer, only blew on his golden horn, which was so loud that it sounded through all the world. At this signal all the Æsir came running to the rainbow bridge, from wherever they happened to be, to find out who it was that was coming to Asgard.

"In three half-years," declared the stranger, "I will build for you a castle so strong that not even the giants, should they swarm hither over Midgard – not even they could enter without your leave."

"Aha!" cried Father Odin, well pleased at this offer. "And what reward do you ask, friend, for help so timely?"

"I will name my price, friends," the stranger said, "a small price for so great a deed. I ask you to give me Freia for my wife, and those two sparkling jewels, the Sun and Moon."

At this demand the gods looked grave, for Freia was their dearest treasure. She was the most beautiful maid who ever lived, the light and life of heaven, and if she should leave Asgard, joy would go with her, while the Sun and Moon were the light and life of the Æsir's children, men, who lived in the little world below.

But Loki the sly whispered that they would be safe enough if they made another condition on their part, so hard that the builder could not fulfil it. After thinking cautiously, he spoke for them all.

"Mighty man," quoth he, "we are willing to agree to your price – upon one condition. We cannot wait three half-years for our castle. See that you finish the fort without help in one winter – one short winter – and you shall have fair Freia with the Sun and Moon. But if, on the first day of summer, one stone is wanting to the walls, then you shall depart without payment."

At first the stranger shook his head and frowned, saying that in so short a time no one unaided could complete the undertaking. At last he made another offer. "Let me have but my good horse, Svadilföri, to help me with the task, and I will try," he urged. "Surely, you will not deny me this little help, from one four-footed friend."

Then again the Æsir consulted, but again Loki urged them to accept. "Surely, there is no harm," he said. "Even with an old horse to help them, no one could build the castle in the promised time. We shall gain a fortress without trouble and with never a price to pay."

Loki was so very eager that, although the other Æsir did not really agree with this crafty way of making bargains, they finally consented. Then the stranger and the Æsir gave solemn promise that the bargain should be kept.

On the first day of winter the strange builder began his work, and wondrous was the way he set about it. His strength seemed as the strength of a hundred men. As for his horse Svadilföri, he did more work by half than even the mighty builder. In the night he dragged the enormous rocks that were to be used in building the castle, rocks as big as mountains of the earth, while in the daytime the stranger piled them into place with his iron arms. The Æsir watched him with amazement, never was seen such strength in Asgard.

As the work went on, the gods began to look at

one another uneasily. Who was this mighty one who had come among them, and what if after all he should win his reward? Freia trembled in her palace, and the Sun and Moon grew dim with fear.

Eventually the Æsir held a meeting upon Ida Plain, a meeting full of fear and anger. At last they realised what they had done – they had made a bargain with one of the giants, their enemies, and if he won the prize, it would mean sorrow and darkness in heaven and upon earth.

"It is your counsels, Loki, that have brought this danger upon us," quoth Father Odin, frowning. "If you cannot save for us Freia and the Sun and Moon, you shall die. This is my word." All the other Æsir agreed that this was just.

Loki was much frightened. "It was my fault, but how was I to know that he was a giant?" he cried. Then his face brightened. "Ha! I have a thought! The builder shall not finish the gate – the giant shall not receive his payment. I will cheat the fellow."

Now it was the last night of winter, and there remained but a few stones to put in place on the top of the wondrous gateway. The giant was sure of his prize, and chuckled to himself as he went out with his horse to drag the remaining stones. However, hardly had he gone to work when out of the wood came running a pretty little mare, who neighed to Svadilföri as if inviting the tired horse to leave his work and come to the green fields for a holiday. Giving a snort of disobedience, off Svadilföri ran after this new friend toward the grassy meadows. Off went the giant after him, howling with rage, as he saw his chance of success slipping out of reach. It was a mad chase, and all Asgard thundered with the noise of galloping hoofs and the giant's mighty tread. The mare who raced ahead was Loki in disguise, and he led Svadilföri far out of reach, to a hidden meadow that he knew, so that the giant howled and panted up and down all night long, without catching even a sight of his horse.

Now when the morning came the gateway was still unfinished, and night and winter had ended at the same hour. The giant's time was over, and he had forfeited his reward.

The delighted Æsir came flocking to the gateway.

"You have failed, fellow," judged Father Odin sternly, "Leave Asgard quickly, we have seen all we want of you and of your race."

Then the giant knew that he was discovered, and he was mad with rage. "It was a trick!" he bellowed, assuming his own proper form, which was huge as a mountain, and towered high beside the fortress that he had built. "I will demolish your shining city!" Indeed, he would have done so in his mighty rage, but at this moment Thor, the mighty thunder god, came rushing to the rescue in his chariot of goats. Before the giant knew what had happened, his head was rolling upon the ground at Father Odin's feet, for with one blow Thor had saved Asgard.

In this extraordinary way the noble city of Asgard was made safe and complete by the addition of a fortress. But always at the top of the gate were lacking three great stones that no one was mighty enough to lift. This was a reminder to the Æsir that now they had the race of giants for their everlasting enemies. And though Loki's trick had saved them Freia, and for the world the Sun and Moon, it was the beginning of trouble in Asgard which lasted as long as Loki lived to make mischief with his guile.

The Buried Moon

From *Tales of Wonder Every Child Should Know*
by Kate Douglas Wiggin and
Nora Archibald Smith

LONG AGO, the Carland was all in bogs, great pools of black water, and creeping trickles of green water, and squishy mools which squirted when you stepped on them. The Moon up yonder shone just as she does now, and when she shone she lighted up the bogpools, so that one could walk about almost as safe as in the day. But when she didn't shine, out came the Things that dwelled in the darkness and went about seeking to do evil and harm — Bogles and Crawling Horrors, all came out when the Moon didn't shine.

Well, the Moon heard of this, and being kind and

good – as she surely is, shining
for us in the night instead of
taking her natural rest – she
was main troubled. "I'll see
for myself, I will," said
she, "maybe it's not so
bad as folks make out."

Sure enough, at the
month's end down she
stepped, wrapped up in
a black cloak, and a black
hood over her yellow
shining hair. Straight
she went to the
bog edge and
looked

The Buried Moon

about her. Water here and water there, waving
tussocks and trembling mools, and great black snags
all twisted and bent. Before her all was dark – dark
but for the glimmer of the stars in the pools, and the
light that came from her own white feet, stealing
out of her black cloak.

The Moon drew her cloak faster about her and
trembled, but she wouldn't go back without seeing
all there was to be seen, so on she went, stepping
as light as the wind in summer from tuft to tuft
between the muddy, gurgling water holes. Just
as she came near a big black pool her foot
slipped and she was nigh tumbling in. She
grabbed with both hands at a snag nearby, to
steady herself with, but as she touched it, it
twined itself round her wrists, like a pair of
handcuffs, and gripped her so that she
couldn't move. She pulled and twisted
and fought, but it was no good.
She was fast, and must stay fast.

Presently as she stood trembling in the dark, wondering if help would come, she heard something calling in the distance, calling, calling, and then dying away with a sob, till the marshes were full of this pitiful crying sound. Then she heard steps floundering along, squishing in the mud and slipping on the tufts, and through the darkness she saw a white face with great feared eyes.

It was a man strayed in the bogs. Mazed with fear he struggled on toward the flickering light that looked like help and safety. And when the poor Moon saw that he was coming nigher and nigher to the deep hole, farther and farther from the path, she was so mad and so sorry that she struggled and fought and pulled harder than ever. And though she couldn't get loose she twisted and turned, till her black hood fell back off her shining yellow hair, and the beautiful light that came from it drove away the darkness.

Oh, but the man cried with joy to see the light

again. And at once all evil things fled back into the dark corners, for they cannot abide the light. So he could see where he was, and where the path was, and how he could get out of the marsh. And he was in such haste to get away from the Quicks, and Bogles, and Things that dwelled there, that he scarce looked at the brave light that came from the beautiful shining yellow hair, streaming out over the black cloak and falling to the water at his feet. And the Moon herself was so taken up with saving him, and with rejoicing that he was back on the right path, that she clean forgot that she needed help herself, and that she was held fast by the black snag.

So off he went, spent and gasping, and stumbling and sobbing with joy, flying for his life out of the terrible bogs. Then it came over the Moon, she would main like to go with him. So she pulled and fought as if she were mad, till she fell on her knees, spent with tugging, at the foot of the snag. And as she lay there, gasping for breath, the black hood fell forward over her head. So out went the blessed light and back came the darkness, with all its Evil Things, with a screech and a howl. They came crowding round her, mocking and snatching and beating, shrieking with rage and spite, and swearing and snarling, for they knew her for their old enemy, that drove them back into the corners, and kept them from working their wicked wills.

They caught hold of her, with horrid bony fingers, and laid her deep in the water at the foot of the snag. And the Bogles fetched a strange big stone and rolled it on top of her, to keep her from rising. And they told two of the Will-o-the-wykes to take turns in watching on the black snag, to see that she lay safe and still, and couldn't get out to spoil their sport. And there lay the poor Moon, dead and buried in the bog till someone would set her loose – and who'd know where to look for her?

Well, the days passed, and it was the time for the new moon's coming, and the folk looked about, for

the Moon was a good friend to the marsh folk, and
they were main glad when the dark time was gone,
and the paths were safe again, and the Evil Things
were driven back by the blessed Light into the
darkness and the waterholes.

But days and days passed, and the new Moon
never came, and the nights were aye dark, and the
Evil Things were worse than ever. And still the days
went on, and the new Moon never came. Naturally
the poor folk were strangely feared and mazed.

One day, as they sat in the inn, a man from the far
end of the bog lands was smoking and listening to
the talk about the Moon, when all at once he sat up
and slapped his knee. "I'd clean forgot, but I reckon I
kens where the Moon be!" he said, and he told them
of how he was lost in the bogs, and how, when he
was nigh dead with fright, the light shone out, and
he found the path and got home safe.

So come the next night in the darklings, out they
went all together, everyone feeling, thou may'st

reckon, main feared and creepy. And they stumbled and stottered along the paths into the midst of the bogs. They saw naught, though they heard sighings and flutterings in their ears, and felt cold wet fingers touching them, but all together, looking around, while they came nigh to the pool beside the great snag, where the Moon lay buried. And all at once they stopped, quaking and mazed and skeery, for there was the great stone, half in, half out of the water, for all the world like a strange big coffin, and at the head was the black snag, stretching out its two arms in a dark gruesome cross, and on it a tiddy light flickered, like a dying candle. And they all knelt down in the mud, and said, "Our Lord".

Then they went nigher, and took hold of the big stone, and shoved it up, and afterward they said that for one minute they saw a strange and beautiful face looking up at them glad-like out of the black water, but the Light came so quick and so white and shining, that they stepped back mazed with it, and

the very next minute, when they could see again, there was the full Moon in the sky, bright and beautiful and kind as ever, shining and smiling down at them, and making the bogs and the paths as clear as day, and stealing into the very corners, as though she'd have driven the darkness and the Bogles clean away if she could.

Do You Believe in Fairies?

An extract from *Peter Pan* by J M Barrie

The home of the Darling children — Wendy, John and Michael — is often visited by a flying boy called Peter Pan. One night, Peter whisks the children to his home — Neverland — so Wendy can mother his gang, the Lost Boys. But Neverland is a dangerous place and, unfortunately, Wendy and her brothers are captured by Captain Hook and his evil band of pirates. Peter's best friend, a mischievous fairy called Tinker Bell, comes to break the bad news to him…

PETER SLEPT ON. The light guttered and went out, leaving the tenement in darkness, but still he slept. It must have been not less than ten o'clock, when he sat up in his bed, wakened by a soft, cautious tapping on the door of his tree.

Soft and cautious, but in that stillness it was sinister. Peter felt for his dagger till his hand gripped it. Then he spoke: "Who is that?"

For a long time there was no answer, but then he heard the knock again.

"Who are you?"

No answer.

Peter was thrilled, and he loved being thrilled. In two strides he reached the door.

"I won't open unless you speak," Peter cried.

Then at last the visitor spoke, in a bell-like voice.

"Let me in, Peter."

It was Tink, and quickly he unbarred to her. She flew in excitedly, her face flushed and her dress stained with mud.

"What is it?"

"Oh, you could never guess!" she cried, and offered him three guesses.

"Out with it!" he shouted, and in one ungrammatical sentence, as long as the ribbons that magicians pull from their mouths, she told of the capture of Wendy and the boys.

Peter's heart bobbed up and down as he listened. Wendy bound, and on the pirate ship – she who loved everything to be just so!

"I'll rescue her!" he cried, leaping at his weapons. As he leaped he thought of something he could do to please her. He could take his medicine.

His hand closed on the fatal draught.

"No!" shrieked Tinker Bell, who had heard Hook mutter about his deed as he sped through the forest.

"Why not?"

"It is poisoned."

"Poisoned? Who could have poisoned it?"

"Hook."

"Don't be silly. How indeed could Hook have got down here?"

Alas, Tinker Bell could not explain this.

Nevertheless Hook's words had left no room for doubt. The cup was poisoned.

"Besides," said Peter, quite believing himself, "I never fell asleep."

He raised the cup. No time for words now, time for deeds, and with one of her lightning movements Tink got between his lips and the draught, and drained it to the dregs.

"Why, Tink, how dare you drink my medicine?"

But she did not answer. Already she was reeling in the air.

"What is the matter with you?" cried Peter, suddenly afraid.

"It was poisoned, Peter," she told him softly, "and now I am going to be dead."

"O Tink, did you drink it to save me?"

"Yes."

"But why, Tink?"

Her wings would scarcely carry her now, but in reply she alighted on his shoulder and gave his nose

a loving bite. She whispered
in his ear, "You silly ass,"
and then, tottering to her
chamber, laid on the bed.

His head almost filled
the fourth wall of her
little room as he knelt near
her in distress. Every moment
her light was growing fainter, and
he knew that if it went out she would be no more.
She liked his tears so much that she put out her
finger and let them run over it.

Her voice was so low that at first he could not
make out what she said. Then he made it out. She
was saying that she thought she could get well again
if children believed in fairies.

There were no children there, and it was night
time, but Peter addressed all who might be
dreaming of the Neverland, and who were therefore
near to him: boys and girls everywhere.

"Do you believe in fairies?" he cried.

Tink sat up in bed almost briskly to listen intently to her fate.

She fancied she heard answers in the affirmative, and then again she wasn't sure.

"What do you think?" she asked Peter.

"If you believe," he shouted to them, "clap your hands – don't let Tink die."

Many clapped.

Some didn't.

A few beastly ones hissed.

The clapping stopped suddenly, as if countless mothers had rushed to their children's bedrooms to see what on earth was happening, but already Tink was saved. Her voice grew strong, then she popped out of bed, then she was flashing through the room more merry and impudent than ever. She never thought of thanking those who believed, but she would have like to get at the ones who had hissed.

"And now to rescue Wendy!"

Arndt's Night Underground

From *Tales of Wonder Every Child Should Know*
by Kate Douglas Wiggin and
Nora Archibald Smith

I T WAS ON A DREARY winter's night that two poor children were coming home from their daily work. Arndt and Reutha were very tired, and as they came across the moor the wind blew in their faces.

"Dear Arndt, let me sit down and rest for a minute, I can go no farther," said Reutha, as she sank down on a little mound that seemed to rise up invitingly, with its shelter of bushes.

It was not a cold night, so Arndt wrapped his sister up in her woollen cloak, and she sat down.

"I will just run a little farther and try if I can see

the light in Father's window," said Arndt. "You will not be afraid, Reutha?"

"Oh, no! I am never afraid," said Reutha, and leaned her head against a branch which seemed to her as soft and inviting as a pillow.

Arndt went a little way, until he saw the light which his father always placed to guide the children over the moor. Then he felt quite safe, and went back cheerfully to his sister.

Reutha was not there! Beside the little mound and among the bushes did poor Arndt search in terror, but he could not find his sister. He called her name loudly – there was no answer. Not a single trace of her could be found, and yet he had not been five minutes away.

"Oh! What shall I do?" sobbed the boy, and there for a long time did Arndt sit by the hillock, wringing his hands in vain.

At last there passed by an old man, who travelled about the country selling ribbons and cloths. Arndt burst into tears and told him of all that had happened that night.

The peddler's face grew graver and graver. "Arndt," whispered he, "did you ever hear of the Hill-men? It is they who have carried little Reutha away." And then the old man told how in his youth he had heard tales of this same moor, for that the little mound was a fairy-hill, where the underground dwarfs lived, and where they often carried off young children to be their servants, taking them under the hill, and only leaving behind their shoes. "For," said the peddler, "the Hill-people are very particular, and will make all their servants wear beautiful glass shoes instead of clumsy leather."

So he and Arndt searched about the hill, and there, sure enough, they found Reutha's tiny shoes hidden under the long grass. At this her brother's tears burst forth afresh.

"Oh! What shall I do to bring back my poor sister? The Hill-men and women will kill her!"

"No," said the old man, "they will keep Reutha with them a hundred years, and when she comes back you will be dead and buried, while she is still a beautiful child." And then, to comfort the boy, the peddler told him wonderful stories of the riches and splendour of the Hill-people, how that sometimes they had been seen dancing at night on the mounds, and how they wore green caps, which, if any mortal man could get possession of, the dwarfs were obliged to serve him and obey him in everything.

All this Arndt drank in with eager ears, and when the peddler went away he sat a long time thinking.

"I will do it," at last he said aloud. "I will try to get my dear Reutha safe back again."

And the boy stole noiselessly to the mound where the Hill-men were supposed to dwell. He hid himself among the surrounding bushes, and there he lay in the silence and darkness. At last a sudden brightness flashed upon the boy's eyes, the grassy hill opened, and the boy saw a palace underground, glittering with gold and gems. The Hill-men danced about within it, dressed like tiny men and women. One by one they rose out of the opening, and gambolled on the snow-covered mound, but wherever they trod flowers sprang up, and the air grew light and warm as summer. After a while they ceased dancing and began ball-playing, tossing their little green caps about in great glee. And lo and behold! One of these wonderful caps, being tossed farther than usual, lighted on the very forehead of the peeping boy! In a moment he snatched it and held on to it fast, with a cry of triumph. The light faded – the scene vanished – only Arndt heard a small weak voice whispering, humbly and beseechingly in his ear.

"Please, noble gentleman, give me my cap again."

"No, no, good Hill-man," answered the boy, in a strong, courageous voice. "You have got my little sister, and I have got your cap, which I shall keep."

"I will give you a better cap for it – all gold and jewels – oh, so beautiful!" said the Hill-man, persuasively.

"I will not have it. What good would it do me? No, no, I am your master, good dwarf, as you very well know, and I command you to take me down in the hill with you, for I want to see Reutha."

Then Arndt saw the elfin mound open again, but this time the palace was at the bottom of what looked like a dim, gloomy staircase. On the top stair stood the little Hill-man, holding a glowworm lamp, and making many low bows to his new master. Arndt glanced rather fearfully down the staircase, but then he thought of Reutha, and his love for her made him grow bold. He took upon himself a lordly air, and bade his little servant lead the way.

The Hill-man took him through beautiful galleries, and halls, and gardens, until the boy's senses were overwhelmed with these lovely things.

Every now and then he stopped, and asked for Reutha, but then there was always some new chamber to be seen, or some dainty banquet to be tasted, until, by degrees, Arndt's memory of his little sister grew dimmer. When night came, the boy felt himself lulled by sweet music to a soft dreaminess, which was all the sleep that was needed in that fairy paradise.

Thus, day after day passed in all gay delights, the elfin people were the merriest in the world, and they did all their little master desired. And Arndt knew not that while they surrounded him with delights it was only to make him forget his errand.

But one day, when the boy lay on a green dell in the lovely fairy-garden, he heard a low, wailing song, and saw a troop of little mortal children at work in the distance. Some were digging ore, and others making jewellery, while a few stood in the stream that ran by, beating linen, as it seemed. And among these poor little maidens, who worked so hard and sang so mournfully, was his own sister Reutha.

"No one cares for me," she murmured, and her song had in it a plaintive sweetness, very different from the way in which the little maiden spoke on earth. "Poor Reutha is quite alone!"

Even amidst the spells of fairyland that voice went to the brother's heart. He called the Hill-people and bade them bring Reutha to him. Then he kissed her, and wept over her, and dressed her in his own beautiful robes, while the Hill-men dared not interfere. Arndt took his sister by the hand, and said: "Now, let us go — we have stayed here long enough. Good Hill-man, you shall have your cap again when you have brought Reutha and me to our own father's door."

But the Hill-man shook his tiny head, and made his most obsequious bow. "Noble master, anything but this! This little maid we found asleep on our hill, and she is ours for a hundred years."

Here Arndt got into a passion, for, convinced of

the power the little green cap gave him over the dwarfs, he had long lost all fear of them. He stamped with his foot until the little man leaped up a yard high and begged and pleaded with his master to be more patient.

"How dare you keep my sister!" cried the boy, his former companion becoming at once hateful to him. And Arndt folded his arms around Reutha and walked with her through all the gorgeous rooms, the Hill-men and women following behind and luring him with their sweetest songs, most bewitching smiles and promises of great riches and treasures. But Reutha's voice and Reutha's smile had greatest power of all over her brother's heart.

They climbed the gloomy staircase, and stood at the opening in the hillock. Arndt felt the breezes of earth playing on his cheek. How sweet they were, even after the fragrant airs of elfin-land!

"Kind master, give me my cap!" piteously implored the Hill-man.

"Take it, and goodbye for ever more!" cried Arndt, as he clasped his sister in his arms and leaped out. The chasm closed, and the two children found themselves lying in a snow-drift, with the grey dawn of a winter's morning just breaking over them.

"Where have you been all night, my children?" cried the anxious mother, as they knocked at the door.

Had it, indeed, been only a single night – the months that seemed to have passed while they were under the hill? They could not tell, for they were now like all other children, and their wisdom learned in fairyland had passed away. It seemed only a dream, save that the brother and sister loved each other better than ever, and so they continued to do as long as they lived.

A Grin Without a Cat

An extract from *Alice's Adventures in Wonderland*
by Lewis Carroll

Alice follows a talking, clothed White Rabbit down a rabbit hole and falls into a dreamlike place where anything can happen. She drinks a drink which shrinks her and eats a cake which makes her grow. She weeps a sea of tears and talks to animals and birds who are washed away. A caterpillar helps her return to her proper size, whereupon she meets a Duchess whose baby turns into a pig and runs away. Then, high in a nearby tree, a strange cat appears...

THE CAT ONLY GRINNED when it saw Alice. It looked good-natured, she thought. Still it had VERY long claws and a great many teeth, so she felt that it ought to be treated with respect.

"Cheshire Puss," she began, rather timidly, as she did not at all know whether it would like the name, however, it only grinned a little wider. 'Come, it's pleased so far,' thought Alice, and she went on.

"Would you tell me, please, which way I ought to go from here?"

"That depends a good deal on where you want to get to," said the Cat.

"I don't much care where—" said Alice.

"Then it doesn't matter which way you go," said the Cat.

"—so long as I get SOMEWHERE," Alice added as an explanation.

"Oh, you're sure to do that," said the Cat, "if you only walk long enough."

Alice felt that this could not be denied, so she tried another question. "What sort of people live about here?"

"In THAT direction," the Cat said, waving its right paw round, "lives a Hatter, and in THAT direction," waving the other paw, "lives a March Hare. Visit either you like – they're both mad."

"But I don't want to go among mad people," Alice remarked.

"Oh, you can't help that," said the Cat, "we're all mad here. I'm mad. You're mad."

"How do you know I'm mad?" said Alice.

"You must be," said the Cat, "or you wouldn't have come here."

Alice didn't think that this proved it at all, however, she went on, "And how do you know that you're mad?"

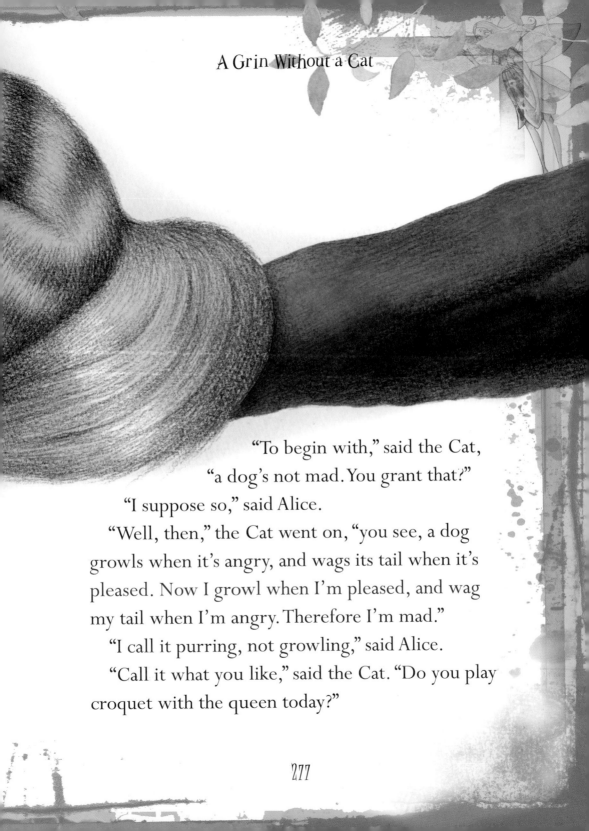

"To begin with," said the Cat, "a dog's not mad. You grant that?"

"I suppose so," said Alice.

"Well, then," the Cat went on, "you see, a dog growls when it's angry, and wags its tail when it's pleased. Now I growl when I'm pleased, and wag my tail when I'm angry. Therefore I'm mad."

"I call it purring, not growling," said Alice.

"Call it what you like," said the Cat. "Do you play croquet with the queen today?"

"I should like it very much," said Alice, "but I haven't been invited yet."

"You'll see me there," said the Cat, and vanished.

Alice was not much surprised at this, she was getting so used to queer things happening. While she was looking at the place where it had been, it suddenly appeared again.

"By-the-bye, what became of the baby?" said the Cat. "I'd nearly forgotten to ask.'

"It turned into a pig," Alice quietly said, just as if it had come back in a natural way.

"I thought it would," said the Cat, and vanished again.

Alice waited a little, half expecting to see it again, but it did not appear, and after a minute or two she walked on in the direction in which the March Hare was said to live. "I've seen hatters before," she said to herself, "the March Hare will be much the most interesting, and perhaps as this is May it won't be raving mad – at least not so mad as it was in March."

As she said this, she looked up, and there was the Cat again, sitting on a branch of a tree.

"Did you say pig, or fig?" said the Cat.

"I said pig," replied Alice, "and I do wish that you wouldn't keep appearing and vanishing so very suddenly – you make one quite giddy."

"All right," said the Cat, and this time it vanished quite slowly, beginning with the end of the tail, and ending with the grin, which remained some time after the rest of it had gone.

'Well! I've often seen a cat without a grin,' thought Alice, 'but a grin without a cat! It's the most curious thing I ever saw in my life!'

The Three Golden Apples

An ancient Greek tale from *A Wonder-Book for Girls and Boys*
by Nathaniel Hawthorne

DID YOU EVER hear of the golden apples that grew in the garden of the Hesperides? Long ago, adventurous young men who desired to do a brave thing, set out in quest of this fruit. Many of them returned no more, and none of them brought back the apples. No wonder that they found it impossible to gather them! For there was a dragon beneath the tree, with a hundred terrible heads, fifty of which were always on the watch, while the other fifty slept.

Once, a hero came wandering through the pleasant land of Italy, a bow and quiver slung across his shoulders. He was wrapped in the skin of the biggest and fiercest lion ever seen, and which he himself had killed, and though, on the whole, he was kind, and generous, and noble, there was a good deal of the lion's fierceness in his heart. As he went on his way, he continually enquired whether that were the right road to the famous garden. He journeyed on and on until, at last, he came to the brink of a river where some beautiful young women sat twining wreaths of flowers.

"Can you tell me, pretty maidens," asked the stranger, "whether this is the right way to the garden of the Hesperides?"

On hearing the stranger's

question, they dropped all their flowers on the grass and gazed at him with astonishment.

"The garden of the Hesperides!" cried one. "We thought mortals had grown weary of seeking it, after so many disappointments. And pray, adventurous traveller, what do you want there?"

"A certain king, who is my cousin," replied he, "has ordered me to get him three of the golden apples. It is my destiny to obey him."

"And do you know," asked the second damsel, "that a terrible dragon with one hundred heads keeps watch under the golden apple tree?"

"I know it well," answered the stranger, calmly. "But, from my cradle upward, it has been my business, and almost my pastime, to deal with serpents and dragons."

Then he sat down on the grass and told them the story of his life, from the day when he was first cradled in a warrior's brazen shield. While he lay there, two immense serpents came gliding over the floor and opened their hideous jaws to devour him, and he, a baby of a few months old, had gripped one of the fierce snakes in each of his little fists, and strangled them to death. When he was but a stripling, he had killed a huge lion, almost as big as the one whose vast and shaggy hide he now wore upon his shoulders. Next he had fought a battle with an ugly sort of monster, called a hydra, which had no less than nine heads, with exceedingly sharp teeth in every one. Then he had chased a very swift stag for a twelvemonth together, without ever stopping to take breath, and had at last caught it by the antlers, and carried it home alive. And he had fought with a very odd race of people, half-horses and half-men, and had conquered them all. Besides all this, he took to himself great credit for having cleaned out a gigantic stable by changing the course of a river so it ran through it and washed it out. Next he told the maidens how he had shot some monstrous birds, and also how he had caught a wild bull alive and let him go again, and had tamed a number of very wild horses, and had conquered Hippolyta, the queen of a race of warlike women called the Amazons. Lastly, he informed the maidens that as strange an adventure as ever happened was when he fought with Geryon, the six-legged giant!

When the stranger had finished the story of his adventures, he looked around at the attentive faces of the maidens. "Perhaps you may have heard of me before," said he, modestly. "My name is Hercules!"

"We had already guessed it," replied the women, "for your deeds are known all over the world."

"Dear maidens," said he, "now that you know my name, will you not tell me how I am to reach the garden of the Hesperides?"

"We will then give you the best directions we can," replied the damsels. "You must go to the seashore, and find out the Old Man of the Sea, and compel him to inform you where the golden apples are to be found."

Hercules thanked them and immediately set forth upon his journey. But, before he was out of hearing, one of the maidens called after him. "Keep fast hold of the Old One, when you catch him!" cried she. "Hold him fast, and he will tell you what you wish to know."

Hercules travelled over hill and dale, and through the solitary woods. Hastening forward, without ever pausing or looking behind, he by and by heard the sea roaring at a distance. At this sound, he increased his speed, and soon came to a beach, where the great surf waves tumbled themselves upon the hard sand, in a long line of snowy foam. At one end of the beach, however, there was a pleasant spot, where some green shrubbery clambered up a cliff. And what should Hercules espy there but an old man, fast asleep!

But was it really and truly an old man? Certainly, at first sight, it looked very like one, but on closer inspection it rather seemed to be some kind of a creature that lived in the sea. For on his legs and arms there were scales, such as fishes have. He was web-footed and web-fingered, after the fashion of a duck, and his long beard, being of a greenish tinge, had more the appearance of a tuft of seaweed than of an ordinary beard.

Hercules was convinced that it could be no other than the Old One, who was to direct him on his way. Thanking his stars for the lucky accident of finding the old fellow asleep, he stole on tiptoe toward him, and caught him by the arm and leg. "Tell me," cried he, before the Old One was well awake, "which is the way to the garden of the Hesperides?"

As you may easily imagine, the Old Man of the Sea awoke in a fright. But his astonishment could hardly have been greater than was that of Hercules, the next moment. For, all of a sudden, the Old One seemed to disappear out of his grasp, and he found himself holding a stag by the fore and hind leg! But still he kept fast hold. Then the stag disappeared, and in its stead there was a sea bird, fluttering and screaming, while Hercules clutched it by the wing and claw! But the bird could not get away. Immediately afterward, there was an ugly three-headed dog, which growled and barked at Hercules, and snapped fiercely at the hands by which he held him! But Hercules would not let him go. In another minute, instead of the three-headed dog, there was a gigantic serpent, and it twisted and twined about the hero's neck and body, and threw its tail high into the air, and opened its deadly jaws as if to devour him outright, so that it was really a very terrible spectacle! But Hercules was no whit disheartened, and squeezed the great serpent so tightly that he soon began to hiss with pain.

As Hercules held on so stubbornly, and only squeezed the Old One so much the tighter at every change of shape, and really put him to no small torture, he finally thought it best to reappear in his own figure. So there he was again, a fishy, scaly, web-footed sort of personage, with something like a tuft of seaweed at his chin.

"Pray, what do you want with me?" cried the Old One, as soon as he could take breath, for it is quite a tiresome affair to go through so many false shapes.

"My name is Hercules!" roared the stranger. "And you will never get out of my clutch until you tell me the nearest way to the garden of the Hesperides!"

When the old fellow heard who it was that had caught him, he saw with half an eye that it would be necessary to tell Hercules everything that he wanted to know.

"You must go on till you come in sight of a giant, who holds the sky on his shoulders," said the Old Man of the Sea. "And the giant, if he happens to be in the humour, will tell you exactly where the garden of the Hesperides lies."

Thanking the Old One, Hercules continued on his journey.

After many more adventures, he came across a giant so vast that the clouds rested about his midst, like a girdle, and hung like a hoary beard from his chin, and flitted before his huge eyes. Most incredible of all, the giant held up his great hands and appeared to support the sky. Poor fellow! He had evidently stood there for a long while. An ancient forest had been growing and decaying around his feet.

"I am Hercules!" roared the hero. "And I am seeking the garden of the Hesperides!"

"There is nobody but myself, Atlas," thundered the giant, "that can go to the garden of the Hesperides, and gather the golden apples. If it were not for this little business of holding up the sky, I would make half a dozen steps across the sea and get them for you."

"You are very kind," replied Hercules. "And cannot you rest the sky upon a mountain?"

"None of them are quite high enough," said Atlas, shaking his head. "But you seem to be a fellow of some strength. What if you should take my burden on your shoulders, while I do your errand for you?"

Hercules considered for a moment then, without more ado, the sky was shifted from the shoulders of Atlas and placed upon his shoulders.

When this was safely accomplished, the first thing

that the giant did was to stretch himself. Then, all at once, he began to caper, and leap, and dance, and laugh for joy at his freedom. When his elation had a little subsided, he stepped into the sea – ten miles at the first stride, which brought him mid-leg deep, and ten miles at the second, when the water came just above his knees, and ten miles more at the third, by which he was immersed nearly to his waist. Hercules watched the giant as he still went onward. At last the gigantic shape faded entirely out of view.

I know not how long it was before Hercules beheld the huge shape of the giant, like a cloud, on the far-off edge of the sea, returning. At his nearer approach, Atlas held up his hand, in which Hercules could perceive three magnificent golden apples, as big as pumpkins, all hanging from one branch.

"I heartily thank you for your trouble," bade Hercules. "And now, as I have a long way to go, and am rather in haste – and as the king, my cousin, is anxious to receive the golden apples – will you be kind enough to take the sky off my shoulders again?"

"Why, as to that my good friend," said the giant, "I could carry the golden apples to the king, your cousin, much quicker than you could. And, besides, I have no fancy for burdening myself with the sky, just now."

"What!" shouted Hercules, very wrathfully. "Do you intend to make me bear this burden for ever?"

"Well, after a thousand years, if I happen to feel in the mood, we may possibly agree to shift about again," shrugged the giant. "You are certainly a very strong man, and can never have a better opportunity than this to prove it. You'll become even more famous than ever!"

"Pish!" cried Hercules, impatiently. "Just take the sky upon your head one instant, will you? I want to make a cushion of my lion's skin, for the weight to rest upon. It really chafes me, and will cause unnecessary inconvenience in so many centuries as I am to stand here."

"That's no more than fair, and I'll do it!" quoth the giant.

Ah, the thick-witted old rogue! He threw down the golden apples and took back the sky. And Hercules picked up the golden apples and set out on his journey homeward, without paying the slightest heed to the thundering tones of the giant, who bellowed after him to come back.

And there stands the giant to this day – or, at any rate, there stands a mountain as tall as he, and which bears his name. And when the thunder rumbles about its summit, we may imagine it to be the voice of the giant Atlas, bellowing after Hercules!

Shipwreck on Lilliput

An extract from *Gulliver's Travels*
by Jonathan Swift, adapted by John Lang

Lemuel Gulliver is a young surgeon who falls on hard times. He takes work on board ships making long sea voyages to strange, distant lands. On one such journey, far from home, a terrible storm wrecks his ship, washing away all the crew and leaving Gulliver at the mercy of the waves...

GULLIVER SWAM till no strength or feeling was left in his arms and legs. He swam bravely, his breath coming in sobs, his eyes blinded with the salt seas that broke over his head. Still he struggled on, until at last, in a part where the wind seemed to have less force, on letting down his legs he found that he was within his depth. But the shore shelved so gradually that for nearly a mile he had to wade wearily through shallow water, till, almost fainting with fatigue, he reached dry land.

By this time darkness was coming on, and there were no signs of houses or of people. He staggered forward but a little distance, and then, on the short, soft turf, sank down exhausted and slept.

When he woke, the sun was shining. He tried to rise, but not by any means could he stir hand or foot. Gulliver had slept lying on his back, and now he found that his arms and legs were tightly fastened to the ground. Across his body were numbers of thin but strong cords, and even his hair, which was very long, was pegged down so securely that he could not turn his head.

All round about him there was a confused sound of voices, but he could see nothing except the sky, and the sun shone so hot and fierce into his eyes that he could scarcely keep them open.

Soon he felt something come gently up his left leg, and forward on to his breast almost to his chin. Looking down as much as possible, he saw standing there a very little man, not more than six inches high, armed with a bow and arrows.

Then many more small men began to swarm over him. Gulliver let out such a roar of wonder and fright that they all turned and ran, many of them getting bad falls in their hurry to get out of danger. But very quickly the little people came back again. This time, with a great struggle Gulliver managed to break the cords that fastened his left arm, and at the same time, by a violent wrench that hurt him dreadfully, he slightly loosened the strings that fastened his hair, so that he was able to turn his head a little to one side. But the little men were too quick for him, and got out of reach before he could catch any of them.

Then he heard a great shouting, followed by a shrill little voice that called sharply, "*Tolgo phonac*," and immediately, arrows like needles were shot into his hand, and another volley struck him in the face. Poor Gulliver covered his face with his hand, and lay groaning with pain.

Again he struggled to get loose. But the harder he fought for freedom, the more the little men shot arrows into him, and some of them even tried to run their spears into his sides.

When he found that the more he struggled the more he was hurt, Gulliver lay still, thinking to himself that at night at least, now that his left hand was free, he could easily get rid of the rest of his bonds. As soon as the little people saw that he struggled no more, they ceased shooting at him, but he knew from the increasing sound of voices that more and more of the little soldiers were coming round him.

Soon, a few yards from him, on the right, he heard a continued sound of hammering, and on turning his head to that side as far as the strings would let him, he saw that a small wooden stage was being built. On to this, when it was finished, there climbed by ladders four men, and one of them (who seemed to be a very important person, for a little page boy attended to hold up his train) immediately gave an order. At once about fifty of the soldiers ran forward and cut the strings that tied Gulliver's hair on the left side, so that he could turn his head easily to the right.

Then the person began to make a long speech, not one word of which could Gulliver understand, but it seemed to him that sometimes the little man threatened and sometimes made offers of kindness.

Shipwreck on Lilliput

As well as he could, Gulliver made signs that he submitted. Then, feeling by this time faint with hunger, he pointed with his fingers many times to his mouth, to show that he wanted something to eat.

They understood him very well. Several ladders were put against Gulliver's sides, and about a hundred little people climbed up and carried to his mouth all kinds of bread and meat. There were things shaped like legs, and shoulders, and saddles of mutton. Very good they were, Gulliver thought, but very small, no bigger than a lark's wing, and the loaves of bread were about the size of bullets, so that he could take several at a mouthful. The people wondered greatly at the amount that he ate.

When he signed that he was thirsty, they slung up two of their biggest casks of wine, and having rolled them forward to his hand they knocked out the heads of the casks. Gulliver drank them both and asked for more, for they held only about a small tumblerful each. But there was no more to be had.

As the small people walked to and fro over his body, Gulliver was sorely tempted to seize forty or fifty of them and dash them on the ground, and then to make a further struggle for liberty. But the pain he had already suffered from their arrows made him think better of it, and he wisely lay quiet.

Soon another small man, who from his brilliant uniform seemed to be an officer of very high rank, marched with some others on to Gulliver's chest and held up to his eyes a paper which Gulliver understood to be an order from the king of the country. The officer made a long speech, often pointing towards something a long way off, and (as Gulliver afterwards learned) told him that he was to be taken as a prisoner to the city, the capital of the country.

The city was not reached till the following day, whereupon Gulliver was brought to a very large building which had once been used as a temple. Inside the building the king's blacksmiths fastened many chains, which they then brought through one of these little windows and padlocked round Gulliver's left ankle. Gulliver found that he could easily creep through the door, and that there was room inside to lie down. He could also get a little exercise by walking backwards and forwards outside. Then the king gave orders that food should be brought for Gulliver, twenty little carts full, and ten of wine, and he and his courtiers, all covered with gold and silver, stood around and watched him eating. After the king had gone away, the people of the city crowded round, and some of them began to behave very badly, one man even going so far as to shoot an arrow at Gulliver which was not far from putting out one of his eyes. But the officer in command of the soldiers who were on guard ordered his men to bind and push six of the worst behaved of the crowd within reach of Gulliver, who at once seized five of them and put them in his coat pocket. The sixth he held up to his mouth and made

as if he meant to eat him,
whereupon the wretched little
creature shrieked aloud with
terror, and when Gulliver
took out his knife, all the
people, even the
soldiers, were
dreadfully alarmed.
But Gulliver only cut
the man's bonds and
let him run away,
which he did in a
great hurry. And when
he took the others out
of his pocket, one by
one, and treated them in
the same way, the crowd
began to laugh.

After that the people
always behaved very well to

Gulliver, and he became a great
favourite. From all over the kingdom
crowds flocked to see the Great
Man Mountain.

The Deliverers of Their Country

An extract from the tale in *The Book of Dragons*
by E Nesbit

THERE WAS no one about in the streets
except dragons, and the place was swarming
with them. Fortunately none were just the right size
for eating little boys and girls. There were dragons
on the pavement, and dragons on the roadway,
dragons basking on the front doorsteps of public
buildings, and dragons preening their wings on
the roofs in the hot afternoon sun. The town
was quite green with them. Even when the
children had got out of the town and
were walking in the lanes, they
noticed that the fields on each side

were greener than usual with the scaly legs and tails, and some of the smaller sizes had made themselves asbestos nests in the flowering hawthorn hedges.

Effie held her brother's hand tight, and when a fat dragon flopped against her ear she screamed out, and a whole flight of green dragons rose from the field at the sound, and sprawled away across the sky.

"Oh, I want to go home," said Effie.

"Don't be silly," said Harry. "People who are going to be their country's deliverers never scream and say they want to go home."

"Are we?" asked Effie, "Deliverers, I mean?"

"You'll see," said her brother, and on they carried on their way.

When they came to St George's Church they walked around the churchyard, and presently they found the large stone tomb, with the great figure of St George carved in marble, wearing his armour and helmet,

305

and with his hands folded across his breast.

"However can we wake him?" they said. Then Harry spoke to St George and tried to waken the great dragon-slayer by shaking his marble shoulders. But St George took no notice.

Then Effie began to cry, and she put her arms around St George's neck and she kissed the marble face, and she said: "Oh, dear, good, kind St George, please wake up and help us."

And at that St George opened his eyes sleepily, and stretched himself and said: "What's the matter, little girl?"

So the children told him all about it, but when he heard that there were so many dragons he shook his head.

"It's no good," he said. 'One man one dragon' was my motto."

At that moment

a flight of dragons passed overhead and St George half drew his sword.

"By the way, what sort of weather have you been having lately?"

Effie said patiently, "It has been very fine. Father says it is the hottest weather there has ever been in this country."

"Ah, I guessed as much," said the champion, thoughtfully. "Dragons can't stand wet and cold. If only you could find the taps…"

St George was beginning to settle down again on his stone slab.

"Goodnight, very sorry I can't help you," he said, yawning behind his marble hand.

"Oh, but you can," cried Effie. "Tell us – what taps do you mean?"

"Oh, like in the bathroom," said St George, still more sleepily. "I'm sorry I can't – goodnight."

And he fell back into his marble and was fast asleep again in a moment.

ENCHANTMENTS AND TRANSFORMATIONS

The Star and the Lily

From *Indian Myths*
by Ellen Russell Emerson

AN OLD CHIEFTAIN was sitting in his
wigwam, quietly smoking his favourite pipe,
when a crowd of Indian boys and girls suddenly
entered and begged him to tell them all a story, and
he did so.

There was once a time when this world was filled
with happy people, when all the nations were as
one, and the crimson tide of war had not begun to
roll. Plenty of game was in the forest and on the
plains. Every tree and bush yielded fruit. Flowers

carpeted the earth. Birds flew from branch to branch, fearing none, for there were none to harm them. The beasts of the field were tame, and they came and went at the bidding of man. One long unending spring gave no place for winter, and sickness was unknown.

It was at such a time, when Earth was a paradise and humans worthy to be in charge, that the Indians were the only dwellers in the American wilderness. They numbered millions, and, living as nature designed them to live, enjoyed its many blessings. At night they met on the wide green beneath the heavenly worlds. They watched the stars – they loved to gaze at them, for they believed them to be the homes of the good, who had been taken home by the Great Spirit.

One night they saw one star brighter than all others. It was far away in the south, near a mountain peak. For many nights it was seen, till at length many began to doubt that the star was as far distant as it seemed to be. People began to think it must be only a short distance away, near the tops of some trees. A number of warriors went to see what it was, and on their return said it appeared strange and somewhat like a bird. A committee of wise men feared that it might be the omen of some disaster – perhaps the star spoken of by their forefathers as the forerunner of a dreadful war. However, others thought it foretold good.

One moon had nearly gone by, and yet the mystery remained unsolved. One night a young warrior had a dream, in which a beautiful maiden came and stood at his side She told him, "Young brave! Charmed with the land of my forefathers, its flowers, its birds, its rivers, its beautiful lakes, and its mountains, I have left my sisters in yonder world to dwell among you. Young brave! Ask your wise and your great men where I can live and see the happy race continually. Ask them what form I shall assume in order to be loved."

When the young man awoke, he assembled the
wise men of the nation and related his dream. They
concluded that the star that had been seen in the
south had fallen in love with mankind and that it
wanted to live with them.

The next night, five tall, noble-looking and
adventurous braves were sent to welcome the
stranger to earth. They went and presented to it a
pipe of peace, filled with sweet-scented herbs, and
were rejoiced that it took it from them. As they
returned to the village, the star, with expanded
wings, followed, and hovered over their homes till
the dawn of day.

Again it came to the young man in a dream and
desired to know where it should live and what form
it should take. Places were named — on the top of
giant trees, or in flowers. At length it was told to
choose a place itself. At first it dwelled in the white
rose of the mountains, but there it could not be
seen. It went next to the prairie, but it feared the

hoof of the buffalo. It then sought the rocky cliff, but there it was so high that the children, whom it loved most out of everything, could not see it.

"I know where I shall live," said the bright fugitive, "where I can see the gliding canoe of the race I most admire. Children! Yes, they shall be my playmates. I will kiss their slumber by the side of cool lakes. The nation shall love me wherever I am."

These words having been said, she alighted on the waters, where she saw herself reflected. And the next morning thousands of white flowers were seen on the surface of the lakes.

This star lived in the southern skies. Her brethren can be seen far off in the cold north, hunting the Great Bear, whilst her sisters watch her in the east and west.

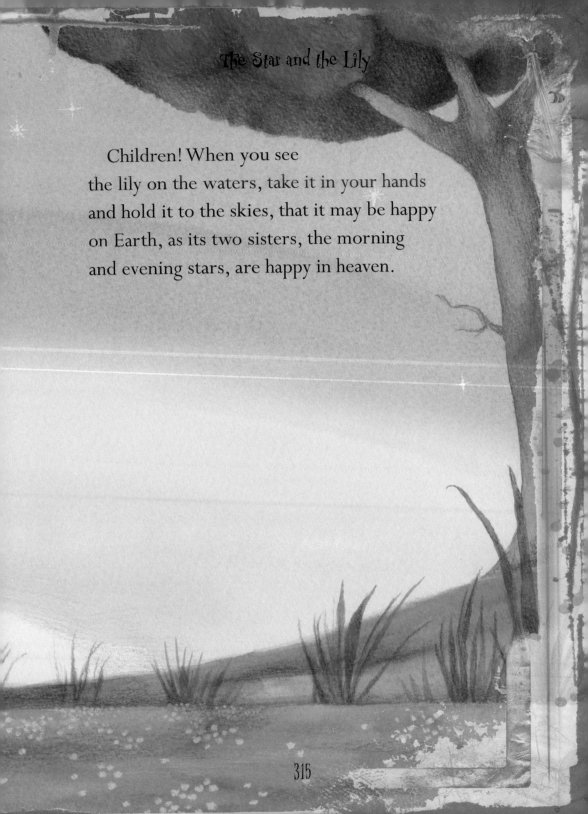

Children! When you see
the lily on the waters, take it in your hands
and hold it to the skies, that it may be happy
on Earth, as its two sisters, the morning
and evening stars, are happy in heaven.

The Enchanted Horse

From *The Arabian Nights Entertainments*,
adapted by Amy Steedman

I TWAS NEW YEAR'S day in Persia, and the king had been entertained by many wonderful shows prepared for him by his people. Evening was drawing on when an Indian appeared, leading a horse he wished to show to the king. It was not real, but it was so wonderfully made that it looked alive.

"Your Majesty," cried the Indian, bowing low, "I beg thou wilt look upon this wonder. Nothing thou hast seen today can equal my horse. I have only to mount upon its back and wish myself in any part of the world, and it carries me there in a few minutes."

"Show us what it can do," the king commanded. He pointed to a distant mountain, and bade the Indian to fetch a branch from the palm trees there.

The Indian vaulted into the saddle, turned a little peg in the horse's neck, and in a moment was flying so swiftly through the air that he soon disappeared from sight. In less than a quarter of an hour he reappeared, and laid a branch from a palm tree at the king's feet.

"Thou art right," cried the king. "Thy enchanted horse is the most wonderful thing I have seen. What is its price? I must have it!"

"Your Majesty," the Indian replied, "it shall be thine only if thou wilt give me your daughter, for my wife."

At these words the king's son sprang to his feet.

"Sire," he cried, "thou wilt never dream of granting such a request."

"My son," answered the king, "at whatever cost I must have this wonderful horse. But before I agree, try the horse, and tell me what thou thinkest of it."

The Indian began to tell the prince how to work the horse. But as soon as the prince was in the saddle, he turned the screw and went flying off through the air.

"Alas!" cried the Indian, "he has gone off without learning how to come back!"

"Wretch," the king cried, "thou shalt be cast into prison, and unless my son returns in safety, thou shalt be put to death."

Meanwhile the prince had gone gaily sailing up into the clouds, and could no longer see the Earth below. This was very pleasant, and he felt that he had never had such a delicious ride in his life before. But presently he began to think it was time to descend.

He screwed the peg round and round, backwards and forwards, but it seemed to make no difference. Instead of coming down he sailed higher and higher, until he thought he was going to knock his head against the blue sky. What was to be done? The prince began to grow a little nervous, and he felt over the horse's neck to see if there was another peg to be found anywhere. To his joy, just behind the ear, he touched a small screw, and when he turned it, he felt he was going slower and slower, and gently turning round. Then the Enchanted Horse flew downwards through the starry night, and he saw, stretched out before him, a beautiful city gleaming white through the purple night.

He let the horse go where it would, and presently it stopped on the roof of a great marble palace. He descended some white marble steps and found himself in a great hall where a row of slaves were sleeping soundly, guarding the entrance to a room beyond. Very softly the prince crept past the guards, and lifting the curtain from the door, looked in. And there he saw a splendid room lighted by a thousand lights and filled with sleeping slaves, and in the middle, upon a sofa, was the most beautiful princess his eyes had ever gazed upon. He went softly to her side, and, kneeling by the sofa, gently touched her hand. The princess sighed and opened her eyes, but before she could cry out, he begged her in a whisper to be silent and fear nothing.

"I am a prince," he said, "the son of the King of Persia."

Now this princess was no other than the daughter of the King of Bengal.

Never before had the princess seen anyone so

gallant and handsome as this strange young prince.
She gave him her hand, awoke her slaves and bade
them give him refreshment. While the prince
rested, she dressed herself in her loveliest robes, and
twined her hair with her most precious jewels, that
she might appear as beautiful as possible. And when
the prince saw her again, he thought her the most
charming princess in all the world, and he loved her
with all his heart. When he had told her all his
adventures she sighed to think that he must now
leave her and return to his father's court.

"My princess," he said, "since it is so hard to part,
wilt thou not ride with me upon the Enchanted
Horse? Then when we arrive once more in Persia
we will marry."

So together they mounted the Enchanted Horse
and the prince placed his arm around the princess
and turned the magic peg. Up and up they flew over
land and sea, and then the prince turned the other
screw, and they landed just outside his father's city.

He left the princess at a palace outside the gates, for he wished to go alone to prepare his father.

"My beloved son!" cried the king, full of joy at his safe return.

And the prince told the king all about his adventure and the Princess of Bengal.

"Let her be brought here instantly," cried the king, "and the marriage shall take place today." Then he ordered that the Indian should be set free at once and allowed to depart with the Enchanted Horse.

Great was the surprise of the Indian when he was released instead of having his head cut off, as he had expected. But when he heard about the prince's adventure, a wicked plan came into his head. He flew on the Enchanted Horse to the palace where the princess was waiting, arriving before the king's messengers could reach her. "Tell the princess," he said to the palace slaves, "that the Prince of Persia has sent me to bring her to his father's palace upon the Enchanted Horse."

The princess was very glad when she heard this message – but alas! As soon as the Indian turned the peg and the horse flew away, she found she was being carried off, far away from Persia and her beloved prince. All her prayers and entreaties were in vain. The Indian only mocked her and said he meant to marry her himself.

When the prince discovered what had happened, he was beside himself with grief. He set off to seek for her, vowing that he would find her, or perish in the attempt.

By this time the Enchanted Horse had travelled many hundreds of miles. The Indian descended into a wood close to the town of Cashmere, where he went in search of food. As soon as the princess had eaten a little she felt stronger and braver, and as she heard horses galloping past, she called out loudly for help. The men on horseback came riding at once to her aid. The leader of the horsemen, who was the Sultan of Cashmere, cut off the Indian's head, placed

the princess upon his horse and led her to his palace.
He had made up his mind to marry her himself!

In vain the princess begged and pleaded to be sent
back to Persia. But the sultan only smiled and began
the wedding preparations. Then she thought of a
plan to save herself. She began talking all the
nonsense she could think of and behaving as if she
were mad. So well did she pretend, that the
wedding was put off, and all the doctors were called
in to see if they could cure her. Of course, none of
them could.

All this time the Prince of Persia was searching
for his princess, and when he came to one of the
great cities of India, he quickly learned that
everyone was talking about the sad illness of the
Princess of Bengal who was to marry the sultan. He
at once disguised himself as a doctor and went to the
palace. The sultan received him with joy, and led
him at once to where the princess sat alone,
weeping and wringing her hands.

"Your Majesty," said the disguised prince, "no one must enter the room with me, or the cure will surely fail and the princess will never recover."

So the sultan left him, and the prince went to the princess, and gently touched her hand. "My beloved princess," he said, "dost thou not know me?"

As soon as the princess heard that dear voice she threw herself into the prince's arms.

"We must at once plan our escape," said the prince. "Canst thou tell me what has become of the Enchanted Horse?"

"Naught can I tell thee of it, dear prince," answered the princess, "but since the sultan knows its value, no doubt he has kept it in some safe place."

"Then first we must persuade the sultan that thou art almost cured," said the prince. "Put on thy costliest robes and dine with him tonight, and I will do the rest."

The sultan was charmed to find the princess so much recovered, and his joy knew no bounds when the new doctor informed him that he hoped by the next day to have complete the cure.

"I find that the princess has somehow been infected by the magic of the Enchanted Horse," he said. "If thou wilt have the horse brought out into the great square, and place the princess upon its back, I will prepare some magic perfumes which will dispel the enchantment."

So next morning the Enchanted Horse was brought out into the square, which was crowded with onlookers, and the princess was mounted upon its back. Then the disguised prince placed four braziers of burning coals round the horse and threw into them a perfume of a most delicious scent. The smoke of the perfume rose in thick clouds, almost hiding the princess, and at that moment the prince leaped into the saddle behind her, turned the peg, and sailed away into the blue sky.

The Enchanted Horse did not stop until it had carried the two of them safely back to Persia, and there they were married amid great rejoicings.

But what became of the Enchanted Horse? Ah! That is a question which no one can answer.

The Princess on the Glass Hill

From Andrew Lang's *Blue Fairy Book*

ONCE UPON A TIME there was a man who had a meadow which lay on a mountain, and in the meadow there was a barn in which he stored hay. But there had not been much hay for the last two years, for every St John's eve, when the grass was highest, it was all eaten clean up, as if a whole flock of sheep had gnawed it during the night. The man became tired of losing his crop, and said to his sons – he had three of them, and the third was called Cinderlad – that one of them must sleep in the barn on St John's night and keep a sharp look-out, to stop whatever was destroying the grass.

The eldest was quite willing to go to the meadow. He would watch so well, he said, that neither man, nor beast, nor even the Devil himself should have any of it. So when evening came he went to the barn and lay down to sleep, but when night was drawing on there was such a rumbling and earthquake that the walls and roof shook. The lad took to his heels as fast as he could, never even looking back, so the barn remained empty that year too.

Next St John's eve, the next oldest son was willing to show what he could do. He went to the barn and lay down to sleep, as his brother had done, but when night was drawing near there was a great rumbling, and then an earthquake even worse than that on the former St John's night. When the youth heard it he was terrified and went running off.

The year after, it was Cinderlad's turn, but when he made ready to go the others mocked him. "Well, you are just the right one to watch the hay, you who have never learned anything but how to sit among the ashes!" said they.

Cinderlad, however, did not trouble himself about what they said, but when evening drew near rambled away to the outlying field. When he got there he went into the barn and lay down, but in about an hour's time the rumbling and creaking began, and it was frightful to hear it. 'Well, if it gets no worse than that, I can manage to stand it,' thought Cinderlad. In a little time the creaking began again, and the earth quaked so that all the hay flew about. 'Oh! If it gets no worse than that I can manage to stand it,' thought Cinderlad. But then came a third rumbling, and a third earthquake, so violent that the boy thought the walls and roof had fallen down, but when that was over everything suddenly grew as still. 'I am pretty sure that it will come again,' thought Cinderlad, but no, it did not. Everything was quiet, and everything stayed quiet, and when he had lain still a short time he heard something that sounded as if a horse were standing chewing just outside the barn door.

He stole away to the door, which was ajar, to see what was there, and a horse was standing eating. It was so big, and fat, and fine a horse that Cinderlad had never seen one like it before, and a saddle and bridle lay upon it, and a complete suit of armour for a knight, and everything was of copper, and so bright that it shone. 'Ha, ha! It is thou who eatest up our hay then,' thought the boy. 'I will stop that'.

331

So he made haste, and took out his steel for striking fire, and threw it over the horse, and then it had no power to stir from the spot, and became so tame that the boy could do what he liked with it. So he mounted it and rode away to a place which no one knew of but himself, and there he tied it up.

When he went home again his brothers sniggered and asked how he had got on.

"I lay in the barn till the sun rose, but I saw nothing and heard nothing, not I," said the boy. "God knows what there was to make you two so frightened."

And when the puzzled brothers went to check the meadow, the grass was all standing just as long and as thick as it had been the night before.

The next St John's eve, Cinderlad went again, and three earthquakes happened exactly as before. This time the horse that arrived was far larger and fatter than the first horse, and it had a saddle on its back, and a bridle was on it too, and a full suit of armour for a knight, all of bright silver, and as beautiful as anyone could wish to see. Again the boy took out his steel for striking fire, and threw it over the horse's mane, and the beast stood there as quiet as a lamb. Then the boy rode the horse away to where he kept the other, and then went home again.

Once more, in the morning, the astounded brothers found the meadow grass standing as high and as thick as ever, but that did not make them any kinder to Cinderlad.

When the third St John's night came, once more Cinderlad dared to go, and everything happened just the same. There were three earthquakes, each worse than the last, and then there was a horse standing outside the barn, much larger and fatter than the two others he had caught. Again the boy pulled out his steel for striking fire, and threw it over the horse, and the boy could do just what he liked with it. He mounted it and rode to the place where he had the two others, and then he went home again.

The brothers hated him, for again the grass was standing, looking as fine and as thick as ever.

Now, the king of the country in which Cinderlad's father dwelled lived in a palace close to a high, high, hill of glass, slippery as ice. One day, the king sent out a proclamation saying that he would give his daughter's hand in marriage – and half the kingdom – to any man who could ride up to the top of the glass hill, to where his daughter was to sit, and take one of three gold apples she would hold in her lap. On the appointed day, princes and knights came riding thither from the very end of the world to win the beautiful princess, and everyone else thronged to the glass hill to see who won her. Cinderlad's two brothers went along too, but they would not hear of letting him go with them, for he was so dirty with sleeping among the ashes that they said everyone would laugh at them if they were seen in the company of such an oaf.

"Well, then, I will go all alone by myself," said Cinderlad.

When the two brothers got to the glass hill, all the princes and knights were trying to ride up it – but in vain, for no sooner did the horses set foot upon the hill then down they slipped, and there was not one which could get even so much as a couple of yards up.

At last all the horses were so tired that they could do no more, and their riders were forced to give up the attempt.

When suddenly a knight in copper armour came riding up on a horse with copper bridle and saddle, shining like the dawn. He rode straight to the hill and began going up as if it were nothing at all. The princess thought that she had never seen so handsome a knight, and hoped that he might make it to the top. But when the knight had got about a third of the way up, he suddenly turned his horse round and rode down again. The disappointed princess threw one of the golden apples down after him, and it rolled into his shoe. But when he had come down from off the hill he rode away, and that so fast that no one knew what had become of him.

That night, Cinderlad's brothers returned home with a long story to tell about the copper knight and his horse riding up the glass hill.

"Oh! I should have liked to see him too, that I should," said Cinderlad, who was as usual sitting by the chimney among the cinders.

Next day the brothers set out again, and once

more refused to let Cinderlad go with them.

All the princes and knights were beginning to ride again, and this time they had taken care to roughen the shoes of their horses – but that did not help them. They rode and they slipped as they had done the day before, and not one of them could get even so far as a yard up the hill. When they had tired out their horses, they again had to stop altogether.

But all at once a knight in silver armour came riding on a steed that was much, much finer than the horse in copper tack. This one had a silver bridle and saddle, and he and his rider shone like the moon. He rode straight to the glass hill and began to go up. The princess liked this knight even better than she had liked the other, and sat longing that he might be able to get all the way up. But when the knight had ridden two-thirds of the way up he suddenly turned his horse around and rode down again. The dismayed princess threw an apple after him, and it rolled into his shoe, and as soon as he had got down the glass hill he rode away so fast that no one could see what had become of him.

At night the two brothers went home full of news of the knight in silver armour.

"Oh, how I should have liked to see him too!" said Cinderlad, from the dirt of the woodpile.

On the third day everything went just as on the former days. Cinderlad wanted to go with them to look at the riding, but the two brothers would not have him, and when they got to the glass hill there was no one who could ride even so far as a yard up it. Then there came thundering a knight in golden armour, riding a stallion without equal, wearing a golden saddle and bridle, and they blazed like the noonday sun. The knight rode straight away to the glass hill, and galloped up it as if it were no hill at all, so that the princess had not even time to wish that he might get up the whole way before he was at the top. The golden knight took the third golden apple from the lap of the princess and then turned his horse about and rode down again, and vanished from their sight before anyone was able to say a word to him.

When the two brothers returned home again, they told Cinderlad all about the knight in the golden armour.

"Oh, if only I could have seen him!" said Cinderlad, scrubbing the scullery floor.

Next day all the knights and princes were to appear before the king and princess, in order that he who had the golden apple might produce it. One after the other they all came, but no one had the golden apple. First princes, then knights went… then all the other young men of the kingdom. Cinderlad's two brothers were the last of all, and the king enquired of them if there was no one else left to come.

"We have a brother," said the two, "but he never got the golden apple! He never left the kitchen on any of the three days."

"Never mind that," said the king. "As everyone else has come to the palace, let him come too."

So Cinderlad was made to go to the king's palace.

"Hast thou the golden apple?" asked the king.

"Yes, here is the first, and here is the second, and here is the third, too," said Cinderlad, and he took all three apples out of his pocket, and with that drew off his sooty rags, and appeared there before them in his bright golden armour, which gleamed as he stood.

"Thou shalt have my daughter, and the half of my kingdom, and thou hast well earned both!" said the king. So there was a wedding, and Cinderlad got the king's daughter, and everyone made merry at the wedding, for all of them could make merry, even though they could not ride up the glass hill. And if they have not left off their merry-making they must be at it still.

The Storks and the Night Owl

From *Tales of Wonder Every Child Should Know*
by Kate Douglas Wiggin and Nora Archibald Smith

CHASID, THE CALIPH OF BAGDAD, was comfortably seated upon his sofa one beautiful afternoon. He smoked from a long pipe made of rosewood, sipped now and then a little coffee, which a slave poured out for him, and stroked his beard very contentedly. So it was very plain that the caliph was in a good humour.

Just then, his grand vizier, Manzor, brought in a merchant with a chest which contained very interesting wares: pearls and rings, richly inlaid pistols, goblets and combs. The caliph and his vizier looked at them and purchased some trinkets. As the merchant was about to pack up his chest the caliph noticed a small, strange box. On opening it, he found it was filled with blackish powder and a paper with strange writing upon it, which neither the caliph nor Manzor could read. "I received these things from a trader who found them in the streets of Mecca," explained the merchant. "I know not what they contain. They are at your service for a trifling price, for I can do nothing with them."

The caliph, who was a great collector of old manuscripts for his library, even if he could not read them, purchased box and writings, and dismissed the merchant. Then, in the hope of finding out what the writings meant, he sent for a man called 'Selim the Wise'.

For a long time Selim examined the writing, before pronouncing the translation: "Oh man, thou who findest this, praise Allah for His great goodness to thee. Whoever snuffs of the powder contained in this box, and says thereupon 'Mutabor', will have the power to change himself into any animal he may choose, and will be able to understand the language of that animal and all others. Should he wish to return to his human form he must bow himself three times to the East, and in the direction of our holy Mecca, and repeat the same word. But beware, when thou art transformed that thou laughest not, otherwise the magic word will disappear completely from thy memory and thou wilt remain a beast."

The caliph was delighted beyond measure. He made Selim vow that he would not disclose the secret to anyone, and dismissed him. Then he commanded the grand vizier to return early next morning, when they would go out into the fields and try out the magic.

Next day, not long after dawn, the caliph and his grand vizier went through the spacious gardens of the caliph to a quiet pond, where they would be alone. When they arrived they saw a stork walking gravely up and down looking for frogs, and now and then clacking something to himself. Far above in the air, another stork hovered.

"I am pretty sure," said the grand vizier, "that these two long-legged fellows are carrying on a fine conversation with each other. What if we should become storks?"

"Well said!" replied the caliph. "But first let us consider, once more, how we are to become men again. True! Three times must we bend toward the East and in the direction of Mecca, and say 'Mutabor', then I am caliph again and thou vizier. But we must take care whatever we do, not to laugh, or we are lost."

While the caliph was thus speaking he saw the other stork hover over their heads and slowly descend towards the earth. He drew the box quickly from his girdle, took a good pinch, offered it to the grand vizier, who also snuffed it, and both cried out "Mutabor!"

At once their legs
began to shrivel up, and
soon became thin and red.
The beautiful yellow slippers
of the caliph and of his
companion were changed into
the strange-shaped feet of the
stork, while their arms were
changed to wings, and their necks
were lengthened out from their
shoulders and became a yard long. Their
bodies were covered with feathers which
were soft, fine and graceful, and finally
their beards disappeared, and their faces
changed, one after the other.

"You have a very beautiful beak,"
said the caliph after a long
pause of astonishment.
"I thank you most
humbly," replied the grand

vizier, while he made his obeisance. "And I must say that Your Highness looks even more handsome as a stork than as a caliph. But come, if it please you, let us listen to our comrades yonder, and find out whether we really understand the language of the storks."

In the meantime the other stork had reached the ground. He trimmed his feet with his beak, put his feathers in order, and advanced towards his companion. The two new storks hastened to get near them, and to their surprise they heard the following conversation:

"Good morning, Lady Longlegs, already so early in the meadow."

"Thank you, dear Clatterbeak, I have had only a slight breakfast."

"Would you like, perhaps, a piece of a duck or the leg of a frog?"

"Much obliged, but I have no appetite today. I have come into the meadow for a very different purpose. I am to dance today before some guests of my father's, and I wish to practise here a little quietly by myself."

The young stork immediately jumped about the field with singular motions. The caliph and Manzor looked on with wonder, but as she stood in a picturesque attitude upon one foot, and fluttered her wings gracefully, they could no longer contain themselves – an irresistible laughter burst forth from their beaks, from which they could not recover themselves for a long time.

Suddenly it occurred to the grand vizier that laughter had been specially forbidden them during their transformation. He told his anxiety to the caliph. "Dear me, dear me, it would indeed be a sorrowful joke if I must remain a stork. Pray bethink thyself of the magic word. For the life of me I can't remember it."

"Three times must we bow to the East and to Mecca, and then say, 'Mu, mu, mu'."

They turned toward the East, and bowed and bowed, so that their beaks almost touched the earth. But alas! The magic word would not come. All recollection of it had vanished, and the poor caliph and vizier remained storks.

They knew not what to do in their great distress. Very mournfully, they wandered about, eating only fruit, for they had no appetite for ducks and frogs. Then they flew upon the roofs of Bagdad to see what passed in the city.

During the first days they observed great mourning in the streets, but on the fourth day, they saw a splendid procession. Drums and fifes sounded, and a man in a scarlet mantle, embroidered with gold, rode a fine steed, surrounded by a brilliant train of attendants.

Half Bagdad leaped to meet him, and all cried: "Hail, Mirza, Lord of Bagdad!" The two storks looked at each other, and the caliph said: "All this must have been a plot – and we fell for it! This

Mirza is the son of my deadly enemy, the mighty magician Cachnur, who, in an evil hour, swore revenge upon me. But still I will not give up hope. Come with me to the grave of the Prophet. Perhaps on that holy spot this spell will vanish." And they at once soared from the roof of the palace and flew toward Mecca.

They flew until evening began to draw in, then looked for a place to shelter for the night. Spotting a ruin in the valley below, they swooped down and found themselves in what was formerly a castle. The storks wandered through the crumbling passages and halls to find a dry spot for themselves. Suddenly the stork Manzor stopped. "My lord and master," he whispered softly, "I am sure that something nearby us sighed and groaned."

The caliph also stood still, and heard very distinctly a low weeping. Bravely, he hastened through a dark passageway and into a ruined chamber. It was dimly lighted by a small grated window, and he saw a night owl upon the floor. Big tears rolled from her large round eyes, and with a hoarse voice she sent forth her cries from her curved beak. As soon, however, as she saw the caliph and vizier she gave a loud scream of joy. Gracefully she wiped the tears from her eyes with her brown-spotted wing, and to the great astonishment of both she exclaimed, "Welcome, ye storks! Ye are a good sign of my rescue, for it has been told me that by a stork I shall attain to great happiness."

When the caliph had recovered from his astonishment he related his own story, and the owl told the two storks hers. "My father is King of India. I, his only daughter, am called Lusa. That magician Cachnur, who has enchanted you, has also plunged me into this misery," she explained.

"There must be a secret connection between our fates," pondered the caliph. "But where can I find the key to this riddle?"

The owl replied: "The magician comes once in every month to these ruins. Not far from this chamber is a hall. There he is accustomed to feast with many of his companions. I have often listened there. They tell one another their histories, and what they have been doing since last they met. Perhaps on the next occasion they may talk over your story, and let fall the magic word that you have forgotten."

"Oh, dearest princess," exclaimed the caliph, "tell me when does he come and where is the hall?"

The owl was silent for a moment and then spoke. "I will tell you on one condition."

"Speak out! " cried the caliph. "Command, and whatever it is, I will obey."

"It is this: I also would gladly be free of my enchantment, and this can only happen if one of you offer me his hand in marriage."

The caliph agreed at once. Of course, the owl was overjoyed, and she said they could not have come at a better time, for the magicians would most likely meet that very night. She then led them to the hall entrance, advising them to keep perfectly quiet. From the opening near where they stood they had a good view. The hall had many pillars, and was richly decorated. In the middle was a round table covered with a feast, and round the table sat eight men. The storks recognised one man as the merchant who had sold them the magic powder! The one who sat next to him asked him to relate his history and what had been done during the last few days. He did so, and among the other things he told the story of his visit to the caliph and grand vizier of Bagdad.

"What kind of a word hast thou given them?" asked the other magician.

"A very hard Latin one – it is 'Mutabor'."

As the storks heard this from their place of concealment they became almost beside themselves for joy. They ran so quickly with their long legs to the door of the ruin that the owl could scarcely follow them. There, the caliph addressed the owl with much emotion.

"Saviour of my life, and the life of my friend, as an eternal thanks for what thou hast done for us, accept me as thy husband," then he turned himself toward the east and towards Mecca. Three times the storks bent their long necks toward the sun, which, by this time, was rising above the distant hills: "Mutabor!" they exclaimed. In a twinkling they were changed, and in the delight of newly restored life, master and servant were laughing and weeping in each other's arms. But who can describe their astonishment as they looked about them?

A beautiful maiden in a the most splendid of dresses stood before them. She held out her hand to the caliph saying: "Do you no longer recognise your night owl?"

The caliph looked with wonder at her beauty and

grace, and said: "It is my greatest happiness that I have been a stork."

The three travelled together to Bagdad, where the caliph's people – who had supposed him dead – were overjoyed to have their beloved lord again. And long and happily the caliph lived with his wife, the princess, with many pleasant hours when the grand vizier visited him in the afternoon. They never tired of talking about their storks' adventure, and when the caliph was more than usually merry he would imitate the grand vizier, and show how he looked when he was a stork. He walked gravely up and down the chamber with slow and solemn steps, made a clacking noise, flapped his arms like wings, and showed how he, to no purpose, bowed himself to the east and called out: "Mu—Mu—Mu." This was always a great delight to the princess and the children, which were afterwards born to her, until they also took delight in calling out to one another: "Mu—Mu—Mu."

The Feast of the Lanterns

From *Tales of Wonder Every Child Should Know*
by Kate Douglas Wiggin and Nora Archibald Smith

WANG CHIH was only a poor man, but he had a wife and children to love, and they made him so happy that he would not have changed places with the emperor himself.

One morning, as he was setting off to work in the fields, his wife sent Han Chung, his son, running after him to ask him to bring home some firewood.

"I shall have to go up into the mountain for it at noon," he said. "Bring me my axe, Han Chung."

Han Chung ran back for his father's axe, and Ho-Seen-Ko, his little sister, came out of the cottage with him.

"Remember it is the Feast of Lanterns tonight, Father," she said. "Don't fall asleep up on the mountain, we want you to come back and light them for us."

She had a lantern in the shape of a fish, painted red and black and yellow, and Han Chung had got a big round one, all bright crimson, to carry in the procession, and, besides that, there were two large lanterns to be hung outside the cottage door as soon at it grew dark.

Wang Chih was not likely to forget the Feast of Lanterns, for the children had talked of nothing else for a month, and he promised to come home as early as he could.

At noon, when his fellow-labourers sat down to rest and eat, Wang Chih took his axe and went up the mountain to find a small tree he might cut down for fuel. He walked a long way, and at last saw one growing at the mouth of a cave. "This will be just the thing," he said to himself. Before striking a blow, he peeped into the cave to see if it were empty.

To his surprise, two old men, with long, white beards, were sitting inside playing chess, as quietly as mice, with their eyes fixed on the chessboard. Wang Chih knew something of chess, and he stepped in and watched them for a few minutes. "As soon as they look up I can ask them if I may chop down a tree," he said to himself. But they did not look up, and by and by Wang Chih got so interested in the game that he put down his axe, and sat on the floor to watch it better.

The two old men sat crosslegged on the ground, and the chessboard rested on a slab, like a stone table, between them. On one corner of the slab lay a heap of small, brown objects which Wang Chih took at first to be date stones, but after a time the chess-players ate one each, and put one in Wang Chih's mouth, and he found it was not a date stone at all. It was a delicious kind of sweetmeat, the like of which he had never tasted before, and the strangest thing

about it was that it took his hunger and thirst away.
He sat there some time longer, and noticed that as

the old men frowned over the
chessboard, their beards grew longer and
longer, until they swept the floor of the cave, and
even found their way out of the door.

"I hope my beard will never grow as quickly," said Wang Chih, as he rose, took up his axe again, and went down the mountain.

To his great shock, he found the fields where he had worked covered with houses, and a busy town where his own little village had been. In vain he looked for his house, his wife, and his children. There were strange faces everywhere, and although when evening came the Feast of Lanterns was being held once more, there was no Ho-Seen-Ko carrying her red and yellow fish, or Han Chung with his flaming red ball.

At last he found a woman, a very, very old woman, who told him that when she was a tiny girl she remembered her grandmother saying how, when she was a tiny girl, a poor young man had been spirited away by the genii of the mountains, on the day of the Feast of Lanterns, leaving his wife and little children with only a few handfuls of rice in the house. "Moreover, it has become a tradition in the procession for two children to be dressed to represent Han Chung and Ho-Seen-Ko, and a woman as their mother carrying the empty rice bowl between them, to remind people to take care of the widow and fatherless," she said.

Poor Wang Chih's heart was very heavy and he walked away out of the town. He slept out on the mountain, and early in the morning found his way back to the cave where the two old men were playing chess.

"You must go to the White Hare of the Moon, and ask him for a bottle of the elixir of life. If you drink that you will live forever," said one of them.

"But I don't want to live for ever," objected Wang Chih. "I wish to go back and live in the days when my wife and children were here."

"Ah, well! For that you must mix the elixir of life with some water out of the sky-dragon's mouth."

"And where is the sky-dragon to be found?" enquired Wang Chih.

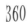

"In the sky, of course. He lives in a cloud-cave. And when he comes out of it he breathes fire, and sometimes water. If he is breathing fire you will be burned up, but if it is only water, you will easily be able to catch some in a little bottle. What else do you want?"

For Wang Chih continued to linger at the mouth of the cave.

"I want a pair of wings to fly with, and a bottle to catch the water in," he replied boldly.

So they gave him a little bottle, and before he had time to say 'Thank you!' a white crane came sailing past and lighted on the ground close to the cave.

"The crane will take you wherever you like," said the old men. "Go now, and leave us in peace."

So Wang Chih sat on the white crane's back, and was taken up, and up, and up through the sky to the cloud-cave where the sky-dragon lived. When he got there, he sat down on the grass near the cave, and considered how to bring the dragon out, and how to

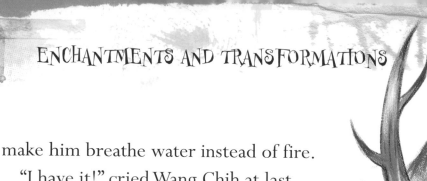

make him breathe water instead of fire.

"I have it!" cried Wang Chih at last. He struck a light and set the grass on fire, and it was so dry that the flames spread all around the entrance to the cave, and made such a smoke and crackling that the sky-dragon put his head out to see what was the matter. And the dragon had the head of a camel, the horns of a deer, the eyes of a rabbit, the ears of a cow and the claws of a hawk. Besides this, he had whiskers and a beard, and in his beard was a bright pearl.

"Ho ho!" cried the dragon, when he saw what Wang Chih had done, "I can soon put this to rights." And he breathed once, and the water came out his nose and mouth in three mighty rivers.

Wang Chih, who had taken care to fill his bottle when the first stream

began to flow, sailed away on the white
crane's back as fast as he could, to escape
being drowned.

The rivers poured over the cloud rock,
until there was not a spark of fire left
alight, and rushed down through the sky
into the sea below.

Meanwhile, Wang Chih was on his way to
the moon, and when he got there he went
straight to the hut where the hare of the moon
lived, and knocked at the door.

The hare was busy pounding the drugs which
make up the elixir of life, but he left his work, and
opened the door, and invited Wang Chih to come in.

He was not ugly, like the dragon. His fur
was quite white and soft and glossy,
and he had lovely, gentle brown
eyes. As soon as he heard what
Wang Chih wanted, he opened
two windows at the back of the

hut, and told him to look through each of them in turn. "Tell me what you see," said the hare, going back to the table where he was pounding the drugs.

"I can see a great many houses and people," said Wang Chih, "and streets – why, this is the town I was in yesterday, the one which has taken the place of my old village."

"Do you want to go back there?" asked the wise old hare.

Wang Chih shook his head.

"Then close the window. It is the window of the Present. And look through the other, which is the window of the Past."

Wang Chih obeyed, and through this window he saw his own dear little village, and his wife, and Han Chung and Ho-Seen-Ko jumping about her as she hung up the coloured lanterns outside the door.

Wang Chih turned, and looked eagerly at the White Hare. "Let me go to them," he said. "I have water from the sky-dragon's mouth, and——"

"Yes, that's all right," said the White Hare. "Give it to me."

He opened the bottle and mixed the contents carefully with a few drops of the elixir of life, which was clear as crystal, and of which each drop shone like a diamond as he poured it in.

"Now, drink this," he said to Wang Chih, "and it will give you the power of living once more in the past, as you desire."

Wang Chih held out his hand and drank every drop of the mixture.

The moment he had done so, the window grew larger, and he saw some steps leading from it down into the village street. Thanking the hare, he rushed through it and ran toward his own house, arriving in time to take the taper from his wife's hand with which she was about to light the red and yellow lanterns which swung over the door.

"What has kept you so long, Father? Where have you been?" asked Han Chung, while little

Ho-Seen-Ko wondered why he kissed and embraced them all so eagerly.

But Wang Chih did not tell them his adventures just then, and only when darkness fell, and the Feast of Lanterns began, he took his part in it with a merry heart.

The Enchanted Waterfall

From *Tales of Wonder Every Child Should Know*
by Kate Douglas Wiggin and Nora Archibald Smith

ONCE UPON A TIME, there lived a simple young woodcutter. He worked all day on the hillside, or in the forest. But he was still very poor, and could bring home but little money to his old parents. This grieved him sorely, for he was an affectionate and dutiful son.

For himself he had but few wants. His mother, too, was always cheerful and contented. The old father, however, was selfish, and often grumbled at the poor supper of rice, washed down with weak tea. "If we had but a little saké," he would say, "it would warm one up, and do one's heart good." And then he would reproach the simple young fellow, telling him that in his younger days he had always been able to afford a nice cup of saké for himself and his friends.

Heavy-hearted, the young man would work harder than ever and think: 'How shall I earn some more money? How shall I get a little saké for my poor father?'

One day as he was at work on the wooded hills, the sound of rushing water caught his ear. He could not remember a waterfall near, so he was surprised when he followed the sound and came upon a beautiful little cascade. The water looked so clear and cool that he stooped down and drank a little of it. Instead of water, it was the most excellent saké!

Overjoyed, he quickly filled the gourd which was hanging at his girdle, and hurried home.

His old father was so delighted with the saké that he drank cup after cup. A neighbour happened to drop in, the story was told to him, and a cup of saké offered and drunk with many words of astonishment and gratitude. Soon the news spread through the village, and before night there was hardly a man who had not paid a visit, been told the tale, and smelled the gourd, which, alas, was now empty.

Next morning the young woodcutter set off to work even earlier, this time carrying a larger gourd, for of course the enchanted waterfall was to be visited again.

Imagine his surprise when he came to the spot to find several of his neighbours already there, all armed with buckets, jars, pitchers, anything that would carry saké. Each man had come secretly, believing that he alone had found his way to the magic waterfall.

One bold man took the lead, saying: "Here we are, all bent on the same task. Let us fill our jars and go home. But first let us taste the magic saké." He stooped drank, with a face of astonishment which soon gave place to anger. "Water!" he shouted in a rage. "Nothing but cold water! We have been tricked and deceived! Where is that young fellow? Let us duck him in his fine waterfall!"

But the young man had been wise enough to slip behind a big rock when he saw the turn things were taking, and was nowhere to be found.

First one and then another tasted of the stream. It was but too true – no saké, but clear, cold water was there. Crestfallen and out of temper, the covetous band returned to their homes.

When they were fairly gone the good young woodcutter crept from his hiding-place. Could this be true? he thought. Was it all a dream? He drank – and sure enough, there was the same fine-flavoured saké he had tasted yesterday.

And so it remained. To the good, dutiful son the cascade flowed with the finest saké, while to all others it yielded only cold water.

The emperor, hearing this wonderful story, sent for the good young woodcutter, rewarded him for his kindness to his father, and even changed the name of the year in his honour as an encouragement to children in all future times to honour and obey their parents.

The Iron Casket

From *Tales of Wonder Every Child Should Know*
by Kate Douglas Wiggin and
Nora Archibald Smith

THERE ONCE LIVED in Bagdad a merchant named Kalif. He was a quiet, retiring man, who sat early and late in his little shop, and went but once a year to Mosul or Shiraz, where he bought embroidered robes in exchange for rose oil.

On one of these journeys, he heard roarings and trampling of a horse's hoofs in the thicket close by the roadside. He entered the thicket and saw a little green, where there was a horseman wearing a blue mantle and a turban fastened by a flashing diamond. His horse was rearing with a piercing neigh while it struggled vainly to dislodge an enormous panther, which had fixed its great claws in its flanks. Kalif sprang boldly out, drew his sword, and with a mighty stroke split the panther's skull.

The horseman calmed his trembling animal then begged his rescuer to follow him. "I wish to reward you well for your bravery," he explained.

"I expect no reward," answered Kalif simply. "But if you so will it, I will accompany you to your tents."

The merchant walked with the stranger till they arrived at an opening in the trees. Here, surrounded by several smaller ones, stood one large tent of purple linen. A number of richly clad men threw themselves on their faces before the newcomer. Then Kalif knew whom he had saved: it was the shah himself. He was about to fall at his feet, but the shah seized his hand and led him into the tent. Inside, standing on five stools, were five caskets, the first of gold alone, the second of gold set with jewels, the third silver, the fourth copper, and the fifth of iron. "Choose one of these caskets," said the shah.

Kalif hesitated. At length he said: "What I did is not worthy of any reward, but if you will it, O King of Kings, I will take one of these caskets to remind me of the day when my eyes were permitted to behold the Light of Asia." He stooped and took the iron casket.

The shah started. "Stranger," he said, "your modesty has met with its own reward. You have chosen the most valuable casket — for, look, the others are empty, but this one contains two jewels which possess the magic gift of bestowing undreamed-of power to their owner." He raised the lid and showed the wondering Kalif the two stones. "This one," he said, "is a lapis lazuli. Whosoever winds it in the folds of his turban, to him everything is known that has happened since the world began, and no secret can be hidden from him. But this stone," and he took a diamond the size of a dove's egg from the casket, "this stone brings all the riches he can think of to its owner. He has but to rub the stone and repeat his wish aloud." He replaced the stones in the casket, closed the lid, and handed it to the merchant, who thanked the shah, hid the treasure in his robes, and hastened on his way.

Kalif never spoke of his adventure, neither could he ever make up his mind to test the stones, being nervous of both too much wealth and wisdom. But at length the news of the shah's rescue by the merchant reached even Bagdad, together with the account of the royal reward, and people jostled one another to call on the merchant and see with their own eyes the wonderful casket. In consequence Kalif had more customers in one day than he generally had in ten years. For many years he enjoyed the reward of his bravery, and at his death Ali Haitam, the eldest son, proposed that they should draw lots for the magic stones. He had great ideas of his own cleverness, and hoped from the bottom of his heart to win the lapis lazuli. Ali Hassuf, the greedy second son, was plotting how to obtain the diamond, to use it for his own greedy purposes. But just as they were about to draw, Abdul Kassim, the youngest son, said: "Dear brothers, we are three, and there are but two stones. To avoid us falling out, I give up my claim on them."

The other two were delighted and, as it happened, each got the stone he desired.

"But in order that I may have a keepsake of my

dear father," continued Abdul Kassim, "permit me to take home the casket. It will be of no use to you, since you have divided the contents."

The three brothers agreed and each went out into the world to seek his fortune in his own way.

Ali Haitam sewed the lapis lazuli inside a turban – and lo! His mind was filled with knowledge! He knew the origin of all things, and his eyes could see through walls five feet thick! He passed the caliph's palace, and he could see that in the recesses of the cellars were hidden nine thousand sacks of gold, and that Fatma, the daughter of the caliph, was the most lovely maiden in the east, and an idea occurred to him that dazzled him. 'How would it be,' he thought, 'if I placed my wisdom at the caliph's disposal, became his first adviser, and finally married the lovely Fatma?'

But together with this dream came the longing to display to an admiring crowd some proofs of his wisdom. He hurried back to the bazaar, mounted the highest steps at the gates, and cried: "You people of Bagdad, who believe that the sun moves round the earth, you are ignorant fools and sons of fools! Hear now what I preach to you. The sun stands still, but the earth moves!"

He intended to continue, but the cries of the bystanders interrupted him.

"Ali Haitam has gone mad," they cried. "Listen to the nonsense he is talking!" A fruit dealer grabbed an orange and threw it at him, whereupon everyone joined in, pelting him with fruit. Sorely bruised, Alie fled away home, leaving his turban with its priceless jewel knocked off his head and lying on the ground, lost to him for ever.

The second brother started out more cautiously. He visited the bazaar to search for treasures that he might use the diamond to buy. There he found a rare Turkish sword, studded thickly with gems on handle and sheath. The dealer asked fifteen hundred golden coins for it, and the bystanders stared with open eyes at the man who dared to bargain for such costly possessions. Just then, a procession passed by bearing a palanquin through the crowd, and through the drawn curtains Ali Hassuf caught a glimpse of the beautiful caliph's daughter. The desire awoke in his soul to marry this lovely creature, and he realised that the caliph might well give him her hand if he used the diamond to become incredibly wealthy.

He turned and went home and waited till it grew dark. Then he went out into the desert with his donkey – not noticing three dark forms, who had never lost sight of him since his visit to the bazaar. He halted by a group of stunted palms, spread out a large cloth, and with trembling fingers began to rub the diamond, crying at the same time, "Spirit of the Stone! Send me at once twenty shekels of golden coins!" He waited a moment and heard a noise as of the falling of soft, heavy weights, and, on stooping, found twenty sacks full of gold money! With haste he slung the sacks on the donkey's back, and turned its head homeward. Suddenly he felt himself seized by heavy hands and thrown to the ground. His clothes were torn off him and he was given a good kicking. As he lay groaning in pain, the robbers disappeared with the donkey and all his gold. But what pained him most was the loss of his diamond, which he had hidden in one of his pockets. And so, left in only his underpants, he returned home.

In the meantime, as the two elder brothers were mourning their losses, Abdul Kassim, the youngest, sat at home in his little house by the gardens, thinking with regret of his father, and wondering what he should do to earn himself his daily bread. Before him, on a little stool, stood the iron casket. There came a knock at the door, and a man to whom he owed money walked in. The moneylender looked grave and said, "Abdul Kassim, times are bad, and ready money gets scarcer and scarcer. You know I lent you ten golden coins, and I have come to ask…" his eyes fell on the casket and he started, but collecting himself, went on: "I have come to tell you that I am not in an immediate hurry for the return of the loan. If you like you can keep it, or, as it is hardly worth mentioning, keep it for some months, or even years if you like. I only wanted to tell you needn't trouble about it, there is no hurry at all." He bowed low to his debtor and withdrew.

Abdul Kassim marvelled at the change in the

moneylender's manner, but as he thought of the looks that the man had cast at the casket he couldn't help smiling.

A week later, Abdul Kassim was utterly stunned to find the grand vizier himself knocking at his door, announcing that the caliph himself was giving him a palace to live in and awaited his visit!

Putting his astonishment aside, that evening Abdul Kassim packed up his few belongings, took his precious iron casket under his arm, and amid a crowd of cheering onlookers, made his way to his luxurious new home. Inside the palace, a banquet and a sumptuous bedroom awaited him. Next morning he put on the gorgeous robe that was provided, bound on the magnificent sword laid out for him, and rode to visit the caliph.

The Commander of the Faithful descended from his throne and took the young man's hand.

"Are you Abdul Kassim," he said, "son of Kalif, the merchant?"

"I am he, Caliph," answered Abdul. "Permit me to express my thanks for the palace with which you have endowed your most humble servant."

"I have heard much good of you," said the caliph, when he had ordered his slaves to retire, "and pray you to show me the magic jewels."

"Of which jewels are you speaking?" asked Abdul Kassim, amazed.

"Well," smiled the caliph, "which other jewels should I mean but those you have inherited from your father?"

The young man stared. So the caliph, too, took him for the possessor of the magic stones? Without reserve he confessed that, to avoid family disputes, he had voluntarily retired and left both of the stones to his brothers.

"But," said the caliph, "news reached my ears that my chief moneylender saw the casket in your house with his own eyes!"

"The casket he may have seen," answered Abdul

Kassim. "I begged it of my brothers in memory of my father."

The caliph seemed still in doubt. He sent a slave to Abdul Kassim's palace to bring the casket. It was in truth empty! So Abdul Kassim was not a man of great wealth and wisdom, deserving of special treatment, as he had been led to believe! …But then the caliph thought hard… Maybe he was, after all…

"Abdul Kassim," he said, "I think you must have jewels in your heart more precious than all the treasures of the earth. For love of your brothers you gave up the stones, and for love of your father you have preserved this seemingly worthless casket. Allah himself has obviously blessed you for your virtues and has arranged to have you raised to power and wealth. I will continue to do Allah's work and help you further. I will give you the most priceless gift at my disposal – the hand of my only daughter."

Then the grand vizier entered the throne room, leading in the beautiful Fatma.

So Fatma was married to Abdul. But neither she nor any other ever knew that the iron casket connected with her young lord's rise and power was empty. The caliph advised his son-in-law to maintain his silence as to the absence of the magic jewels.

In the fifth year of their wedded life the caliph, feeling the weight of advancing years, abdicated in Abdul Kassim's favour. He reigned many, many years over Bagdad, the best and wisest ruler who had ever ascended the throne.

The Old Man and the Gift

From *Japanese Fairy Tales* by Yei Theodora Ozaki

Long ago there lived an old man and his wife who supported themselves by farming a small plot of land. Their life had been happy and peaceful save for one great sorrow — they had no child. They lavished all their affection on their pet dog, Shiro — even giving him more to eat than they had themselves.

ONE DAY THE OLD man heard Shiro barking in the field at the back of the house. He hurried out to see what was the matter with him. Shiro ran to meet him, and, seizing the end of his kimono, dragged him under a large yenoki tree. Here he began to dig as fast as he could, yelping with joy. The old man ran back to the house, fetched his spade and joined Shiro in digging. Imagine his astonishment when he came upon a heap of old and valuable coins. He and his wife were rich!

Now, the old man had a horrible next-door neighbour, and he did not notice that this nasty man

was peering in through the bamboo hedge and had seen everything. This neighbour began to think that he, too, would like to find a fortune. So a few days later he sneaked into the old man's house and stole Shiro. He then took his spade and hastened to his own field. As soon as he reached a yenoki tree, he said to Shiro, threateningly: "If there were gold coins under your master's tree, there must also be gold coins under my tree. You must find them for me! Where are they?" And catching hold of Shiro's neck he held the dog's head to the ground, so that Shiro began to scratch and dig in order to free himself from the horrid old man's grasp.

The old man was very pleased, for he at once supposed that some gold coins also lay buried under his tree. He pushed Shiro away and began to dig. Soon there was a foul smell and he came upon a stinking, rotting, rubbish heap. The old man was utterly disgusted! But this soon gave way to anger. He stormed back on to his neighbour's land and set fire to the yenoki tree under which Shiro had found the coins.

Imagine Shiro's master's horror when he saw that

his tree was ablaze! In a panic, he and his wife ran to fetch water to put out the flames. But by the time they quenched the fire, the tree was charred and dead. The old man cut it down and saved an unburned, thick, sturdy branch. He hollowed it out and made a bowl. He thought that his wife could use it for making rice cakes in, to offer to the gods in thanks for their blessings.

But no sooner had his wife begun to pound the rice, than it began to grow and grow till it was about five times the original amount, and the cakes were turned out of the bowl as if an invisible hand were at work. The old man and his wife tasted the cakes and found them nicer than any other food. So from this time they never troubled about food, they lived upon the cakes with which the bowl never ceased to supply them.

The greedy neighbour, hearing of this new piece of good luck, was filled with envy as before, and called on the old man to borrow the wonderful bowl. The old man was too kind to refuse.

Several days passed and the neighbour did not bring the bowl back, so Shiro's master went to ask for it. He found his neighbour sitting by a wood fire. The wicked neighbour said haughtily: "Have you come to ask me for your bowl? When I tried to pound cakes in it only some horrid smelling stuff came out. So I broke it into pieces and now I am burning it."

The good old man calmly said: "If you had asked me for the cakes, I would have given you as many as ever you wanted. Now please give me my bowl — even though it is but ashes."

The neighbour grudgingly agreed, and the old man carried home a basket full of ashes. Just as he reached his garden, a gust of wind blew some onto his trees. It was late autumn and all the trees had shed their leaves, but no sooner did the ashes touch their branches than the cherry trees, the plum trees, and all other blossoming shrubs burst into bloom,

so that the old
man's garden was
suddenly transformed into
a beautiful picture of spring.

   The story of the old man's beautiful
garden spread far and wide. It even reached the
ears of a great earl, who had a prized cherry
tree which was mysteriously withering and
dying. The earl summoned the old man
to his palace to see if he could cure
the tree. Of course, as soon as the
old man scattered some ashes over
it, it at once burst into full bloom!
The earl was so overjoyed that he
rewarded Shiro's master with
many riches. He
also gave him the
title of Hana-Saka-
Jijii, or 'The Old
Man who makes

the Trees to
Blossom', and
sent him home
with great honour.
The wicked
neighbour heard of the
good old man's fortune and
was filled with jealousy. He
gathered together all the ashes which
remained in the fireplace from the
burning of the wonderful bowl and
went to the palace to tell the earl
that he could revive dying plants
too. The curious earl put him to the
test — but the nasty neighbour's
ashes did nothing to cure dying
plants. In fact, they caused
blossoming plants to die! The furious
earl ordered the liar to be thrown
into prison — and

thus the nasty neighbour met with punishment at last for all his evil doings.

The good old man, however, with the treasure of coins and with all the gold and the silver which the earl had showered on him, became a rich and prosperous man in his old age, and lived a long and very happy life, with his good wife and his faithful dog, Shiro.

The Well of the World's End

From *English Fairy Tales* by Joseph Jacobs

ONCE UPON A TIME, there was a girl whose mother had died, and her father married again. And her stepmother hated her because she was more beautiful than herself. She used to make her do all the work, and never let her have any peace. One day, the stepmother thought to get rid of her altogether, so she handed her a sieve and said: "Go, fill it at the Well of the World's End and bring it home to me full, or woe betide you." For the stepmother thought the girl would never be able to find the Well of the World's End, and, if she did, how could she bring home a sieve full of water?

Well, the girl started off, and asked everyone she met where the Well of the World's End was. But nobody knew, and she didn't know what to do, when a little old woman, all bent double, told her how to get to it. So at last she arrived there, but when she dipped the sieve in the cold, cold water, it all ran out again. She tried and tried, but every time it was the same, and at last she sat down and cried as if her heart would break.

Suddenly she heard a croak, and she looked up and saw a great frog with goggle eyes looking at her.

"What's the matter, dearie?" it said.

The girl explained, and the frog replied: "If you promise me to do whatever I bid you for a whole night long, I'll tell you how to fill the sieve."

The girl didn't like the idea, but she had no choice, so she agreed. And the frog said:

Stop it with moss and daub it with clay,
And then it will carry the water away

Then it gave a hop, skip, and jump, and jumped –

flop – back into the Well of the World's End.

So the girl lined the sieve with moss, and over that she put some clay, and then she dipped it once again into the Well of the World's End, and this time, the water didn't run out.

Quite forgetting her promise to the frog, she went back to her stepmother, who was angry as angry, but said nothing at all.

That very evening they heard something tap-tapping at the door low down, and a voice cried out: "Open the door, my darling!"

The girl went and opened the door and, to her dismay, there was the frog from the Well of the World's End. She explained about the agreement, and her stepmother said: "Girls must keep their promises!" For she was quite gleeful that the girl would have to obey a nasty frog.

And it hopped, and it hopped, and it jumped, till it was right inside and then it said: "Let me sit on your knee, my dear!"

But the girl didn't like to, till her stepmother said: "Lift it up this instant! Girls must keep their promises!"

So at last she lifted the frog up on to her lap, and it lay there for a time, till at last it said: "Give me some supper, my sweetheart!"

Well, she didn't mind doing that, so she got it a bowl of milk and bread, and fed it well. And when the frog had finished, it said: "Now, go with me to bed, my own one!"

But that the girl wouldn't do, till her stepmother said: "Do what you promised, or out you go, you and your froggie."

So the girl took the frog with her to bed, and kept it as far away from her as she could. Well, just as the day was beginning to break what should the frog say but: "Chop off my head, my true love. Remember the promise you made to me!"

At first the girl wouldn't, for she thought of what the frog had done for her at the Well of the World's

End. But when the frog said the words over again, she took an axe up and chopped off its head.

Lo and behold! There stood before her a handsome young prince, who told her that he had been enchanted by a wicked magician, and he could never be unspelled till some girl would do his bidding for a whole night, and chop off his head at the end of it.

So the prince and the girl were married and went away to live in the castle of the king, his father, and the stepmother hated every bit of it!

The Crystal Coffin

From Andrew Lang's *Green Fairy Book*

A YOUNG TAILOR once found himself lost in a wood. Evening came on and, for fear of wild beasts, he climbed a tall oak tree. After passing several hours in fear, he noticed a light shining in the distance. Cautiously, he climbed down and went towards it.

The tailor found it came from a house, and he knocked bravely at the door. It was opened by an old man who said roughly: "Who are you, and what do you want?"

"I beg you to let me shelter in your hut till morning," replied the youth.

Very grudgingly, the old man let him come in, and after giving him some bread and water, showed him to a bed in one corner of the room.

The weary tailor slept sound till early morning, when he was roused by a thunderous, bellowing noise. The tailor hurried out to find a huge black bull fighting with a fine large stag. At length, the stag drove his antlers with such force into his opponent's body that the bull fell to the ground, finished. Then, to the tailor's great amazement, the stag bounded up to him, forked him up with its great antlers, and set off at full gallop over hill and dale. The tailor could do nothing but hold on tight and hope for the best!

At length the stag paused before a steep rock and let the tailor down

to the ground. With his antlers, he struck such a
blow on a door in the rock that it flew open. Flames
of fire rushed forth and clouds of steam. The tailor
was quite frozen with fear, but a voice from the rock
cried: "Step in, no harm shall befall you."

Passing through the door, the tailor was amazed
to find himself in a hall, whose ceiling, walls, and
floor were covered with carved tiles. Full of
wonder, he heard the same voice saying: "Tread
on the stone in the middle of the hall, and good
luck will attend you."

Hardly had he stepped on the stone than
it began to sink with him into the depths
below. He found himself in an even
more splendid hall, whose walls were
lined with shelves on which stood
glass vessels filled with bright-
coloured smokes. On the floor
were two large crystal
boxes opposite each

other, and these attracted his curiosity at once.

Stepping up to one, he saw within it a model castle surrounded by farms, barns, stables, and a number of other buildings. Everything was quite tiny, but perfect.

He was even more amazed at what was in the other crystal box. Lying there was a beautiful girl. She looked asleep, but though her eyes were closed, the bright colour in her face, and the movement of a ribbon, which rose and fell with her breath, left no doubt as to her being alive.

Suddenly the maiden opened her eyes and started with delight. "Help me!" she cried. "Only push back the bolt of this coffin and I am free from my prison."

The tailor promptly obeyed, and the girl quickly pushed back the crystal lid and stepped out. After giving her rescuer a kiss to thank him, she explained: "I am the daughter of a wealthy nobleman. My parents died when I was very young, and they left me to the care of my eldest brother, whom I love very much. One evening, a stranger rode up to the castle and asked for shelter. Of course, we took him in. But that night, I woke to find the stranger entering my room, even though the door had been securely locked. He was softly singing a strange song, and I found I could neither move nor cry out! Then I must have fainted, for I remember nothing more until I opened my eyes to find myself lying here, in this crystal coffin. The magician – for that is indeed what the stranger was – appeared again and told me that he had transformed my brother into a wild stag. He had shrunk our castle and the surrounding village to miniature and locked them up in another glass box. And after turning everyone in our household into smoke, had banished them into glass jars. He told me that if I agreed to marry him, he would undo all the spells! He said he would leave me time to ponder my fate and he vanished. Now, to my great joy, you are here – and now I beg you to help me

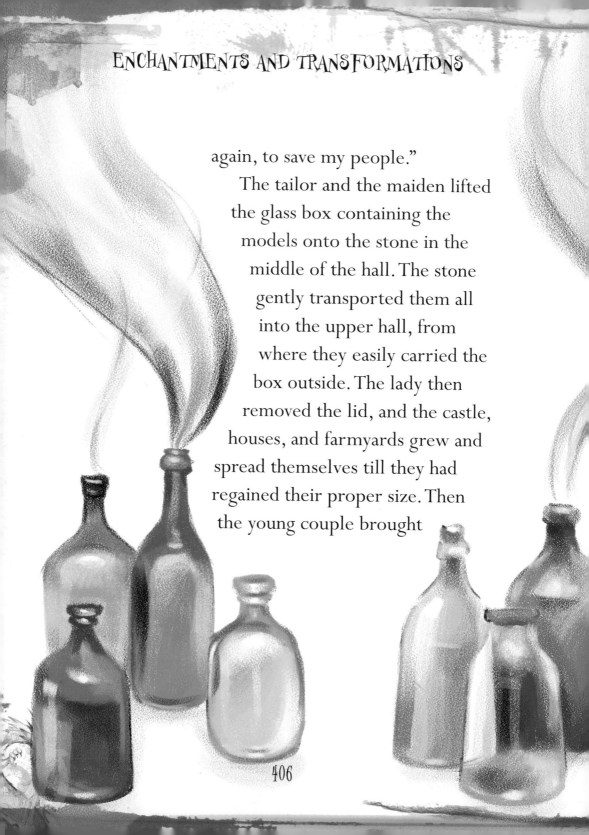

again, to save my people."

The tailor and the maiden lifted the glass box containing the models onto the stone in the middle of the hall. The stone gently transported them all into the upper hall, from where they easily carried the box outside. The lady then removed the lid, and the castle, houses, and farmyards grew and spread themselves till they had regained their proper size. Then the young couple brought

up all the glass vessels filled with smoke.
No sooner were they uncorked than
brightly-coloured clouds billowed out of
them and became all the lady's servants and
attendants.

The maiden's joy was complete when her brother
came from the forest in his proper shape. Of course,
he had been the stag, and he had killed the magician
– who had been in the form of the bull. That very
day, the lady gave her hand in marriage to the young
tailor, and they lived happily ever after.

MYSTERIOUS MORALS

The Baker's Daughter

From *Folk-lore and Legends*
by Charles John Tibbits

A LONG TIME AGO, there lived a baker who was a mean, greedy man. He sought in every way to put money by, and cheated people whenever he was able when they came to his shop. He had a daughter who helped him in his business, and seeing how her father treated the people, and how he succeeded in getting money by his bad practices, she, too, in time came to do the like.

One day when her father was away, and the girl remained alone in the shop, an old woman came in. "My pretty girl," said she, "give me a bit of dough I beg of you, for I am old and very hungry."

The girl at first told her to be off, but as the old woman would not go, and begged harder than before for a piece of bread, at last the baker's daughter took up a piece of dough, and giving it to her, said: "There now, be off, and do not trouble me any more."

"My dear," said the woman, "you have given me a piece of dough, let me bake it in your oven, for I have no place of my own to bake it in."

"Very well," replied the girl, and, taking the dough, she placed it in the oven, while the old woman sat down to wait till it was baked.

When the girl thought the bread should be ready she looked in the oven expecting to find there a small cake, and was very much amazed to find instead a very large loaf of bread. She pretended to look about the oven as if in search of something. "I cannot find the cake," said she. "It must have tumbled into the fire and got burned."

"Very well," said the old woman, "give me another

piece of dough instead and I will wait while it bakes."

So the girl took another piece of dough, smaller than the first piece, and having put it in the oven, shut the door. At the end of a few minutes or so she looked in again, and found there another loaf, larger than the last. "Dear me," said she, pretending to look about her, "I have surely lost the dough again. There's no cake here."

"Tis a pity," said the old woman, "but never mind. I will wait while you bake me another piece."

So the baker's daughter took a piece of dough as small as one of her fingers and put it in the oven, while the old woman sat near. When she thought it ought to be baked, she looked into the oven and there saw a loaf, larger than either of the others.

"That is mine," said the old woman.

"No," replied the girl. "How could such a large loaf have grown out of a little piece of dough?"

"It is mine, I am sure," said the woman.

"It is not," said the girl. "You shall not have it."

Well, when the old woman saw that the girl would not give her the loaf, and saw how she had tried to cheat her – for she was a fairy, and knew all the tricks that the baker's daughter had put upon her – she drew out from under her cloak a stick, and just touched the girl with it. Then a wonderful thing occurred, for the girl became all of a sudden changed into an owl, and flying about the room, at last, made for the door, and, finding it open, she flew out and was never seen again.

Grasp All, Lose All

From Andrew Lang's *Olive Fairy Book*

ONCE, IN FORMER TIMES, there lived in a city in India a poor oil-seller, called Déna, who had borrowed from a banker, of the name of Léna, the sum of one hundred rupees, which, with the interest Léna charged, amounted to a debt of three hundred rupees. Now Déna had no money to pay his debt, so Léna was angry and threatened to punish him in all sorts of ways. One day, Déna decided that he had no choice but to run away. So that evening, he told his wife, and slipped out of the city without knowing very well where he was going.

At about ten o'clock that night Déna came to a

well by the wayside, near which grew
a giant peepul tree. As he was very
tired, he climbed up into it and
settled down to rest there for
the night. Whilst he slept,
some spirits, who roam about
such places on certain nights,
picked up the tree and flew away
with it to a faraway shore where no
creature lived, and there, long
before the sun rose, they set it
down. Just then the oil-seller
awoke, and was amazed to behold
nothing but waste shore and wide
sea, and was dumb with horror and
astonishment. Whilst he sat up,
trying to collect his senses, he
began to catch sight here and
there of twinkling, flashing
lights, like little fires, that moved

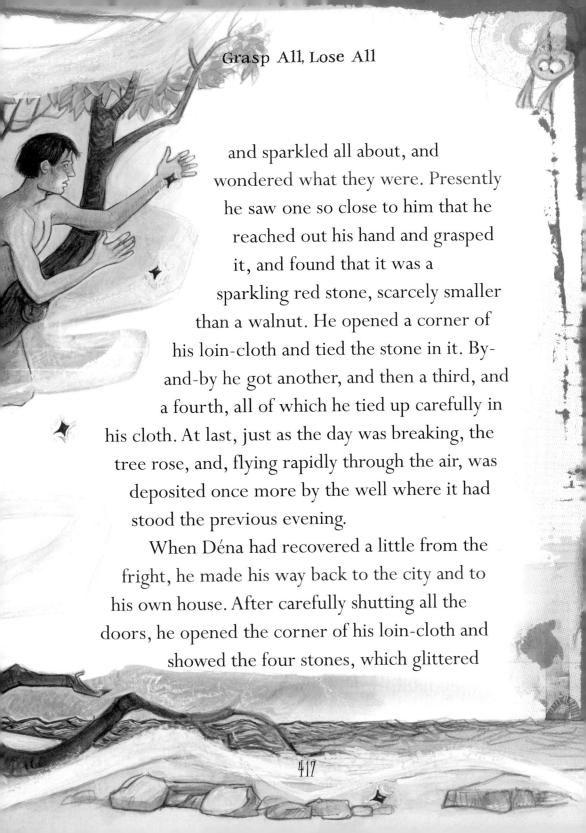

and sparkled all about, and wondered what they were. Presently he saw one so close to him that he reached out his hand and grasped it, and found that it was a sparkling red stone, scarcely smaller than a walnut. He opened a corner of his loin-cloth and tied the stone in it. By-and-by he got another, and then a third, and a fourth, all of which he tied up carefully in his cloth. At last, just as the day was breaking, the tree rose, and, flying rapidly through the air, was deposited once more by the well where it had stood the previous evening.

When Déna had recovered a little from the fright, he made his way back to the city and to his own house. After carefully shutting all the doors, he opened the corner of his loin-cloth and showed the four stones, which glittered and flashed as he turned them over and over.

"Pooh!" said his wife. "What use are such silly, small pebbles! Now if you had found food or money, there'd be some sense in it!" And she turned away with a sniff.

Just then, Léna threw open the door and demanded his money.

Déna politely invited the moneylender in, carefully shut the door as before, and then showed him the four great flashing stones. "This is all," said he, "that I have in the world to set against my debt, for, as your honour knows, I haven't a penny, but the stones are pretty!"

Now Léna saw at once that the stones were in fact magnificent rubies, and his mouth watered for want of them, but as it would never do to show what was in his mind, he went on: "What do I care about your stupid stones? It is my money I want, my lawful debt which you owe me, and I shall get it out of you yet somehow or another, or it will be so much the worse for you."

And so Léna went on and on, while Déna begged
for mercy – until, at length, Léna very grudgingly
announced that he would take the stones instead of
the money. Whilst Déna nearly wept with gratitude,
he wrote out a receipt for the three hundred rupees,
and, wrapping the four stones in a cloth, he put
them into his jacket. He hurried off to the house of
the chief wazir to do a deal to exchange them for
money. Before long, he had given the rubies to the
chief wazir and was striding home with ten
thousand rupees in his pocket, quite overjoyed.

The chief wazir was quite stunned by the beauty
of the rubies and went straight away to the palace,
to show them to his royal master, the rajah.

"Oh, ho!" said the rajah. "These are priceless
gems, and you have done well to give them to me.
In return I will make you the master of ten villages."

Whilst the rajah put the rubies into his turban,
the chief wazir hurried away beaming with

happiness at the thought that for ten thousand rupees he had become lord of ten villages.

The rajah was also equally pleased, and strolled off with his new purchases to the women's quarters and showed them to the queen, who was nearly out of her mind with delight. Then, as she turned them over and over in her hands, she said: "Ah! If I had eight more such gems, what a necklace they would make! Get me eight more of them or I shall die!" And then she fell to weeping and wailing until the rajah promised that in the morning he would make arrangements to get some more such rubies.

In the morning the rajah sent for the wazir, and said that he must manage to get eight more rubies like those he had brought him the day before, "And if you don't I shall hang you," cried the rajah, for he was very cross.

The wazir left the palace, much troubled in mind, and bade his slaves bring Léna before him. "Get me eight more such rubies as those you brought yesterday," commanded the wazir. "Eight more, and be quick, or I am a dead man."

"But how can I?" wailed Léna. "I got them from Déna, the oil-seller, and they were all he had."

"Well, send for him and ask him where he got them," answered the wazir. And more slaves were sent to summon Déna.

When Déna arrived he was closely questioned, and then all three went to see the rajah, and to him Déna told the whole story.

"What night was it that you slept in the peepul tree?" demanded the rajah.

"I can't remember," said Déna, "but my wife will be able to tell you."

Then Déna's wife was sent for, and she explained that it was on the last Sunday of the new moon. Now everyone knows that it is on the Sunday of the new moon that spirits have special power to play pranks upon mortals. So the rajah forbade them all, on pain of death, to say a word to anyone, and declared that, on the next Sunday of the new moon, they four – the rajah, the wazir, Léna and Déna – would go and sit in the peepul tree and see what happened.

The days dragged on to the appointed Sunday, and that evening the four met secretly, and entered the forest. They had not far to go before they reached the peepul tree, into which they climbed as the rajah had planned. At midnight the tree began to sway, and presently away it flew, with the four men clinging tightly to its branches, until at last it was set down by the waste sea-shore where a great wide sea came tumbling in on a desert beach. Presently, as before, they began to see little points of light that glistened like fires all around them.

Then Déna thought to himself: 'Think! Last time I only took four that came close to me, and I got rid of all my debt in return. This time I will take all I can get and be rich!'

'If I got ten thousand rupees for four stones,'

thought Léna, 'I will gather forty now for myself, and become so wealthy that they will probably make me a wazir at least!'

'For four stones I received ten villages,' the wazir was silently thinking. 'Now I will get stones enough to purchase a kingdom, become a rajah, and employ wazirs of my own!'

And the rajah thought: 'What is the good of only getting eight stones to make one necklace? Why, here are enough to make twenty necklaces, and wealth means power!'

Full of greed, each scrambled down from the tree, spread his cloth, and darted hither and thither picking up the precious jewels, looking the all the while over his shoulder to see whether his neighbour fared better than he. So engrossed were they in the business of gathering wealth that the dawn came upon them unawares, and before they knew it the tree rose up again and flew away, leaving them upon the seashore staring after it, each with his cloth heavy with priceless jewels.

Morning broke in the city, and great was the
worry in the palace when the chamberlains declared
that the rajah had gone out the evening before and
had not returned.

In vain they waited, and searched – but none of
the four men ever returned to their homes, and the

confused tale which was told by Déna's wife was the only clue to their fate.

To this day, in that country, people warn greedy folk: "If you reach for more, you may well lose everything!"

The Paradise of Children

From *A Wonder-Book for Girls and Boys*
by Nathaniel Hawthorne

LONG, LONG AGO, there was a boy named Epimetheus who didn't have a best friend — until he met a girl called Pandora. The first time Pandora went to Epimetheus's house, she noticed a curious, great box. And almost the first question she put to him, after crossing the threshold, was: "Epimetheus, what have you in that box?"

"That is a secret," answered Epimetheus, "and you must not ask any questions about it. The box was left here to be kept safely, and I do not myself know what it contains."

"But who gave it to you?" asked Pandora. "And

where did it come from?"

"That is a secret, too," replied Epimetheus.

"How vexing!" exclaimed Pandora, pouting.

"Oh, come, don't think of it any more," cried Epimetheus. "Let's go and play with the other children."

It is thousands of years since Epimetheus and Pandora were alive, and the world, nowadays, is very different from in their time. Then, everybody was a child. They needed no fathers and mothers because there was no danger, nor trouble of any kind, and no clothes to be mended, and there was always plenty to eat and drink. It was a very pleasant life indeed. No jobs to be done, no schoolwork to be studied – there was nothing but games and dancing and singing and laughter. For what was most wonderful of all, the children never quarrelled or cried or sulked. The truth is, those ugly little winged monsters, called Troubles, which are now almost as numerous as mosquitoes, had never yet been seen on the earth. It is probable that the very greatest annoyance which a child had ever experienced was Pandora's vexation at not being able to discover the secret of the mysterious box. This was at first only the faint shadow of a Trouble, but every day it grew more and more.

"Where can the box have come from?" Pandora continually kept saying to herself. "And what in the world can be inside it?" One day she begged Epimetheus to tell her more about how the box came to be in his house.

"It was just left at the door," replied Epimetheus, "by a person dressed in an odd kind of a cloak, and a cap that seemed to be made partly of feathers, so that it looked almost as if it had wings. He had a curious walking staff – it was like two serpents twisting around a stick, and was carved so naturally that I, at first, thought the serpents were alive. He told me very sternly that until he comes back and gives permission, no one has any right to lift the lid of the box."

Then, quite fed up of thinking about the box, Epimetheus went out to play.

Pandora, who had refused to go with him, was left gazing at the box. It was made of a beautiful kind of wood, so highly polished that she could see her face in it. The edges and corners were carved with most wonderful skill. There were figures of graceful men and women, and the prettiest children ever seen, surrounded by a tangle of flowers and leaves. Once or twice as Pandora examined it, she fancied that she saw a face not so lovely, or something or other that was disagreeable. Nevertheless, on looking more closely, and touching the spot with her finger, she could discover nothing of the kind.

The most beautiful face of all was in the centre of the lid. Pandora thought that, had it been able to speak, it looked just as if it would have said: "Do not be afraid, Pandora! What harm can there be in opening the box? Never mind that poor, simple Epimetheus! You are wiser than he, and have ten times as much spirit. Open the box, and see if you do not find something very pretty!"

The box was fastened by a very intricate knot of gold cord. There appeared to be no end to this knot, and no beginning. But Pandora was not one to give up easily. She stood for a while, turning it this way and that, and then murmured to herself: "I really believe that I begin to see how it was done. I am sure that if I undid it, I could do it up again afterwards."

She took the golden knot in her fingers, and was soon busily engaged in attempting to undo it. Meanwhile, the bright sunshine came through the open window, as did likewise the merry voices of the children, playing at a distance, and perhaps the voice of Epimetheus among them. Pandora stopped to listen. What a beautiful day it was! Would it not be wiser if she were to let the troublesome knot alone, and think no more about the box, but run and join her little playfellow and be happy?

All this time, however, her fingers were half unconsciously busy with the knot, and just then, by the merest accident, she gave the knot a kind of twist. The gold cord untwined itself, as if by magic, and left the box without a fastening.

Suddenly Pandora seemed to hear the murmur of

small voices within. "Let us out, dear Pandora – pray, let us out!"

'What can it be?' thought Pandora. 'Is there something alive in the box? Maybe I should take a peep – just one peep – and then the lid shall be shut down as safely as ever! There cannot possibly be any harm in having just one little peep!'

As Pandora raised the lid, the cottage grew very dark and dismal, for a black cloud had swept quite over the sun, and seemed to have buried it alive. There had for a little while past been a low growling and muttering, which all at once broke into a heavy peal

432

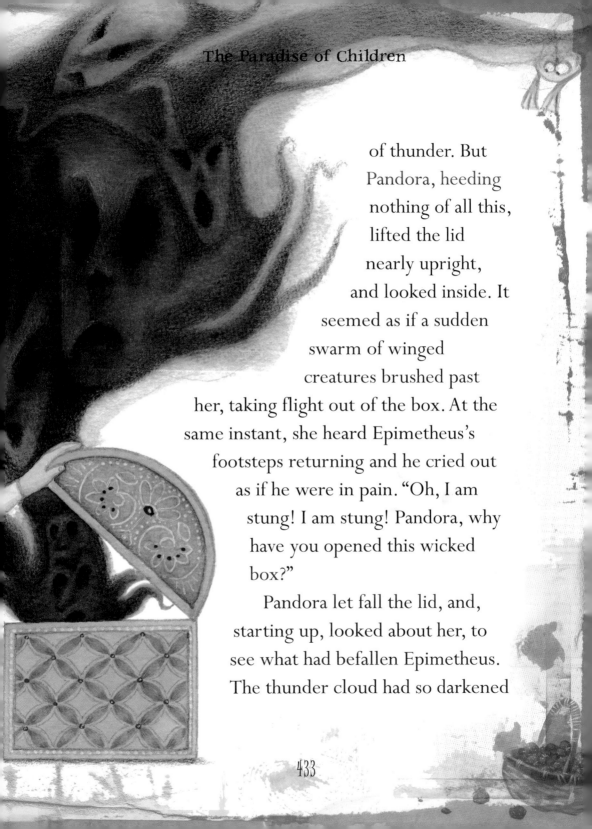

of thunder. But Pandora, heeding nothing of all this, lifted the lid nearly upright, and looked inside. It seemed as if a sudden swarm of winged creatures brushed past her, taking flight out of the box. At the same instant, she heard Epimetheus's footsteps returning and he cried out as if he were in pain. "Oh, I am stung! I am stung! Pandora, why have you opened this wicked box?"

Pandora let fall the lid, and, starting up, looked about her, to see what had befallen Epimetheus. The thunder cloud had so darkened the room that she could not very clearly discern what was in it. But as her eyes grew more accustomed to the imperfect light, she saw a crowd of ugly little shapes, with bats' wings, looking horribly spiteful, and armed with terribly long stings in their tails. It was one of these that had stung Epimetheus. Nor was it a great while before Pandora herself was stung and she too began to scream in pain.

The ugly things which had made their escape out of the box were the whole family of earthly Troubles. There were evil Passions, there were a great many species of Cares, there were more than a hundred and fifty Sorrows, there were Diseases (in a vast number of miserable and painful shapes), there were more kinds of Naughtiness than it would be of any use to talk about. And now the evil Troubles flew out of the windows and doors, to pester and torment the children all over the world – who from that moment on began to grow old and die.

Meanwhile, Epimetheus sat down sullenly in a corner while Pandora flung herself upon the floor, sobbing as if her heart would break.

Suddenly there was a gentle little tap on the inside of the lid.

"What can that noise be?" cried Pandora, lifting her head.

Epimetheus made no answer.

Again the tap! It sounded like the tiny knuckles of a fairy's hand, knocking lightly and playfully on the inside of the box. "Let me out!" came a sweet voice. "I am not like those wicked creatures that have stings in their tails. They are no brothers and sisters of mine, as you would see at once, if you were only to get a glimpse of me. Come, come, my pretty Pandora! I am sure you will let me out!"

"Shall I lift the lid again?" whispered Pandora to Epimetheus.

"Just as you please," replied the boy. "You have done so much mischief already, that perhaps you may as well do a little more. One other Trouble, in such a swarm as you have set adrift about the world, can make no very great difference."

So the two children again lifted the lid. Out flew a sunny and smiling little personage, and hovered about the room, throwing a light wherever she went. She flew to Epimetheus, and laid the least touch of her finger on the inflamed spot where the Trouble had stung him, and immediately the anguish of it was gone. Then she kissed Pandora on the forehead, and her hurt was cured likewise.

"Who are you, beautiful creature?" enquired Pandora, shyly.

"I am called Hope!" answered the sunshiny figure. " I was packed into the box, to make amends to the human race for that swarm of ugly Troubles, which was destined to be let loose among them. Never fear – we shall do pretty well in spite of them all."

"And will you stay with us," asked Epimetheus, "for ever and ever?"

"As long as you need me," said Hope, "and that will be as long as you live in the world – I promise never to desert you."

And she never has.

He Wins Who Waits

From Andrew Lang's *Olive Fairy Book*

ONCE UPON A TIME there reigned a king who had an only daughter. The girl had been spoiled by everybody from her birth, and, besides being beautiful, was clever and wilful, and when she grew old enough to be married she refused to have anything to say to the prince whom her father favoured, but declared she would choose a husband for herself. By long experience the king knew that when once she had made up her mind, there was no use expecting her to change it, so he enquired meekly what she wished him to do.

"Summon all the young men in the kingdom to

appear before me a month from today," answered the princess. "The one to whom I shall give this golden apple shall be my husband."

"But, my dear——" began the king, in dismay.

"The one to whom I shall give this golden apple shall be my husband," repeated the princess, in a louder voice than before. And with a sigh, the king proceeded to do her bidding.

The young men arrived – tall and short, dark and fair, rich and poor. They stood in rows in the great courtyard in front of the palace, and the princess, passed before them all, holding the apple. Once or twice she stopped and hesitated, but in the end she always passed on, till she came to a youth near the end of the last row. There was nothing specially remarkable about him. A hundred others were handsomer, and all wore finer clothes, but he met the princess's eyes frankly and with a smile, and she smiled too, and held out the apple.

"There is some mistake," cried the king, who had

hoped that none of the candidates would please her. "It is impossible that she can wish to marry the son of a poor widow! Tell her to look again!" and the princess went through the rows a second time, and gave the apple to the widow's son again. "Well, marry him if you will," exclaimed the angry king, "but at least you shall not stay here." And the princess answered nothing, but threw up her head, and taking the widow's son by the hand, they left the castle.

That evening they were married and after the ceremony they went back to the house of the bridegroom's mother, which was not much bigger than a hen-coop. The old woman was not at all pleased when her son entered bringing his bride with him. "As if we were not poor enough before," grumbled she. "I dare say this is some fine lady who can do nothing to earn her living."

But the princess stroked her arm, and said softly: "Do not be vexed, dear mother, I am a famous spinner, and can sit at my wheel all day without breaking a thread."

The little family of three worked hard, but despite their efforts, they became poorer and poorer. At the end of six months it was agreed that the husband should go to a nearby town to get work. Here he met a merchant who was about to start on a long journey with a train of camels laden with goods of all sorts. The merchant took the widow's son as a servant, and gave him his whole year's salary beforehand. The young man returned home with the news, and next day bade farewell to his mother and his wife, who were very sad at parting from him.

"Do not forget me," whispered the princess as she flung her arms round his neck, "and as you pass by the well which lies near the city gate, stop and greet the old man you will find sitting there. Kiss his hand, and then ask him what counsel he can give you for your journey."

Then the youth set out, and when he reached the

well where the old man was sitting he asked the questions as his wife had bidden him.

"My son," replied the old man, "remember three things: 'She whom the heart loves, is ever the most beautiful.' 'Patience is the first step on the road to happiness.' And 'He wins who waits.'"

The young man thanked him and went on his way.

Next morning the caravan set out, and before sunset it had arrived at the first halting place, round some wells, where another company of merchants had already encamped. No rain had fallen for a long while in that country, and both men and beasts were parched with thirst. To be sure, there was another well about half a mile away, where there was always water, but to get it you had to be lowered deep down, and, besides, no one who had ever descended that well had been known to come back.

Till they could store water in their bags of goatskin, the caravans dared not go further, and the merchants had decided to offer a reward to anyone

brave enough to go down into the
enchanted well and bring some up.

"I will go," the youth told them bravely.

"How can we thank you!" all the merchants
exclaimed, pressing round him. "We and our
camels are almost dead of thirst. See! Here is a
rope on which we can let you down."

On reaching the well, the rope was
knotted around him, a big goat-skin
bottle was given him, and he was
lowered to the bottom of the pit.
Here a stream was bubbling over
the rocks. Stooping down, he
was about to drink, when a
huge Arab appeared
before him, saying in a
loud voice: "Come
with me!"

The young man

rose, never doubting that his last hour had come, but as he could do nothing, he followed the Arab into a brilliantly lighted hall, on the further side of the little river. There his guide sat down, and drawing towards him two boys, he said to the stranger: "I have a question to ask you. If you answer it right, your life shall be spared. If not, your head will be forfeit, as the head of many another has been before you. Tell me: which of my two children do I think the handsomer."

The question did not seem a hard one, for while one boy was as beautiful a child as ever was seen, his brother was undoubtably ugly. But, just as the youth was going to speak, the old man's counsel flashed into the youth's mind, and he replied hastily: 'The one whom we love best is always the handsomest.'

"You have saved me!" cried the Arab in great joy. "I was condemned by a powerful, wicked genie to remain here until that riddle was answered correctly! Ah, if you could only guess how long I have suffered from the stupidity of all the people I have had to ask that question to! But what brought you to this place, and how can I reward you for what you have done for me?"

"By helping me to draw enough water for my caravan of eighty merchants and their camels, who are dying for want of it," replied the youth.

"That is easily done," said the Arab. "Take these three apples, and when you have filled your skin, and are ready to be drawn up, lay one of them on the ground. Halfway to the earth, let fall another, and at the top, drop the third. If you follow my directions no harm will happen to you. And take, besides, these three pomegranates, green, red and white. One day you will find a use for them!"

The young man did as he was told, and stepped out on the rocky waste, where the merchants were anxiously awaiting him. Oh, how thirsty they all were! But even after the camels had drunk, the skin seemed as full as ever.

Full of gratitude, the merchants pressed the money into his hands, while his own master bade him choose what goods he liked, and a mule to carry them.

So the widow's son had made his fortune at last, and when the merchant had sold his merchandise, and returned home to his native city, his servant hired a man by whom he sent the money and the mule back to his wife.

'I will send the pomegranates also,' thought he, 'for if I leave them in my turban they may some day fall out,' and he drew them out of his turban. But the fruit had vanished, and in their places were three precious stones, green, white and red.

For a long time he remained with the merchant, who gradually trusted him with all his business, and gave him a large share of the money he made. After twenty years, his master died and the young man set off to return home.

Now, soon after the young man had taken service

with the merchant a little boy had been born to
him, and both the princess and his old mother had
toiled hard all day to get the baby food and clothing.
When the money and the pomegranates arrived
there was no need for them to work any more, for
the princess saw at once that they were not fruit at
all, but precious stones of great value. She went to
the market and bought three of the finest
pomegranates she could find for her little boy to
eat. Then she bought beautiful new clothes for all of
them, and when they were dressed they looked as
fine as could be. Next, she took out one of the
precious stones which her husband had sent her. She
wrapped it up in a beautiful, embroidered
handkerchief and placed it in a small silver box.
Then she filled the old woman's pockets with gold
and silver pieces. "Go, dear mother," she said, "to the
palace, and present the jewel to the king, and if he
asks you what he can give you in return, tell him
that you want a paper, with his seal attached,

proclaiming that no one is to meddle with anything you may choose to do. Before you leave the palace, distribute the money amongst the servants.'

The old woman took the box and started for the palace. No one there had ever seen a ruby of such beauty, and the royal jeweller declared to the king that there wasn't enough money in his treasury to buy it.

The dismayed king asked the old woman: "If I cannot give you its worth in money, is there anything you will take in exchange?"

"A paper signed by your hand, and sealed with your seal, proclaiming that I may do what I will, without let or hindrance," answered she promptly. And the king, delighted to have obtained what he coveted at so small a cost, gave her the paper without delay. Then the old woman took her leave and returned home.

The fame of this wonderful ruby soon spread far and wide, and envoys arrived at the little house to know if there were more stones to sell. Each king was so anxious to gain possession of the treasure that he bade his messenger to outbid all the others, and so the princess sold the two remaining stones for a sum of money so large that if the gold pieces had been spread out they would have reached from here to the moon. The first thing she did was to build a palace by the side of the cottage, and it was raised on pillars of gold, in which were set great diamonds, which blazed night and day. Of course the news of this palace was the first thing that reached the king, her father, on his return from the wars, and he hurried to see it for himself. In the doorway stood a young man of twenty, who was his grandson (though neither of them knew it), and so pleased was the king with the appearance of the youth, that he carried him back with him to his own palace, and immediately made him commander of the whole army.

Not long after this, the widow's son arrived in his native land. There, sure enough, was the tiny cottage where he had lived with his mother, but the gorgeous building beside it was quite new to him. What had become of his wife and his mother? And who could be dwelling in that other wonderful place? These were the first thoughts that flashed through his mind, but not wishing to betray himself by asking questions of passing strangers, he climbed up into a tree that stood opposite the palace and watched, and waited.

By-and-by a lady came out, and began to gather some of the roses and jasmine that hung about the porch. The twenty years that had passed since he had last beheld her vanished in an instant, and he knew her at once to be his own wife, looking almost as young and beautiful as on the day of their parting. He was about to jump down from the tree and hasten to her side, when she was joined by a young man who placed his arm affectionately round her neck. At the sight of this the angry husband drew his bow, but before he could let fly the arrow, the counsel of the wise man came back to him: 'Patience is the first step on the road to happiness.' And he laid it down again.

At this moment the princess turned, and drawing her companion's head down to hers, kissed him on each cheek. A second time blind rage filled the heart of the watcher, and he snatched up his bow from the branch where it hung, when words, heard long since, seemed to sound in his ears: 'He wins who waits.' And the bow dropped to his side.

Then, through the silent air came the sound of the youth's voice: "Mother, last night I dreamed that my father was here," said the youth. "How I wish it were true and I could meet him at last!"

Then the man understood, and he came down from the tree, and clasped his wife and son in his arms. All that night they talked, and when the sun rose it still found them talking. But as soon as it was proper, he went up to the palace to pay his homage

to the king, and to inform him of all that had happened and who they all really were.

The king was overjoyed to think that his daughter, whom he had long since forgiven and sorely missed, was living at his gates, and was, besides, the mother of the youth who was so dear to him. "It was written beforehand," cried the monarch. "You are my son-in-law before the world, and shall be king after me."

And the man bowed his head. He had waited, and he had won.

The Three Dwarves

From Andrew Lang's *Red Fairy Book*

THERE WAS ONCE a man who lost his wife, and a woman who lost her husband. The man had a daughter and so had the woman. The two girls were friends and used often to play together. One day the woman turned to the man's daughter and said: "Go and tell your father that I will marry him, and then he will be better looked after."

The girl went home and told her father what the woman had said.

"What am I to do?" he answered. Not being able to make up his mind, he took off his boot, and handing it to his daughter, said: "Take this boot which has a hole in the sole, hang it up on a nail in the hayloft, and pour water into it. If it holds water I will marry again, but if it doesn't I won't."

The girl did as she was bid, but the water drew the hole together and the boot filled up to the very top. She went and told her father the result, and he got up and went to see for himself. When he saw that it was true and that there was no mistake, he accepted his fate, proposed to the widow, and they were married at once.

On the morning after the wedding, when the two girls awoke, milk was standing for the man's daughter to wash in and wine for her to drink, but for the woman's daughter, only water to wash in and only water to drink. On the second morning, water to wash in and water to drink was standing for the man's daughter as well. And on the third morning, water to wash in and water to drink was standing for the man's daughter, and milk to wash in and wine to drink for the woman's daughter. And so it continued ever after. The woman hated her stepdaughter from the bottom of her heart, and did all she could to make her life miserable. She was as jealous as she could possibly be, because the girl was so beautiful and charming, while her own daughter was both ugly and repulsive.

One winter's day when there was a hard frost, and mountain and valley were covered with snow, the woman made a dress of paper, and calling the girl to her said: "There, put on this dress and go out into the wood and fetch me a basket of strawberries!"

"Now heaven help us," replied her stepdaughter, "strawberries don't grow in winter – the earth is all frozen and the snow has covered everything up. And why send me out in a paper dress? It is so cold outside that one's very breath freezes – the wind will whistle through my dress, and the brambles tear it from my body."

"How dare you contradict me!" said her stepmother. "Be off with you at once, and don't show your face again till you have filled the basket with strawberries." Then she gave her a hard crust of bread, saying: "That will be enough for you today," and she thought to herself: 'The girl will certainly perish of hunger and cold outside, and I shan't be bothered with her any more.'

The girl was so obedient that she put on the paper dress and set out with her little basket. There was nothing but snow far and near, and not a green blade of grass anywhere. When she came to the wood she saw a little house, and out of it peeped three little dwarfs. She wished them good day, and knocked at the door. They called out to her to enter, so she stepped in and sat down on a seat by the fire, wishing to warm herself and eat her breakfast. The dwarfs said at once: "Give us some of your food!"

"Gladly," she said, and breaking her crust in two, she gave them the half.

Then they asked her what she was doing in the depths of winter in her thin dress.

"Oh," she answered, "I have been sent to get a basketful of strawberries, and I daren't show my face again at home till I bring them with me."

When she had finished her bread they gave her a broom and told her to sweep away the snow from the back door. As soon as she left the room to do so, the three little men consulted what they should give her as a reward for being so sweet and good, and for sharing her last crust with them.

The first said: "Every day she shall grow prettier."

The second: "Every time she opens her mouth a piece of gold shall fall out."

And the third: "A king shall come and marry her."

The girl in the meantime was doing as the dwarfs had bidden her, and was sweeping the snow away from the back door, and what do you think she found there? Heaps of fine ripe strawberries that showed out dark red against the white snow.

She joyfully picked enough to fill her basket, thanked the little men for their kindness, shook hands with them, and ran home to bring her stepmother what she had asked for.

When she walked in and said "Good evening", a piece of gold fell out of her mouth. Then she told what had happened to her in the wood, and at every word pieces of gold dropped from her mouth, so that the room was soon covered with them.

"She's surely more money than wit to throw gold about like that," said her stepsister, but in her secret heart she was very jealous, and determined that she too would go to the wood and look for strawberries.

But her mother refused to let her go, saying: "My dear child, it is far too cold, you might freeze to death."

The girl however left her no peace, so she was forced at last to give in, but she insisted on her putting on a beautiful fur cloak, and she gave her bread and butter and cakes to eat on the way.

The girl went straight to the little house in the wood, and as before the three little men were looking out of the window. She took no notice of them, and without as much as 'By your leave' or 'With your leave' she flounced into the room, sat herself down at the fire, and began to eat her bread and butter and cakes.

"Give us some!" cried the dwarfs.

But she answered: "No, I won't, it's hardly enough for myself, so catch me giving you any!"

When she had finished eating they said: "There's a broom for you, go and clear up our back door."

"Do it yourselves, I'm not your servant," she answered rudely.

When she saw that they did not mean to give her anything, she left the house in no amiable frame of mind. Then the three little men consulted about what they should do

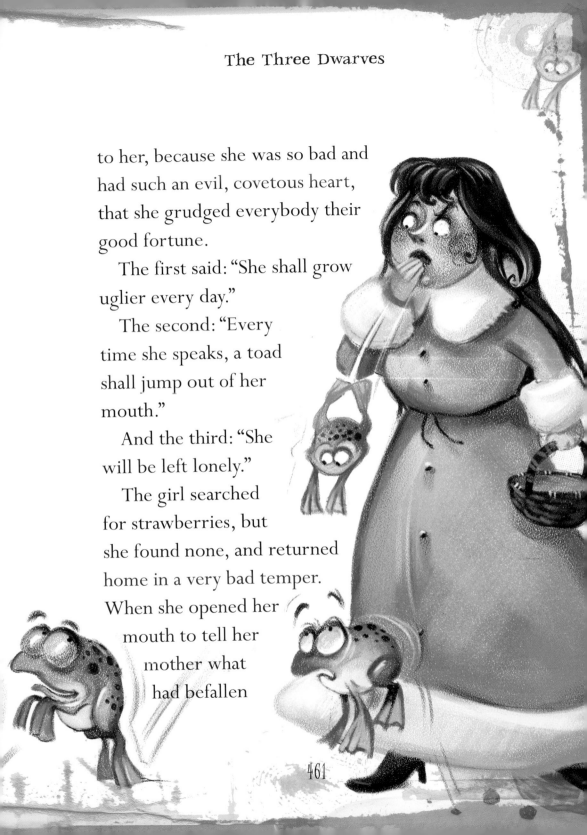

to her, because she was so bad and had such an evil, covetous heart, that she grudged everybody their good fortune.

The first said: "She shall grow uglier every day."

The second: "Every time she speaks, a toad shall jump out of her mouth."

And the third: "She will be left lonely."

The girl searched for strawberries, but she found none, and returned home in a very bad temper. When she opened her mouth to tell her mother what had befallen

461

her in the wood, a toad jumped out, so that everyone was quite disgusted with her.

Then the stepmother was more furious than ever, and from then on she did nothing but plot mischief against the man's daughter, who was daily growing more and more beautiful. At last, one day the wicked woman took a large pot, put it on the fire and boiled some yarn in it. When it was well scalded she hung it round the poor girl's shoulder and, giving her an axe, she bade her break a hole in the frozen river, and rinse the yarn in it. Her stepdaughter obeyed as usual, and went and broke a hole in the ice. While she was busily engaged in wringing out the yarn a magnificent carriage passed, and the king sat inside. The carriage stood still, and the king asked her: "My child, who are you, and what in the wide world are you doing here?'"

"I am only a poor girl," she answered, "and am rinsing out my yarn in the river."

Then the king was sorry for her, and when he saw

how beautiful she was he said: "Will you come away with me?"

"Most gladly," she replied, for she knew how willingly she would leave her stepmother and sister, and how glad they would be to be rid of her.

So she stepped into the carriage and drove away with the king, and when they reached his palace the wedding was celebrated with much splendour. So all turned out just as the three little dwarfs had said.

King Grisly~Beard

The Brothers Grimm

A GREAT KING of a land far away had a daughter who was very beautiful, but so proud and vain that none of the princes who came to ask her in marriage was good enough for her, and she only made fun of them.

The king held a great feast and invited all her suitors, and they all sat in a row – kings, and princes, and dukes, and earls, and counts, and barons, and knights. Then the princess came in, and as she passed them she said something spiteful to every one. The first was too fat: "He's as round as a tub," said she. The next was too tall: "What a maypole!" said she. The next was too short: "What a dumpling!" said she. And thus she had some joke to crack upon every one, but she laughed more than all at a good king who was there. "Look at him," said she. "His beard is like an old mop – he shall be called Grisly-beard." So the king got the nickname of Grisly-beard.

But the old king was very angry when he saw how his daughter behaved, and how she ill-treated all his guests, and he vowed that, willing or unwilling, she should marry the first man, be he prince or beggar, that came to the door.

Two days after there came by a travelling fiddler, who began to play under the window and beg alms, and when the king heard him, he said, "Let him come in." So they brought in a dirty-looking fellow, and when he had sung before the king and the princess, he begged a boon. Then the king said, "You have sung so well, that I will give you my daughter for your wife." The princess begged and pleaded, but the king said, "I have sworn to give you to the first comer, and I will keep my word." So words and tears were no good. The parson was sent for, and she was married to the fiddler. When this was over the king said, "Now get ready to go — you must not stay here, you must travel on with your husband."

Then the fiddler went his way, and took her with

him, and they soon came to a great wood. "Pray," said she, "whose is this wood?"

"It belongs to King Grisly-beard," answered he. "Had you taken him, all this would have been yours."

"Ah! Unlucky wretch that I am!" sighed she. "I wish I had married King Grisly-beard!"

Next they came to some fine meadows. "Whose are these beautiful green meadows?" said she.

"They belong to King Grisly-beard, and they could have been yours too," the fiddler replied.

"Ah! Unlucky wretch that I am!" said she. "I wish I had married King Grisly-beard!"

Then they came to a great city. "Whose is this noble city?" said she.

"It belongs to King Grisly-beard, and it could have been yours."

"Ah! Unlucky wretch that I am!" sighed she. "I wish I had married King Grisly-beard!"

"Why should you wish for another husband?" asked the fiddler. "Am not I good enough for you?"

At last they came to a small cottage. "What a paltry place!" said she. "To whom does that little dirty hole belong?"

Then the fiddler said, "That is your and my house, where we are to live."

"Where are your servants?" cried she.

"What do we want with servants?" said he. "You must do for yourself whatever is to be done. Now make the fire, and put on water and cook my supper, for I am very tired." But the princess knew nothing of making fires and cooking, and the fiddler was forced to help her.

When they had eaten a very scanty meal they went to bed. But the fiddler called her up very early in the morning to clean the house. Thus they lived for two days. When they had eaten up all there was in the cottage, the man said, "Wife, we can't go on thus, spending money and earning nothing. You must learn to weave baskets." Then he went out and cut willows, and brought them home, and she began to

weave, but it made her fingers very sore. "I see this
work won't do," said he. "Try and spin – perhaps
you will do that better." So she sat down and tried to
spin, but the threads cut her tender fingers till the
blood ran. "See now," said the fiddler, "you are good
for nothing – you can do no work! However, I'll try
and set up a trade in pots and pans, and you shall
stand in the market and sell them."

"Alas!" sighed she. "If any of my father's court
should pass by and see me standing in the market,
how they will laugh at me!"

But her husband did not care for that, and said she
must work, if she did not wish to die of hunger. At
first the trade went well. Many people, seeing such
a beautiful woman, went to buy her wares, and paid
their money without thinking of taking away the
goods. They lived on this as long as it lasted, and
then her husband bought a fresh lot of ware, and she
sat herself down with it in the corner of the market,
but a drunken soldier soon came by, and rode his

horse against her stall, and broke all her goods into a thousand pieces. Then she began to cry, and knew not what to do. "What will become of me?" said she. "What will my husband say?" So she ran home and told him all.

"Who would have thought you would have been so silly," said he, "as to put an earthenware stall in the corner of the market, where everybody passes?

But let us have no more crying, I see you are not fit for this sort of work, so I have been to the king's palace, and asked if they did not want a kitchen-maid, and they say they will take you, and there you will have plenty to eat."

Thus the princess became a kitchen-maid, and she helped the cook to do all the dirtiest work, but she was allowed to carry home some of the meat that was left, and on this they were able to live. She had not been working there long before she heard that the king's eldest son was passing by, going to be married, and she went to one of the windows and looked out. Everything was ready, and all the pomp and brightness of the court was there. Then she bitterly grieved for the pride and folly which had brought her so low. And the servants gave her some of the rich meats, which she put into her basket to take home.

All of a sudden, as she was going out, in came the king's son in golden clothes. When he saw a beautiful woman at the door, he took her by the hand, and said she should be his partner in the dance, but she trembled for fear, for she saw that it was King Grisly-beard, who was making fun of her. However, he kept fast hold, and led her in, and the cover of the basket came off, so that the meats in it fell about. Then everybody laughed and jeered at her. She was so embarrassed that she wished herself a thousand feet deep in the earth. She sprang to the door to run away, but on the steps King Grisly-beard overtook her, and brought her back. All at once he smiled at her, and said, "Fear me not! I am the fiddler who has lived with you in the hut. I brought you there because I really loved you. I am also the soldier that overset your stall. I have done all this only to cure you of your silly pride, and to show you the folly of your ill-treatment of me. Now all is over: you have learned wisdom, and it is time to hold our marriage feast."

Then the chamberlains came and brought her the

most beautiful robes, and her father and his whole court were there already, and welcomed her home on her marriage. Joy was in every face and every heart. The feast was grand, they danced and sang, and all were merry – and I only wish that you and I had been at the party.

The Hermit

From *Tales of Wonder Every Child Should Know*
by Kate Douglas Wiggin and
Nora Archibald Smith

IN THE REIGN of King Moabdar there lived
at Babylon a young man named Zadig. He was
handsome, rich, and good-hearted. At the moment
when this story opens, he was travelling to see the
world and learn wisdom. However, he had seen so
many terrible disasters and encountered so much
misery among people that he had begun to think
that the world was very unfair and to doubt that
God existed. In this very unhappy state of mind he
was walking on the banks of the River Euphrates,
when he chanced to meet a holy hermit, whose
snowy beard fell to his belt. He carried a scroll

which he was reading very intently. Zadig stopped, bowed, and inquired what the scroll was.

"It is the Book of Destiny," replied the hermit. "Would you like to read it?"

He handed it to Zadig, but though Zadig knew a dozen languages, he could not understand a word of it. His curiosity increased.

"I can tell from your face that you are a troubled man," said the kindly hermit.

"Alas!" said Zadig. "I do feel very gloomy."

"Allow me to accompany you," said the hermit, "I may be useful to you. I am sometimes able to comfort the sorrowful."

Zadig was impressed by the holy appearance and the mysterious scroll of the old hermit, and thought that he must be very learned and wise. He was delighted that the old man wanted to accompany him. As they walked, the hermit spoke of fairness, of fate, of temptations and human weaknesses, and of all the goodness in life, with so much power that

Zadig was quite captivated and wanted to listen to him for as long as possible. He begged the hermit not to leave him until they returned to Babylon.

"I ask you the same favour," said the hermit. "Promise me that, whatever I may do, you will keep me company for several days."

Zadig gave the promise, and they journeyed onwards together.

That night the travellers arrived at a grand mansion. The hermit begged for food and lodging for himself and his companion. The porter, who was so richly dressed that he might have been mistaken for a prince, ushered them in with a very snooty air. The chief servant showed them the magnificent apartments where they were to spend the night, and they were then admitted to the great hall to dine at the long, long dinner table – albeit they were sat at the very bottom, where the master of the mansion did not even cast a glance at them. They were, however, served with all sorts of delicious morsels, and, after dinner, washed their hands in a golden basin set with emeralds and rubies. After an extremely comfortable night's sleep, the next morning, before they left the castle, a servant brought them each a piece of gold.

"The master of the house," said Zadig, as they went their way, "appears to be a generous man, although he obviously thinks too highly of himself." As he spoke he noticed that a kind of large pouch which the hermit carried appeared much bigger than usual. He asked what was in it and the hermit explained that it was the golden basin, set with precious stones, which he had stolen! Zadig was highly astonished – but he didn't say anything.

At noon the hermit stopped before a little house, in which lived a man who was very wealthy but very mean. An old valet in a shabby coat received them very rudely, showed them into the stable, and set before them a few rotten olives, some mouldy bread, and beer which had turned sour. However, the hermit didn't seem upset at all. In fact, he ate and drank with as much content as he had shown the night before. Then, addressing the old valet, who had kept his eye upon them to make sure that they stole nothing, he gave him the two gold pieces which they had received that morning, and thanked him for his kind attention. "Be so good," he added, "as to let me see your master."

The astonished valet showed them in.

"Most mighty sir," said the hermit, "I can only give you my humble thanks for the noble manner in which you have received us. I beseech you to accept this golden basin as a token of my gratitude."

The mean man almost fell backwards with amazement. The hermit, without waiting for him to recover, set off with speed with his companion.

"What does all this mean?" asked Zadig. "You steal a golden basin set with jewels from a man who receives you generously, and you give it to a curmudgeon who treats you badly."

"My son," replied the hermit, "I can assure you that from now on, the mighty lord who only welcomes travellers in order to display his riches, will grow wiser. However, the mean man will gradually be taught generosity. Be amazed at nothing, and follow me."

Zadig knew not whether he was dealing with the most foolish or the wisest of all men. But the hermit spoke with such faith that Zadig had no choice except to follow him.

That night they came to a simple but comfortable-looking house, with no signs of either showiness nor meanness. The owner was a wise man who had taken himself off to live by himself and study peacefully the rules of goodness and common sense, and who yet was happy and contented. He had built this calm house to suit himself, and he received the strangers in it with openness and straight-forwardness. He led them himself to a comfortable chamber, where he left the travellers to rest awhile. Then he returned to lead them to a dainty little supper. They held an interesting conversation, during which they all agreed that the wisest people are not always the ones in charge of the things that happen in the world. The hermit also made the point that the world is much bigger than we know and things often happen for reasons which we don't understand. Zadig wondered how it was that a person who committed such mad acts could seem to talk so sensibly!

At length, the host led the two travellers to their apartment, and thanked heaven for sending him two visitors who were so wise and good. He offered them some money, but the old man declined with thanks and bade their host goodnight.

At break of day the hermit woke his comrade. "We must be going," he remarked. "But while everyone is still asleep, I wish to leave this worthy man a gift." With these words he took a torch and set the house on fire. Zadig burst forth into cries of horror, and would have stopped the frightful act, but the hermit was somehow stronger and pushed him

away. Beaten back
by both the old man and the
heat, Zadig was forced to leave the house in a blaze
and retreat to a safe distance. When the travellers
were both a good way off, the hermit looked back
calmly at the burning pile. "Heaven be praised!" he
cried. "Our kind host's house is destroyed from top
to bottom." At these words Zadig knew not whether
he should burst out laughing, call the holy man an

old rascal, knock him down, or run away. But he did none of these things. Still overwhelmed by the firm manner of the hermit, he followed him against his will to their next lodging.

This was the dwelling of a good and charitable widow, who had a nephew of fourteen, her only hope and joy. She did her best to treat the travellers well, and the next morning she bade her nephew guide them safely past a certain bridge, which, having recently been broken, had become dangerous to cross over. The youth, eager to oblige them, led the way. "Come," said the hermit, when they were half across the bridge, "I must show my gratitude toward your aunt," and as he spoke he seized the young man by the hair and threw him into the river. The youth fell, reappeared for an instant on the surface, and then was swallowed by the torrent.

"Oh, monster!" exclaimed Zadig. "Ah! Most evil of men——"

"You promised me more patience," interrupted

the old man. "Listen! Beneath the ruins of that house which I set on fire, the owner will discover an enormous treasure, while this young man, whose existence I cut short, would have turned to wickedness and killed his aunt within a year, and you yourself in two."

"Who told you so?" cried Zadig. "Even if you read this in your Book of Destiny, who bestowed upon you the power to drown a youth who never harmed you?"

Once he had spoken, he saw that the old man had a beard no longer, and that his face had become young. His hermit's frock had disappeared, and four white wings covered his back and shone with dazzling light.

"You are an angel of heaven!" cried Zadig.

The Hermit

"People," replied the angel Jezrael, for that's who he was, "judge all things without true knowledge, and you, of all people, most deserved help to become wise. The world imagines that the youth who has just died fell by accident into the water, and that by similar accident the rich man's house was set on fire. But there is no such thing as chance – everything happens to test people or to punish people or because of things which must happen in the future."

As he spoke, the angel flew up to heaven, and Zadig fell upon his knees.

The Elf and the Housewife

Juliana Horatia Gatty Ewing

THERE ONCE LIVED a penny-pinching
Housewife and one day an elf came
knocking at her door.

"Can you lend us a saucepan?" said he. "There's a
wedding in the hill, and all the pots are in use."

The Housewife went to get one, but she thought
to herself: 'I'll give him the old one. It leaks, and the
elves are such nimble workers, they are sure to
mend it. So I'll help the elves and at the same time
I'll save the sixpence that the tinker would have
charged me to repair it.'

She gave the old saucepan to the dwarf, who

thanked her, and went away.

In due time the saucepan was returned, and, as

the Housewife had foreseen, it was neatly mended.

At supper-time she filled the pan with milk, and
set it on the fire to warm for the children's supper.
But in only a few minutes the milk was so burned
and smoked that no one could touch it.

"Oh how infuriating!" cried the Housewife, almost crying at the waste. "There's a whole quart of good milk wasted!"

"And that's sixpence," cried a voice from the chimney. "You didn't save the money after all!"

And with that the elf himself came tumbling down the chimney, and went off laughing through the door.

But from that day forwards, the saucepan was as good as any other.

The Wonderful Weaver

From *Old Greek Stories* by James Baldwin

THERE WAS A YOUNG GIRL in Greece whose name was Arachne. Her face was pale but beautiful, and her eyes were big and blue, and her hair was long and like gold. All that she cared to do from morn till noon was to sit in the sun and spin, and all that she cared to do from noon till night was to sit in the shade and weave.

And oh, how fine and fair were the things which she wove in her loom! Flax, wool, silk – she worked with them all – and when they came from her hands, the cloth which she had made of them was so thin and soft and bright that men came from all parts of the world to see it. And they said that cloth so rare could not be made of flax, or wool, or silk, but that the warp was of rays of sunlight and the woof was of threads of gold.

Then as, day by day, the girl sat in the sun and span, or sat in the shade and wove, she said: "In all the world there is no yarn so fine as mine, and in all the world there is no cloth so soft and smooth, nor silk so bright and rare."

"Who taught you to spin and weave so well?" someone asked.

"No one taught me," she said. "I learned how to do it as I sat in the sun and the shade, but no one showed me."

"But it may be that Athena, the queen of the air, taught you, and you did not know it."

"Athena, the queen of the air? Bah!" said Arachne. "How could she teach me? Can she spin such skeins of yarn as these? Can she weave goods like mine? I should like to see her try to match me. I can teach her a thing or two."

She looked up and saw in the doorway a tall woman wrapped in a long cloak. Her face was fair to see, but stern, oh, so stern! And her grey eyes were so sharp and bright that Arachne could not bring herself to meet her gaze.

"Arachne," said the woman, "I am Athena, the queen of the air, and I have heard your boast. Do you still mean to say that I have not taught you how to spin and weave?"

"No one has taught me," said Arachne, "and I thank no one for what I know." And she stood up, straight and proud, by the side of her loom.

"And do you still think that you can spin and weave as well as I?" said Athena.

Arachne's cheeks grew white, but she said: "Yes. I can weave as well as you."

"Then let me tell you what we will do," said Athena. "Three days from now we will both weave — you on your loom, and I on mine. We will ask all the world to come and see us, and great Jupiter, who sits in the clouds, shall be the judge. And if your work is best, then I will weave no more so long as the world shall last. But if my work is best, then you shall never use loom or spindle or distaff again. Do you agree to this?”

"I agree," said Arachne.

"It is well," said Athena. And she was gone.

When the time came for the contest in weaving, all the world was there to see it, and great Jupiter sat among the clouds and looked on.

Arachne had set up her loom in the shade of a mulberry tree, where butterflies were flitting and grasshoppers chirping all through the livelong day. But Athena had set up her loom in the sky, where the breezes were blowing and the summer sun was shining, for she was the queen of the air.

Then Arachne took her skeins of finest silk and began to weave. And she wove a web of marvellous beauty, so thin and light that it would float in the air,

and yet so strong that it could hold a lion in its meshes, and the threads were of many colours, so beautifully arranged and mingled one with another that all who saw were filled with delight.

"No wonder that the maiden boasted of her skill," said the people.

And Jupiter himself nodded.

Then Athena began to weave. And she took of the sunbeams that gilded the mountain top, and of the snowy fleece of the summer clouds, and of the blue of the summer sky, and of the green of the summer fields, and of the royal purple of the autumn woods – and what do you suppose she wove?

The web which she wove in the sky was full of enchanting pictures of flowers and gardens, and of castles and towers, and of mountain heights, and of men and beasts, and of giants and dwarfs, and of the mighty beings who dwell in the clouds with Jupiter. And those who looked upon it were so filled with wonder and delight, that they forgot all about the beautiful web which Arachne had woven. And Arachne herself was ashamed and afraid when she saw it, and she hid her face in her hands and wept.

"Oh, how can I live," she cried, "now that I must never again use loom or spindle or distaff?" And she kept on, weeping and weeping and weeping, and saying, "How can I live?"

Then, when Athena saw that the poor maiden would never have any joy unless she were allowed to spin and weave, she took pity on her and said: "I would free you from your bargain if I could, but that is a thing which no one can do. You must hold to your agreement never to touch loom or spindle again. And yet, since you will never be happy unless you can spin and weave, I will give you a new form so that you can carry on your work with neither spindle nor loom."

Then she touched Arachne with the tip of the spear which she sometimes carried, and the maiden was changed at once into a nimble spider, which ran into a shady place in the grass and began merrily to spin and weave a beautiful web.

I have heard it said that all the spiders which have been in the world since then are the children of Arachne, but I doubt whether this be true. Yet, for all I know, Arachne still lives and spins and weaves — and the very next spider you see may be she herself.

Peter and the Magic Goose

From *Fairy Stories and Fables* by James Baldwin

THERE WAS ONCE a man who had three sons. The eldest of these sons was called Jacob, the second John, and the youngest Peter. Now Peter was good-natured and not very wise, and so it was easy for his brothers to play tricks on him. When there was hard work to be done, it was Peter that had to do it, and when anything went wrong about the farm, it was Peter that had to bear the blame for it.

One day in summer Jacob wanted to go into the woods to cut down a tree. So his mother gave him a nice cake and a bottle of milk for lunch, and told him that as soon as he felt tired he must come home and let Peter finish the job.

While he was looking at the trees and wondering which one to cut down, a little red-faced man came along. He seemed to be very old and feeble, and he said to Jacob: "Kind sir, will you not give me a piece of that nice cake which is in your pocket? I have not had anything to eat since yesterday."

"Not a bit of it," said Jacob. "I have nothing for beggars. If you want food, you must work for it as I do."

The little man said not a word but hobbled away, and Jacob began to chop his tree. He had hardly made a dozen strokes when his foot slipped. He fell against his axe and cut his arm so badly that he had to go home to have it bound.

The next day John said that he would go out and

498

finish cutting the tree. So his mother baked a nice cake for him, and gave him a bottle of milk for his lunch, and told him to take care and not hurt himself.

John had hardly reached the wood, when he met the little red-faced man, hobbling along among the trees. "Please give me a bite of the nice cake and let me have a taste of the milk in that bottle," said the man, "for I am almost dead with hunger and thirst."

"Why should I give you anything?" said John, "I have no more than I want for myself."

The little man made no answer, and John walked on through the woods, until he found the tree which his brother had begun to chop down. At the very first stroke, his axe glanced and struck his foot, and cut so deep a gash that the blood rushed out in a stream. Some men who were not far off heard his cries and came to him, and if they had not bound his wound and carried him home, he would have died.

The next day Peter's mother said: "Peter, do you

see what you have made your brothers suffer by your idleness? If you had gone into the woods as you should have done in the first place, this would not have happened. So take the axe and go now, and don't come home till you have cut that tree down." And then she gave him a hard crust of bread, and a small flask of sour milk for his lunch.

It was a long time before Peter found the tree, and when he came to it, he was both hungry and tired. He took the crust of bread from his pocket and was just going to taste it, when the little red-faced man stood before him. "Please give me one crumb of your bread and a drop of your milk in, for I am dying of hunger and thirst," said the poor man.

"Come and sit down with me on this log," said Peter, "and I will share it all with you."

So the two sat together, side by side, and ate their lunch, and Peter thought that he had never tasted anything so good.

When they had finished, the little man said: "You

are very kind-hearted, so I'll tell you a secret. When
you have cut the tree down, look in the hollow
stump. There you will find a strange creature which
you must carry to the king. It may be that some
people will try to touch the creature as you are
walking along, and so you must be sure whenever it
cries out, to say, 'Hold fast! Hold fast! Hold fast!'"

After the little man had gone on his way, Peter
took up his axe and began to chop with all his
might. The chips flew, and it was not
long till the tree began to tremble,
and soon it fell with a crash to the
ground. There was a round
hollow place in the stump,
and in it sat – a goose.

Peter thought
that this was
not a very

strange creature after all, for he had seen geese all his life. If he had been wiser, he would have laughed at the idea of carrying it to the king, but, since the little man had told him to do so, he picked the goose up in his arms and started at once.

He made his way out of the woods, and soon came to the great road which led to the king's town. By the side of the road there was an inn, and some men were standing in the wagon yard nearby. When Peter came up with the goose in his arms, the innkeeper's daughter, who was looking out at the door, called to him, and said: "Where did you get that pretty goose? You'll give me one of its feathers, won't you?"

"Come and pull one out," said Peter, kindly.

The girl ran out and tried to get one of the long white feathers from the bird's wing, but the moment that she touched it the goose screamed, and Peter remembered what the little man had told him to say. "Hold fast! Hold fast! Hold fast!" he cried, and the young lady's fingers stuck so fast to the goose that she could not let go. She screamed and tried her best to pull away, but Peter walked along and took no more notice of her at all.

The men who were standing in the yard laughed, for they thought that she was only making believe, but the stable boy, when he heard her cries, ran out into the road to see what was the matter.

"Oh, Tommy, Tommy help me!" cried the poor girl. "Give me your hand and set me free from this horrid goose."

"Of course I will," said Tommy, and he seized the girl's hand.

But at that very moment the goose screamed again, and Peter, without looking back, cried out: "Hold fast! Hold fast! Hold fast!"

The stable boy could not let go of the girl's hand, but was obliged to follow after her, and although he howled loudly and tried to pull away, Peter walked steadily along and seemed not to notice him.

They soon came to a village where there were a great many people out for a holiday. A circus show was about to open, and the clown was in the street doing some of his funny tricks. When he saw Peter and the girl and the stable boy passing by, he cried out: "What's the matter there? Have three more clowns come to town?"

"I am no clown," cried the stable boy, "but this girl holds my hand so tight that I can't get away. Come, set me free, and I will do you as good a turn some day."

The clown, in his droll way, seized the stable boy by the string of his apron. The goose screamed, and Peter cried out: "Hold fast! Hold fast! Hold fast!"

Of course the clown could not let go. But Peter walked on, and looked neither to the right nor to the left. When the people saw the clown trying to pull away, they thought he was only at his tricks again, and everybody laughed.

Just then the mayor of the village came walking

up the street. He was a very grave, sober man who was never known to smile, and the clown's silly actions did not please him at all. "What do you mean by grinning at me?" he said, and he seized the fellow's coat tail and tried to stop him.

But at that moment the goose screamed, and Peter again cried out: "Hold fast! Hold fast! Hold fast!" What could the mayor do but follow Peter with the rest? For, try as hard as he would, he could not let go.

The wife of the mayor, a tall, spare woman, was greatly vexed when she saw her husband marching along and hanging to the clown's coat tail. She ran after him and seized his free arm and tried her best to pull him away.

The goose screamed, and Peter, without looking back, cried out: "Hold fast! Hold fast! Hold fast!"

The good lady could not help herself. She had to walk along whether she would or not, and make the best of it. A great many people followed, laughing and wondering, but none of them wanted to touch the mayor's wife – for she kept her tongue going very fast, you may be sure.

In a little while, Peter came in sight of the king's palace. Just before reaching the gates he met a fine carriage drawn by four white horses, and in the carriage sat a young lady, as beautiful as a summer day, but with a sad and solemn look.

Peter and his train stepped aside to let the carriage pass, and just then the young lady looked out. When she saw the goose, and the funny way in which so many people had to walk behind it, she burst into a loud laugh. Then she ordered the coachman to stop, so that she might see better, and the longer she looked, the harder she laughed.

"The princess has laughed! The princess has laughed!" cried all the servants that were with her, and one of them ran back to tell the king about it.

When the king heard what had happened he was delighted. He ran out to see for himself, and when he saw Peter and his train he was so amused that he laughed louder than anybody else.

"My good friend," he said to Peter, "which

will you choose?"

Peter stared at him and said nothing, for he did not know what the king meant.

"Do you know what I promised to the one who would make my daughter laugh?" said the king.

"No, I don't think I do," said Peter.

"I promised a thousand dollars or a piece of land," said the king. "Which will you choose?"

"I think I'll take the land," said Peter.

Then he stroked the goose's head, and in a moment the girl and the stable boy and the clown and the mayor and the mayor's wife were suddenly free, and they were so glad to get away that they all ran home quickly as though someone had lit a fire behind them.

"What a pretty bird!" said the princess as she stepped out of her carriage and came to look at the goose. Then she reached out her pretty white hand to stroke its neck.

The goose screamed, and Peter cried out: "Hold

fast! Hold fast! Hold fast!"

And the princess thought that Peter was the handsomest lad she had ever seen. The king, too, was pleased with him and gave him a fine suit of clothes, and took him into the palace to be a page and wait on the ladies at the table.

When Peter grew up to be a strong and handsome man, he became a brave knight, and he and the princess were married. But the goose flew up into the air and winged its way back to the forest, and nobody has seen it from that day to this.

About the Authors

Find information below on some of the authors whose stories appear in this book.

HANS CHRISTIAN ANDERSEN 1805–1875

Born in Denmark, Hans Christian Andersen was apprenticed to a weaver and a tailor before working as an actor and singer in Copenhagen. While in the theatre he wrote poetry and stories. He became famous worldwide for his children's tales, many of which have been translated into over 150 languages.

F ANSTEY 1856–1934

Thomas Anstey Guthrie used the pen name 'F Anstey'. He was a barrister in London before becoming a successful comic novelist. Many of his stories have been adapted for theatre and films.

J M BARRIE 1860–1937

James Matthew Barrie grew up in Scotland. After graduating from the University of Edinburgh in 1882 he became a journalist. Barrie eventually moved to London where he became a novelist and playwright, and is best known as the creator of *Peter Pan*.

L FRANK BAUM 1856–1919

Lyman Frank Baum was born in New York, USA. He hated his first name and preferred to be called Frank. He began writing stories as a child, printing them on his own printing press, and later worked as a newspaper and magazine editor. Baum's greatest success was writing *The Wonderful Wizard of Oz*. He went on to write 13 books about the magical land of Oz, and many other short stories, poems and scripts.

LEWIS CARROLL 1832–1898

Lewis Carroll was the pen name of Charles Lutwidge Dodgson. He wrote poetry and short stories from a young age, but proved himself as a brilliant mathematician at Oxford University. He is most famous for his 'Alice' novels.

Sir George Webbe Dasent 1817–1896

After graduating from university, Dasent became a diplomat in Sweden. While there he met Jacob Grimm and became interested in folk tales. He went on to translate and publish several collections of ancient folk and fairy stories.

Brothers Grimm
Jacob Ludwig Karl Grimm 1785–1863
Wilhelm Karl Grimm 1786–1859

Born near Frankfurt in Germany, Jacob and Wilhelm read law at university, then went on to study spoken language and how it changes over time. They collected many European folk tales and published them in several volumes.

Joseph Jacobs 1854–1916

Born in Australia, Jacobs studied in England and Germany as a young man, researching Jewish history. Eventually he settled in America, and, inspired by the Brothers Grimm, went on to edit five collections of fairy tales.

Rudyard Kipling 1865–1936

Born to a British family in India, Kipling lived in England from the age of five. He became one of Britain's best-loved poets and children's writers for works including *Just So Stories* and *The Jungle Book*.

Andrew Lang 1844–1912

Born in Scotland, Lang studied at St Andrew's University in Fife and Balliol College, Oxford. He researched folklore, mythology and religion, and wrote poetry, novels and literary criticism. Lang adapted many folk and fairy tales for children in a series of 12 books.

E Nesbit 1858–1924

Edith Nesbit was born in Surrey, England. She began writing stories in her teens and went on to write and collaborate on over 60 children's books, several of which have been adapted for film and television. Her most famous novels include *The Railway Children* and *Five Children and It*.

Kate Douglas Wiggin 1856–1923
Nora Archibald Smith 1859–1934

Sisters Kate and Nora were born in Philadelphia, USA. Kate started the first free kindergarten in San Francisco. Then she and Nora set up a training school for kindergarten teachers, and raised money for it by writing stories. Together, they retold and edited many collections of tales for children.

About the Artists

Marsela Hajdinjak

Marsela contributes to a number of children's magazines and has also created characters and scenography for several animated films. In 2005, she received the Grigor Vitez Award in recognition of her illustrations for the books *Water Sprite* and *Old Pear Tree*. She lives and works in Zagreb, Croatia.

The Mermaid and the Boy, The Butterfly that Stamped, The Stars in the Sky, The Cinder-Maid, The Tinder-box, The Council with the Munchkins, A Grin Without a Cat, The Star and the Lily, The Storks and the Night Owl, The Iron Casket, The Paradise of Children, The Wonderful Weaver

Alida Massari

Italian illustrator Alida has always been fond of art. She has travelled around Europe visiting old towns and galleries, both of which inspire her ancient-modern style. She has illustrated around 30 books, and works with acrylics, watercolours and collage.

The Crab that Played with the Sea, The Unicorn, Dapplegrim, The Stone-cutter, An Unexpected Opening, The Giant Builder, Do You Believe in Fairies?, The Three Golden Apples, The Deliverers of Their Country, The Enchanted Waterfall, The Well of the World's End, King Grisly-Beard, The Elf and the Housewife

Marcin Piwowarski

From a very young age Marcin began painting, and he now specializes in children's illustration. His style is energetic, with multicultural references. Marcin's work has been published in the UK, Norway and the USA.

The Egg, The Frog, The Three Wishes, The Magical Mug, The Lad Who Went to the North Wind, The Buried Moon, Arndt's Night Underground, The Enchanted Horse, The Feast of the Lanterns, The Crystal Coffin, The Baker's Daughter, The Three Dwarves, Peter and the Magic Goose

Tom Sperling

After working at The Museum of Modern Art, New York, Tom pursued his interest in illustration by studying at The Art Student's League. He has twice been awarded the Paul Revere Award for Graphic Excellence and has won the Small Press Book Award for *The Wish Ring* for Best Illustrated Young Adult Book.

The King of the Polar Bears, The Emperor's Nightingale, The Half-Chick, A Grand Transformation Scene, Beautiful as the Day, The Mines, Shipwreck on Lilliput, The Princess on the Glass Hill, The Old Man and the Gift, Grasp All, Lose All, He Wins Who Waits, The Hermit